Alibi

Lynda La Plante was born in Liverpool. She trained for the stage at RADA and worked with the National Theatre and RSC before becoming a television actress. She then turned to writing and made her breakthrough with the phenomenally successful TV series *Widows*. She has written over thirty international novels, all of which have been bestsellers, and is the creator of the Anna Travis, Lorraine Page and *Trial and Retribution* series. Her original script for the much-acclaimed *Prime Suspect* won awards from BAFTA, Emmy, British Broadcasting and Royal Television Society, as well as the 1993 Edgar Allan Poe Award.

Lynda is one of only three screenwriters to have been made an honorary fellow of the British Film Institute and was awarded the BAFTA Dennis Potter Best Writer Award in 2000. In 2008, she was awarded a CBE in the Queen's Birthday Honours List for services to Literature, Drama and Charity.

✉ Join the Lynda La Plante Readers' Club at
www.bit.ly/LyndaLaPlanteClub
www.lyndalaplante.com
f Facebook @LyndaLaPlanteCBE
🐦 Twitter @LaPlanteLynda

Lynda La Plante

Alibi

ZAFFRE

First published in 1998 by Macmillan

This edition published in 2023 by
ZAFFRE
An imprint of Zaffre Publishing Group
A Bonnier Books UK Company
4th Floor, Victoria House, Bloomsbury Square, London, WC1B 4DA
Owned by Bonnier Books
Sveavägen 56, Stockholm, Sweden

A CIP catalogue record for this book is
available from the British Library.

Trade paperback ISBN: 978-1-80418-294-9
Paperback ISBN: 978-1-80418-247-5

Also available as an ebook and an audiobook

1 3 5 7 9 10 8 6 4 2

Typeset by IDSUK (Data Connection) Ltd
Printed and bound in Great Britain by Clays Ltd, Elcograf S.p.A.

Zaffre is an imprint of Zaffre Publishing Group
A Bonnier Books UK Company
www.bonnierbooks.co.uk

CHAPTER 1

THURSDAY 16 APRIL. EVENING

'Is that nice?' asked Susie lightly.

The client, sprawling face down on the narrow padded table, groaned with pleasure as she kneaded the back of his neck. She felt his whole body pulse at once, and then again, under the stimulus of her probing fingers. Susie immediately let her hands relax, flattening them against the punter's shoulders before starting to work them down each side of his spine towards the small of the back. A tuft of dark body hair sprouted towards the base of his spine which she grasped, giving it a mischievous tug before laying her hands absolutely flat on the lower back over his kidneys. Her fingers were spread like starfish on the white, lightly oiled skin. Sometimes at work she would find herself almost in a trance, her mind detached and her hands moving spontaneously. She watched them now, beginning the familiar slow, sensuous, circular motion that is known in massage by a beautiful name: effleurage. A proper physiological grounding, a knowledge of the bones, muscles and blood circulation, was essential, she knew. But even more you needed these instinctive hands, able to locate the knots and tensions in a body by pure intuition. She had once been told by her massage teacher that the hands of the best masseurs are the hands of an artist, part pianist, part sculptor. It was a thought that made her tingle with pride.

'Turn over,' she ordered, after a few minutes more of the rhythmical effleurage. She raised the towel which lay across the man's buttocks and he rolled onto his back. His cock stood up, rigid and twitching. Demurely Susie covered it with the towel and moved down to attend to the intricate architecture of the man's feet. The other would come later, so long as he was prepared to part with the necessary twenty pounds extra; in the meantime she remained absorbed in her art.

* * *

Susie's shift at Pinkers continued until eleven. She'd done a nail extension, two deep face packs and three massages since seven o'clock. She had also been round the corner to the apartment of a private punter during the mid-shift break. Before that she'd done a lunchtime stint behind the bar at the Slipper pub, collected her daughter from school and taken her to her nana's. Now, in the small room where the girls changed, she was aching with tiredness. After stripping off her short white coat, she stood in her lacy, black half-cup bra and French knickers smoking a cigarette, refreshing her make-up and tidying her braided hair. Shiree was sounding off about a new massage customer and his personal hygiene problem. But Susie was only half listening to her friend's high-pitched complaints and when Shiree's mobile phone started to cheep she was glad enough of the chance to stub out the smoke, open her locker and get on with dressing.

Pulling out a small wad of money from the back of the locker, she hooked the latest crumpled banknote from her cleavage and added it to the stash, then pushed the money into the sole of her shoe. Hand-job money. One day it would pay for another week or so of private schooling for little Justine, but the cash would have to be smuggled out past old Mother Fuller. Officially Pinkers was a legitimate parlour, dedicated to clinical massage. Mrs Fuller was prepared to be complacent about what went on inside the private cubicles, expecting only a fifty per cent cut of the cash generated by these 'extras' – though in reality she rarely collected more than half of her rake-off.

It was just after eleven when Susie signed out and escaped into the unseasonably warm Fulham night. A hundred yards away, the King's Road bustled: the clubs were ready to receive customers who had finished dining but didn't plan to stop enjoying themselves; the restaurants reset tables to receive late-night diners migrating from West End entertainments. Belting her white raincoat tightly around the slim waist that she was so proud of, Susie paused at the kerb looking for a cab. Her mother, Bibi, always babysat Justine at her own flat on the evenings when Susie worked. Rather than disturb the child's sleep, Susie would sleep the night there before taking Justine in to school the next day. She was too knackered now to consider the bus or Tube.

The street was lined on both sides with cars, and between them drivers cruised in search of somewhere to park. No taxis. She had begun to walk speculatively towards the King's Road when she heard Shiree's voice shouting to her from outside the parlour.

'Eh! Susie! You coming down the Slipper for a drink?'

Susie turned and shook her head. 'No. I got to get home.'

Then her ear caught the diesel rattle of an approaching taxi. But it came from Shiree's direction and before Susie could make it to the kerb, her friend was there first, hailing the cab for herself. At the same time, though, she became aware of a deeper-sounding engine coming from the other direction. A white van pulled up.

'Hey, darling! Going our way?'

The young man was resting his chin on his arm, which lay casually over the sill of the rolled-down window. She hesitated. It was always tough to find a cab in this area at this time of night.

She might still be looking in fifteen minutes. The guy flashed a smile and raised his eyebrows.

'Don't fancy a lift then?'

He was eyeing her up and down slowly, noticing the long silky legs, the painted eyelids and red lips, the elaborately braided hair. It wasn't what she fancied that was uppermost in his mind and, suddenly, getting home didn't seem that important. She had two hundred in her shoe but another fifty wouldn't hurt, and nor would it be the first time she'd been late home to her mum's. What the hell? It wasn't as if Justine wasn't safe there. And she had a whacking bill for council tax to pay by the end of the month.

She leaned down into the van window and nonchalantly opened negotiations.

CHAPTER 2
FRIDAY 17 APRIL

With every year that passed it seemed to Bibi Harrow that she woke earlier. In her younger days she'd enjoyed the precious interval between sleeping and waking, but now, just past sixty, she could no longer simply lie in bed and blissfully doze. As her eyes opened, so the day began and there was no going back.

Unlike her granddaughter, Justine, who also woke early, Bibi did not much look forward to the day. Not for her to bounce out of bed and go looking for cartoons on the telly – there seemed so much to do and so little time. Bibi had her self-imposed routine of morning duties: making the beds, a little cleaning and tidying up around the flat. If Susie and Justine were both staying, she got the child breakfasted, dressed and ready for school before waking Susie. Then she went off, always a little anxiously, to work.

The supermarket checkout is a hard taskmaster, as Bibi could tell you. It is bad enough that the customers have sour faces and snap at you if there's the smallest delay. They can be so stupid sometimes and dishonest too. (Who says the customer is always right? Bibi would say different.) But on top of all this, Mrs Davis, the staff supervisor, was a proper tartar about timekeeping. She enjoyed humiliating the checkout staff, which was all the more reason to arrive at work on time: nine on the dot for her shift. There was no point in giving that woman the satisfaction.

'Come on, darlin',' she called out as she arranged the Teletubbies cereal bowl and shook out a portion of Choco-Flakes. 'Your breakfast's ready! I can't be late.'

Justine came wandering in with a bleeping hand-held computer game. Sliding into her chair, she didn't once shift her eyes from the tiny screen as her grandmother poured the milk. Sometimes Bibi thought the child should be made to do a little more for herself. Not being able to pour her own cereal at five! But then, five was young yet, and found its own world so fascinating.

'Nana, I got two spacemen and if I just get three . . .'

Justine's voice faded as her concentration returned to the quest for more spacemen. Bibi looked at her watch. Twenty to nine. She had better go into the sitting room and wake Susie.

'There's a clever girl. Can you tell Nana the time?'

There was a clock on the wall, a colourful modern design with hands, not digital. Bibi had got it recently with Justine in mind, making sure it had proper numbers, not those daft Roman ones that no child could be expected to read. Justine looked up and squinted at the clock face.

'Is it eight? Eight o'clock?'

Bibi clicked her tongue as she buttered a piece of toast. Spreading it rapidly with jam, she dropped it in front of Justine and stroked the child's long springy curls.

'No, sweetheart. It's nearly nine, so you eat up fast because Mummy has to get you off to school – and first of all I've got to wake up Mummy.'

Down the hall from the kitchen it was a couple of steps to the lounge, where Susie slept on the sofa-bed. Bibi stood outside the door and knocked on the ribbed glass.

'Susie, love. It's a quarter to nine. She's had her breakfast but I've got to be at work.'

She pushed down the handle and the door swung open. The sofa-bed stood just as she had left it when she got it ready last night. The duvet was turned back, the sheets beautifully smooth underneath. The bed had never been slept in. Bibi looked at it and sighed, then went to the phone to dial. Susie's end purred a few times, then there was a click and a fizzing sound, followed by Susie's voice, bright and artificial for the recording.

'Hi! Sorry I can't come to the phone right now. If you leave a message, I'll get back to you.'

Bibi frowned.

'Sue!' she said. 'Where are you? It's me. It's time to take Justine to school! So I'll do it myself, but you know how it's trouble for me when I'm late for work. You just pick her up at three, all right? Bye.'

She was going to have to face the wrath of Mrs Davis, old bitch. Bibi straightened her back, replaced the receiver and hurried to Justine, whose little toy was still bleeping.

'Come on, darling. No time for hunting spacemen now. We got to be fast or my guts will be going for apron strings.'

* * *

Six hours later Justine's teacher, Jo Hully, dismissed her class, then stood at the window to watch the stream of miniature humanity flowing out across the playground. A mob of parents waited to receive them by the school gates. The area was usually vacated quickly enough, except for the inevitable stragglers. A few of the more local children deemed old enough to take themselves home would hang around for a while to kick a ball or swap football cards and pop music fanzines. And there was always a scattering of younger ones whose parents were late for collection, which was bound to happen occasionally and usually to the same kids.

Jo went round the tables, picking up the crayon jars which the children had been using and returning them to their own neatly labelled shelf. She made a stack of the pictures they had been working on, placing them on a vacant section of windowsill. They would all have to be pinned up before she went home tonight.

She looked out and saw Justine Harrow with her rucksack strapped on, waiting among the uncollected ones. That was unusual. Her mum was almost always there on the dot to pick up Justine. A beautician, apparently, and obviously very caring towards the child. With a sigh, Jo picked up the stack of drawings and took them out to the corridor where they were to be displayed.

When she returned to her classroom, the shouts and thudding football sounds had died away. There was now just a lone child waiting under the small rain shelter, swinging herself around and around the cast-iron stanchion that held up its roof. Justine. The sight was so unusual that Jo hurried straight outside to talk to her.

'Justine! Has nobody collected you yet? What's the problem, do you think?'

'My mum's late.'

'Well, I can see that, dear. Half an hour late. Come on, let's go inside and call her on the phone, shall we?'

But there was only a pre-recorded reply from Susie Harrow's flat. Jo left a message and looked again in the Harrow file. There wasn't a work number listed under Susie Harrow, but next of kin was Mrs Bibi Harrow, the grandmother, who worked at the superstore. Jo looked up the number and dialled again.

Within five minutes Bibi was in her coat and leaving a message for Mrs Davis to say sorry, she had been called away on urgent family business. If she got the sack, too bad. It was a long way to go to the school, so she arranged for Mrs Hully to send Justine back to her flat in a minicab, then got a taxi herself to make sure she would be there first. It was money she could not really afford.

At home she dialled Susie's number and heard once again the warm-up sounds of the answering machine.

'Oh, come on! Where are you?'

'Hi! Sorry I can't come to the phone right now. If you leave a message, I'll get back to you.'

'Sue, it's me.'

Bibi tried to keep the irritation out of her voice, but it crept in anyway. 'They just called from the school, so she'll be here. You could at least ring me!'

Why didn't Susie have a mobile? Or maybe she did and wouldn't give her the number. Your kids never stopped being your kids, living their own life, taking advantage of yours – even when they got kids of their own. Bibi replaced the receiver. There had been odd times like this before. Sue was usually conscientious, but once or twice she'd been caught up in a house call on the other side of London and couldn't get away. Bibi scrabbled around in the pewter bowl she kept mostly for taxi and pizza numbers and came up with a card: PINKERS BEAUTY AND MASSAGE PARLOUR: MALE AND FEMALE CLIENTS CATERED FOR BY QUALIFIED STAFF. NO APPOINTMENT NECESSARY. She dialled the number.

Bibi had never met Mrs Fuller, Susie's employer, but on the phone she came over as a very superior person. Politely Bibi asked about her daughter.

'Susie?' cooed Mrs Fuller suavely. 'She was working late last night. Left around eleven, but I've not seen hide nor hair of her today. Never phoned in or anything. So, Mrs Harrow, if you do see your daughter, would you ask her to kindly contact me, if she *values* her job at all.'

Bibi said she would and hung up, suddenly wondering if this was something to do with that lump of a boyfriend of Susie's. She remembered Nicky giving her his mobile number once, printed on a card. She found it in the bowl. Very flashy, the card was. He was just a nightclub bouncer, but from this you'd think he was an international superstar. She dialled the number, only to be told that connection was not possible. This didn't surprise her. Whether the phone was switched off, broken, stolen or lost – what was the difference? It was typical of that boy to be out of touch when he was most needed. He should start acting like the father he was, because, even with a caring loving mum like Susie, Justine surely needed her father.

* * *

By seven there was still no sign of Susie. Justine had had her tea and Bibi briefly considered making the child ready for bed. But that would have to wait. Susie must have been in an accident. Got a bang on the head and lost her memory. Or she was lying unconscious in some casualty ward. Whatever had happened, she needed to be found. So Bibi bundled Justine into her padded parka jacket, picked up her bag and keys and banged the door of the flat on their way out.

'Where are we going, Nana?'

'The police. We got to ask them to find your mummy.'

* * *

It was a ten-minute bus ride to South Lambeth Street police station, where Duty Sergeant Morris was feeling considerably harassed. In the last half-hour he felt he had faced a concentration of all the social problems in South Lambeth: the five protagonists of a punch-up at a pub near the Oval, two drunken vagrants, a citizen's arrest of a mugger around the corner, a drug overdose admission phoned through from St Thomas's Hospital and a domestic dispute in the station's own waiting area. Sitting through it all, the little woman with the wide-eyed, mop-headed child in tow waited her turn with imperturbable patience. She had already told him she didn't want to be a nuisance, but she'd a missing person to report.

At last the sergeant was able to attend to the Harrows. He led them into an interview room and opened his report pad.

'OK, Mrs, er—'

'Harrow.'

'Harrow, yes. Your full name and address, please.'

Bibi supplied them.

'And your daughter, is it? The little girl's mother. She didn't turn up to collect Justine from school. That right?'

'Yes. And she was supposed to stay the night with us, only she never came. I had to take Justine to school myself this morning, and it's away over at Wandsworth. I was an hour late for work.'

'So your daughter and Justine don't live with you?'

'No, they live in Wandsworth. It's a nice flat, upstairs in a house. I'm just in a block, see.'

'And you don't know where Susie was last night?'

Bibi shook her head slowly. 'She was at work. And I called the place she worked and they told me she left around eleven. When she has to work late like that, I look after Justine and they both sleep at my place.'

Bibi felt a rush of helplessness which brought her near to tears. She fought them down.

'It's not like Susie, really. She always calls in if she's going to be late. I have to be at work by nine.'

Morris gripped the pen hard as he wrote on his pad, pressing to ensure that the triplicate carbons were impressed.

'Has she ever done this before?' He looked up. 'Not called?'

Bibi knew what the policeman was thinking. But her Susie was a decent girl, not a fly-by-night. She shook her head.

'Never. It's not like her at all. I mean, she's not even phoned me at work, you know, to tell me where she is.'

'And your daughter works at?'

'Like I said, a bar three days a week and four nights at . . . Well, it's a massage place, just off King's Road.'

Morris looked up and Bibi met his gaze. There was something in his expression that goaded her into defending her daughter's name.

'She's a qualified masseuse. Got her certificate as a beautician too. Sometimes she does private clients, at home like. Facials, hair and nail extensions. And, well, this is not like her.'

Bibi watched the sergeant writing further deeply incised words and then looked sideways at Justine. She was sitting on the chair, kicking her legs and looking around the wall at the crime-prevention posters. Bibi leaned forward and spoke with a lowered voice, her head jerking sideways at Justine.

'I have to work and I can't get to pick her up from school. It's too far. I don't want to be a problem, it's just I'm not sure what to do.'

Morris stopped writing and scratched his head. Had he forgotten anything? In missing-persons cases there are so many possible angles and by definition no direct witnesses.

'What about a husband?'

Bibi shook her head.

'Boyfriend?'

'Oh, him! Nicky Burton. I called him, got no reply.'

'Could she be with him, do you think?'

Bibi considered.

'Well, I don't know. It doesn't sound right. Nicky doesn't believe in commitment, you see. Doesn't like to spend more than a few hours at a time with my daughter.'

'Oh? Why's that then?'

Bibi again indicated the preoccupied Justine.

'I'll tell you why. He's afraid Susie'll get her hooks in him. That's what *I* think.'

* * *

Bibi and Justine left the station just after nine thirty. There was a fifteen-minute wait for a bus, so it was not until almost ten that Bibi put her granddaughter into pyjamas, supervised her toothbrushing and tucked her into bed. Ten minutes later, Justine having tumbled into an exhausted sleep, Bibi was negotiating with her friend Marlene on the floor below to come and sit in the flat for a couple of hours. Bibi's eventful evening was not over by any means.

She called another cab. The third today, she remembered ruefully. What on earth would her mother in Trinidad have thought about her Bibi riding around London like this, and paying with her own money what's more? It was lucky enough that today was payday. By the middle of next week, she'd be feeling the pinch, but what could she do? You couldn't rely on the police.

'You know the Snake Pit Club?' she asked the driver. 'I think it's towards the river.'

The driver called his controller, who squawked back the directions. Going noisily up through his gears along the Wandsworth Road and towards Lavender Hill, he smiled to himself. It would be a scruffy dive. What business did a little old lady have in a place like that?

* * *

Nights were 'nites' at the Snake Pit and Friday was a busy one. For Nicky and his mate Alvin, the club's two doormen, it would be non-stop until five or six the next morning. First they'd be on the door turning away undesirables and stamping the desirables' hands as they filed in. Later they would be on what Vernon, the boss, laughably called 'drugs patrol', when his bouncers were expected to spot any deals going down around the heaving, sweaty dance floor. This was a joke, because Nicky and Alvin were doing most of the dealing themselves. And then there was the unceasing need to punch the throats of any rowdy elements. It was demanding work.

The big attraction tonight was a band called Wormhole. They had a big following, possibly on account of the fact that one of them could play guitar with his foot. It certainly wasn't because they were, in Nicky Burton's opinion, any good. Students, that was all. Being black, he preferred Saturday nights when the club had a choice MC from Brixton rapping out street poetry against a wicked drum 'n' bass.

Bibi Harrow came at him out of the darkness and at first he thought she was just a punter jumping the queue. Only when he got a good view did the whole embarrassing truth come to him. The little woman with the determined eyes was Sooze's *mum*. Everyone took the piss out of him about Sooze, how she behaved like she practically owned him, like they were married or something. Well, she didn't and they weren't. Just because they'd been going together off and on for a few years didn't mean her mum had the right to come round to his work like some mother-in-law. He couldn't believe it.

He rounded on Bibi, thinking to get in before she could open her mouth. He was always telling Alvin, no matter how old they be, you got to do that with women or they crawl all over you.

'What *you* doing here, man? I'm working. I can't talk to you. The owner of this club don't like us having personal conversations when we're working. You better scoot, Mrs Harrow!'

But Bibi Harrow was not so easily put off and, when Nicky's attention was momentarily distracted by some words between Alvin and a punter with a bad attitude, she seized her chance.

'No, I won't scoot, Nicky! I'm looking for my Susie. She's not been seen since yesterday. She over at your place? She been in touch with you?'

He drove his rubber stamp rather too hard down on the wrist of a skinny girl whose eyebrows were chained to her earlobes. As she yelped in surprise, he almost snarled at Bibi.

'I've not seen her for days. She threw one of her moods. So don't ask me where she is.'

'Hasn't she called you?'

Nicky waved his hand in the space between himself and the old woman.

'No. And I got to work, so—'

'You understand, Nicky. I can't look after Justine. Not all the time.'

Nicky tried a smile which he hoped looked like mockery.

'Don't look at me.'

He thought for a moment. It was a bit weird Susie dropping out of sight like that. She was so crazy about the kid. She can't have gone far.

'Have you tried the pub?' he asked.

Bibi nodded.

'Yes. She didn't turn up for the lunchtime shift today and they've not seen her since yesterday. She is your kid and it's about time you took responsibility.'

Nicky didn't look at Bibi but went on methodically stamping the hands of the punters as they came through.

'Not my problem. OK?'

CHAPTER 3

SATURDAY 18 APRIL

Detective Inspector Pat North was the most senior woman CID officer at South Lambeth Street, the station serving South Lambeth, Nine Elms and the southern Thames river bank between Vauxhall and Chelsea bridges. The policing of this locality means involvement in the problems of large commercial developments strung along the riverside (such as the huge site of New Covent Garden vegetable market) as well as those of the residential streets and estates arrayed on either side of Wandsworth Road, the A3 trunk road down which traffic surges out of London towards Guildford, Portsmouth and the south coast. Pat North was relatively new to the manor, having transferred there a few months previously. In that time she had seen the very best and the very worst of human nature, always simmering dangerously close to boiling point in the vast, volatile pressure cooker of the inner city.

On the face of it a missing person was another routine occurrence. The woman Susie Harrow had gone AWOL only thirty-six hours previously, which was no time at all in the context of the uncountable daily accumulation of random movements and decisions made by the population of London. When the case had landed on her desk the previous night, after Sergeant Morris brought it to her in the Crime Management Unit, it had not at first seemed one over which to lose a lot of sleep.

'I posted her on the missing-persons log,' Morris told her. 'She's not in any of the local A and E units and I phoned Fulham, Kennington and Battersea nicks myself. If she's got herself nicked somewhere else, something may come through on the computer. Mrs Harrow's worried about the little girl. She can't take care of her, got to work.'

Pat North studied the report.

'That's a social services problem, surely?'

'Well, not exactly, because I've filed the report as a "vulnerable missing persons". It's totally out of character for her to leave the little girl.'

'If you say so.'

But North wanted to know more. Morris was sometimes mocked around the station for his earnestness, but he was nothing if not diligent.

'Go on,' she said.

'There's no husband – but there is a boyfriend, Nicky Burton. He's a bouncer at a local nightclub. She works at a bar and a massage parlour – Pinkers, off King's Road.'

PC Phelps, sitting at a computer, pricked up his ears.

'That's a knocking-shop – or it used to be.'

North looked at him sharply. She and Phelps had worked together before. She knew him.

'How do you know?'

Phelps grinned.

'Just a wild guess!'

North thought for a moment, pulling at her lip.

'Well, let's look into it.'

She yawned. It had been another long day and this would keep, until tomorrow anyway. The Harrow woman would probably have turned up by then. She stood up and dropped the file in front of Phelps, who seized it and began riffling through Bibi Harrow's statement.

'I'll do the massage parlour,' he said a shade too eagerly.

Morris leaned over and snatched the file back.

'I bet you will, sunshine!'

Pat North had pulled her coat from the rack. Phelps was a cheeky sod, none too tactful, and if Susie Harrow really was a hooker, they'd better give her disappearance a touch more priority than a couple of uniforms.

'No, Simon. I'll handle that particular visit myself.'

She had spoken as she walked to the door. When she got there she turned, jabbing a finger at the constable.

'But I'll tell you what. You find the boyfriend. She may be with him or he may know where she is. And keep your eyes open, right?'

*   *   *

North and Detective Sergeant Lawrence Brown found that Pinkers was not the sleazy clip joint of Phelps's fevered imagination but a clean, businesslike establishment, its ambience floating somewhere halfway between an alternative health clinic and a beauty salon. The bright, recently painted walls displayed advertisements for reflexology, acupuncture, electrolysis and 'non-surgical' face-lifts.

Monica Fuller sat demurely behind reception, a carefully made-up middle-aged woman in a white coat. Not a hair of her elaborate coiffure was out of place and she seemed unworried by the arrival of the police.

'To be honest,' she was saying, 'Susie really let me down. I mean, she was supposed to be in last night. But she's not called and she has some clients who won't go with anyone else.'

Pat North looked around. At a second glance there was the merest hint that sexual services were not out of the question here. An exceptionally glamorous young staff member had walked into reception with an exaggerated swing to her hips. She was wearing full make-up and stiletto heels. The shortness of her white coat was not what you would see around Harley Street. Brown's eyes noted this; his brain was thinking, 'And what's she wearing underneath?'

'So when was the last time you saw her?' asked North.

Mrs Fuller shrugged.

'Thursday night. Is she in trouble?'

Choosing not to respond to the question, Pat North met the woman's eyes.

'Is there anyone I can talk to who saw her on Thursday?'

The short-coated girl looked brightly at North, batting her coloured-up and spikily false-lashed eyelids.

'You here about Susie?' she asked in a bright, high voice.

Mrs Fuller stood up. Suddenly she was flustered, for the girl's appearance and demeanour had tended to blow her cover. She began to protest just a bit too much.

'Listen, I don't want any trouble. This is a legitimate business. If she's got problems, I don't want to know. I mean, what the girls do in their spare time is their business – know what I mean?'

Pat maintained eye contact. This sounded like the first hint of non-cooperation. It would have to be stamped on.

'How about I look into just what kind of business you do run here, Mrs Fuller? If you want cars and uniforms, you'll get them. That would make your clients run.'

The Fuller woman was about to speak, but North forestalled her with a raised hand. Time to be reasonable again. She spoke firmly but in a gentler voice.

'Now, I *just* want to ask you a few questions – all right?'

Mrs Fuller let her eyes fall shut and she sighed. She spoke to the other girl.

'Shiree, take them into the back room.'

*   *   *

Phelps and PC Julian Henshaw got to Nicky Burton's place about two. It took ten minutes of ringing the bell to get the man himself to the door. Burton was wearing nothing but a pair of baggy jogging-bottoms, but though his face was sleep-sodden and he scowled none too prettily, his worked-out body was a sculpture of muscles and gleamed with health. Henshaw cleared his throat.

'Afternoon. I'm PC Henshaw and this is PC Phelps from South Lambeth Street police station. We're making inquiries into the whereabouts of Miss Susan Harrow. Any ideas, sir?'

Burton glowered.

'I don't know where she is and, to be honest, I don't give a shit.'

He looked the constables up and down, from their shiny shoes to their gleaming helmet badges. Then he looked up and down the street before ushering them into his hallway.

'And you guys coming round here don't do me no favours.'

Phelps slipped the strap from under his chin and took off his helmet.

'Do you have a sexual relationship with Miss Harrow, sir?'

Burton sneered.

'No, we play Monopoly.'

'Mr Burton,' said Henshaw, hurriedly butting in before Phelps said something even more stupid. 'Mr Burton, no one has seen Susan Harrow since Thursday night and—'

'Well, they're a day ahead of me, because the last time I saw her was Wednesday.'

'And she has made no contact since?'

'No.'

It was all they got out of him and all they *would* get for now. Even if Nicky Burton knew where his girlfriend was, his hatred of the police would not let him reveal it without the exertion of considerably greater pressure. When, a few minutes later, Phelps and Henshaw left, they had penetrated no further into Nicky Burton's busy, self-absorbed life than the first ten feet of his hallway.

* * *

Driving back to the station from Fulham, Pat North felt she now knew a good deal more about Susie Harrow. Monica Fuller had given a polished performance but, underneath the varnished shell of a legitimate businesswoman, she had the soul of a brothelkeeper. And if Shiree was anything like Susie, their missing person was hardly more than a few tricks advanced from a shiny little card in a BT phone box.

At one level this meant that they were dealing with a less than model citizen, and a life that did not run to a predictable pattern. She may have skived off to Brighton for the weekend with a punter. She may have lain down with her bloodstream full of smack in a dark alleyway and never got up. She may have simply walked away from her sordid life. It happened.

But prostitution is dangerous work and as North drove into the car park behind the police station she knew they could not treat Susie Harrow's disappearance lightly. The more days that went by, the more ways there were that she could be in deep trouble.

* * *

She was pleased to be stopped on her way through reception and told by Duty Sergeant Morris about the foray to Susie Harrow's flat in Wandsworth. He handed her an envelope with something rectangular inside.

'What's this?'

'From the answering machine. See what you make of it.'

She took the cassette to her desk, slotted it into a playback machine and turned to the log of the calls appended to the report. Then she started the tape. The first voice was a young man's, sounding nervous.

'Hello. I, er, got your name from a friend who says you do hotel visits. But you're obviously not there so I'll, erm—'

The voice broke off, the tape fizzed briefly, then whistled and Bibi's voice was heard.

'Sue, where are you? It's me. It's time to take Justine to school. So I'll do it myself but you know how it's trouble for me when I'm late for work. You just pick her up at three, all right? Bye.'

Next up was a woman.

'Susie, it's Barbara. Just ringing to ask if you can take Marcie to school for me on Monday morning. Call me back, OK?'

Then another man, older.

'Hello, Susie. Just ringing about Saturday. Be with you at two thirty as usual, OK? See you then.'

The next voice was that of the schoolteacher, Mrs Hully, saying that she was waiting with Justine in the school office. Then the mother, Bibi Harrow, was heard again, giving the first hint of something wrong.

'Sue, it's me. They just called from the school, so she'll be here. You could at least ring me!'

North stopped the tape and pulled out Bibi's statement, referring to her mention of this phone call. Around four in the afternoon on Friday. She noted the time and pressed the 'Play' button.

'Hi, it's Liz. The blonde streaks were nice, but can you do more? It's just that I don't think they're sort of obvious enough. So can you call me?'

'Hi. Be free lunchtime, will you? I'll be with you, say, one fifteen?'

'Susie, it's Jen. Can you do my nail extensions, plus facial? I can be there at six, but I have to leave at seven. See ya!'

'Six o'clock – make sure you wear what I like! Look forward to seeing you.'

She looked up at Morris, who had come to her desk with the report on Susie Harrow's flat.

'They've searched the place,' he said. 'Not found a diary or anything, but the place is spotless and all her clothes seem to be there.'

Pat nodded at the tape player.

'The men never leave their names. Some of these have got to be regular clients. Maybe check with the neighbours for descriptions of blokes coming and going.'

Morris noted North's serious tone. She must be beginning to fear the worst.

'Listen, some of these girls take off for a week with a punter—'

Pat North shook her head.

'Not this one. She has a kid that she takes good care of. Hasn't the boyfriend heard from her yet?'

'Nope.'

Pat North shook her head. It wasn't looking good.

CHAPTER 4

WEDNESDAY 22 APRIL. EVENING

Vernon Reid, the manager of the Snake Pit Club, always did have an acute sense of smell. At primary school, from the very moment the kitchen's first rancid odours began wafting along the corridor, he could tell his classmates what was boiling up for dinner. And even now, at work, he always knew which of his employees was standing behind him from the aftershave they'd been splashing on. For the past few days, his nose had been a conduit for his growing sense of discomfort. Somehow, somewhere, from inside the building or close by, the club was beginning to stink.

On the second evening after he himself had detected it, even his bouncers were complaining of the pong. Vernon told Nicky Burton to see that all the toilets were functioning normally, while he called a plumbing outfit. In the Yellow Pages he found a display advertisement for Clean-a-Drain – 'Minimum Call-out Charge, Blocked Drains Rodded 24 Hours, Fully Trained Operatives'. Predictably, they didn't want to come until tomorrow and, when Vernon insisted, he was informed of their special triple 'minimum' call-out fee for night-time visits. But a club is a place of escape, and nothing destroys escapism faster than a bad stench – never mind the attendance of some environmental-health SWAT squad. Vernon told them never mind the cost, he wanted his drains dealt with ASAP. While Clean-a-Drain couldn't guarantee a time, they promised that two of their fully trained operatives would attend as soon as possible.

Nicky's preference for Lynx aftershave announced his reappearance in the manager's office.

'It's not the fuckin' toilets, Vernon. They flush fine.'

'Plumbers are coming,' Vernon told him. 'The drains got to be taken up, I reckon. Last thing I need is those environmental shitheads nosing around. They can pull my licence like that.'

He swung round in his chair, reached for a panatella cigar and lit up.

'I hope it's not blocked sinks in the kitchen. That's worse than the bloody drains. Can't get at the pipes.'

Nicky was already backtracking to the door. This wasn't his line of work at all and he'd rather punch the heads of a dozen drunk students than open a single manhole. But he wanted to keep Vernon sweet.

'OK, we'll take a look, but it's Indie Nite. The place is rammed.'

Vernon shut his eyes, sighed and ran his hands through his hair.

'Tell me about it.'

In the end Vernon picked up a couple of torches and accompanied his senior bouncer round the back of the club, where the outflow from the kitchen waste dropped into a small grated drain. The row of houses in which the club was situated backed onto a patch of waste ground clogged with urban rubbish: tyres, mattresses, abandoned furniture, the rusty skeleton of a pedal bike, rolls of wire, several oil drums and smashed televisions. For the last six months Vernon had been trying to get his hands on this piece of ground to develop as a car park, but it was owned by a local motor dealer who thought he might one day need it for his own expansion.

They shone their torches into the sink waste sump. The smell was worse out here, but Vernon couldn't be sure if it came from the drain, from inside the soil pipe attached to the wall of the building, from under the square metal drain cover on which they were standing or from somewhere else entirely. He looked at Nicky, who was equally stumped. Neither man had a particularly firm grasp on how domestic plumbing connects to the sewage system. Nicky raised his mobile phone to his ear and spoke to Lee, the assistant barman.

'Flush it now.'

Lee flushed a toilet somewhere inside and they heard a rush of water down the soil pipe.

'Tell him to do the sinks,' said Vernon.

'Lee? Run the washbasins in the toilets . . . What? . . . No, just turn them all on!'

The basin water began to flow and they could hear it gushing into the drain below the metal cover. There didn't seem to be any question of a blockage. Vernon swivelled round. His super-sensitive nose seemed to be giving him a new direction and he was now casting about like a gun dog seeking fallen game.

'Something stinks, Nicky. But where is it?'

At this point two overalled men, lugging toolboxes and drain probes, appeared from around the front of the building. Vernon greeted them dubiously.

'You from Clean-a-Drain?'

In reply he got a nod and a grunt. The club manager gestured vaguely towards the drains and the manhole cover.

'Cop that terrible smell. Doesn't seem to be from the club's drains, though.'

The plumbers walked around, peering and sniffing, while Nicky told Lee to shut off the taps. One of the plumbers, a good twenty years older than the other and projecting all the authority of a seasoned craftsman, straightened up and jerked his thumb out into the darkness.

'What's out there then?'

'Just waste ground that a bastard won't sell me for car parking.'

Vernon was lighting another slim cigar as the younger of the two men switched on a powerful torch and swept the area with its beam. Nicky was bobbing up and down with impatience.

'I should get back out front, Vern. We're going to be packed tonight.'

Vernon nodded to him and followed the Clean-a-Drain men into the dark. They were both using torches now, casting around from side to side and sniffing.

'It's stronger further back,' said the youth. 'You can really smell it out here, Harry.'

'Why do you think I got you guys in?' called Vernon. 'It's been stinking for days but now it's got worse. Is it the drains then?'

There was a pause as Harry considered, without halting his methodical survey of the ground. Finally he pronounced judgement.

'No way. You'd not get drains dug this far from the main sewage pipes under the road. Smell's really bad now, eh, Colin?'

Colin gave out an odd grunt of agreement. Vernon stopped for an instant and drew on his panatella. Were they taking the piss?

'Tell you what I *have* got out here,' he said forcefully, starting after them again but making slow progress in his Italian shoes. 'Bloody rats. I've had the vermin control buggers here, laying down poison pellets. I said to them, you sure these pellets ain't attracting them? Because they look like they been dining out – big mothers. And then we got stray dogs, cats. It's a flaming sanctuary out here. You know, I've offered a good price for this land—'

'What's that over there?' called Harry.

He was moving towards a pile of split plastic bin bags, heaped up beyond the remains of a three-piece suite. The burst sofa and half-burned chairs stood grouped together like the last sad remnants of a bomb-blasted living room.

'I'll tell you what,' said Vernon, still stumbling in the wake of the plumbers. 'Some of the tarts bring their clients back here. I mean, if it was a car park you'd not get that problem. I'd have someone on duty and there'd never be any—'

He was interrupted again by Harry's voice, a husky, trembling kind of shout.

'Here, Colin! Oh, Jesus! Over here. Take a look at this.'

When Vernon finally caught up with them, the two men were standing silently side by side, directing their torches down at the mound of refuse sacks which lay on a burned mattress. Protruding from underneath, pale palm upwards and slim fingers curled, was a human hand.

* * *

Two minutes after Vernon Reid had dialled 999, the news was relayed to South Lambeth Street's Computer Aided Dispatch (or CAD) room: a woman's body had been found on waste ground behind the Snake Pit Club. It was late in Pat North's shift, which ended at ten o'clock, that the report sheet was brought up to the CID office. Phelps wandered in to have a look.

'Anyone we know?'

'Couldn't tell you. We've sent a couple of cars down there but there's not a lot to be done tonight, except cordon off the area.'

Even with the cordon there would be problems with the locals, of course, and nothing caused so much sensation as the discovery of a body. But they had no choice except to leave the dead woman where she was. To remove her from there in the dark would be a forensic disaster.

North had contacted the Area Major Investigation Pool (AMIP). If this was a murder – and all the indications pointed to it – they would be assigning a senior officer to head the investigation. North had also liaised with the Metropolitan Police Crime Scene Coordinator and the Forensic Science Service. The FSS had told her a forensic biologist would be in attendance the next morning and that she must not interfere with the site. Bastards. Did they think she didn't know her job?

On her way home, she dropped by the Snake Pit Club with a copy of Vernon Reid's statement, meaning to ask him a few clarifying questions. The place was locked and in darkness. After the clubbers' names and addresses had been taken, the place had been closed down. Reid had gone home.

North drove around to the waste ground, where she found a couple of squad cars and a uniformed PC whose job it was to guard the murder scene from behind the cordon of blue and white police tape. He also had to log forensic and police visitors in and out. A small knot of gawpers had gathered beyond the perimeter. She recognised the constable – Baker – and told him she wanted to look at the body. The standard procedure, as FSS had indicated, is to cover the body and surrounding area with a plastic tent, secure the perimeter and await the arrival of the experts.

For April it was a warmish night with little wind and the smell around the body was intense and putrid. North looked into the tent. Nothing had been moved. The filthy mattress was still in place, covering most of the body, yet what she saw was enough to make her flinch. She could pick out two feet with shoes still on. Twisted around the ankles was some kind of black material.

Further under the mattress, she could see an area of flesh – part of a leg it seemed. The skin was grey and greasy from decomposition except where parts had been torn away, the holes white and ragged. She grimaced. In places, the flesh looked as if it had been ripped and chewed.

She moved backwards out of the tent and, once in the fresh air, spun sharply around, walking with quick paces away from the forensic tent and the constable hovering near. She was breathing deeply, aware that she might vomit. She fought her retching stomach and felt slightly ashamed. She should have stood her ground. She should have been able to.

She also felt angry. It was a sex crime, she was quite certain. One of the reasons Pat North had joined the police was to help rid the world of men who did things like this. Most of them seemed to be normal and everyday until it turned out they had some kink inside that made them menace women. Like that bloke at the student dance who'd given her a lift home that time and—

'Guv!'

She looked up. The constable was edging to her with his clipboard. He coughed.

'Yes?'

'Will you be wanting access to the tent again? Only I ought to log you out.'

She shook her head.

'No, I've seen all I want to for now. Goodnight, Baker.'

She went back to her car. She had noticed a lottery ticket under the clip of the constable's board. He probably bought those tickets every week in the full expectation of a big win. What followed in his fantasies? A lifetime of perfect sunshine beside some pool in Barbados? Poor idiot, with his getaway dreams.

CHAPTER 5

THURSDAY 23 APRIL

Dr Deirdre Smith of the Forensic Science Service, recently transferred to the London Metropolitan region from rural Huntingdon, arrived on the crime site just ten minutes after sunrise. She knew that the police would be anxious to remove the body as soon as possible. Anyway, she herself much preferred to look at bodies in the early morning when temperatures were low and there were fewer people about.

She was a small, stocky woman of middle age, the type you expect to meet running parish bring-and-buy sales rather than examining the mutilated bodies of murder victims. Smith actually was a regular at the local parish church, but her spiritual and professional lives were kept strictly separate. The methodical, utterly unhurried manner with which she approached a body was legendary in the service.

Smith's first task was a rapid survey of the site in company with Detective Constable Dave Palmer, the exhibits officer assigned to the case. Detective Sergeant Tony Jenetta, the crime scene coordinator, showed them round, pointing out salient features. As he did so, two further officers, the stills photographer and video operator, arrived.

'As you can see,' Jenetta was saying, 'there's a fair amount of bagged refuse and some dumped household furniture. Apparently local prostitutes sometimes used the – er – facilities.'

'And winos?' asked Dr Smith.

'Yes, down-and-outs sometimes come down here, and the local police have nicked them for starting fires and what have you. But we've not heard of any spotted here last night.'

Smith knelt and snapped open her heavy aluminium case. She selected a pair of surgical gloves which she stripped from their packaging and pulled on. She then delved into the case again for her tape recorder and advanced towards the tent, beckoning the waiting cameramen. Pulling aside the flap, she passed inside, where there was room to stand up and move around the body. It lay exactly as it had been found, half concealed by the mattress. Smith seemed impervious to the smell which most civilians would have found overpowering and which became worse as she began gently to ease away the mattress.

'I'll need some help with this,' she observed.

She looked up at Palmer, a black, bespectacled giant of an officer who seemed even more huge in the restricted confines of the forensic tent. The camera clicked and whirred as he jumped forward to grasp the stained and sodden article. Recording every detail, the video operator circled round to get a better angle.

Now that they could see it properly, the wretched state of the corpse was revealed. It lay sprawled, face up, the legs extended at right angles with a once-white mackintosh covering most of the torso. When Smith began to remove the raincoat, it was stiff, resisting her pressure. As she pulled harder, the mackintosh began to come away with a dry tearing sound, like sticky tape pulled off a roll, and then they saw the reason why. Much of the body was covered with a dry black crust which had glued the coat to the body. Smith touched a place where it lay particularly thickly, then probed on the ground beneath the chest, where a great deal more of the thick, black deposit lay in a congealed pool.

'This is blood,' she said. 'The woman probably bled to death right here.'

She clicked on her tape recorder and held it up to her mouth.

'She's been dead some time and the decomposition is . . .'

She gently tested the softness of the arm.

'. . . advanced.'

She moved around to the other side and peered at the dead woman's side.

'But we've no sign of plant life inside the corpse.'

She lightly held the corpse's shoulder and eased it over until she could see the chest.

'Oh dear, oh dear.'

The woman's chest was a mass of matted dried blood. Where her left breast had been there was nothing but a thick plaque of hardened, bloody flesh. Her right breast was slashed and scored, as was the rest of her chest, ribcage and belly, with numerous black-seamed cuts. Meanwhile, a wound had opened up her throat; a slash almost from ear lobe to ear lobe.

'It looks like, er, injuries to the throat, breasts . . .'

Smith momentarily stopped speaking and all that could be heard was the whirr of the two recording devices. Suddenly she clicked off hers, turned to Jenetta and gestured at the area between the body and the tent walls.

'There've been rodents. I need this area cleared for examination. But don't move her yet. I need to look for any blood distribution.'

As her orders were carried out, she walked a little way across the rubble-strewn ground, speaking quietly into her phone.

* * *

All morning the AMIP team had been setting up shop at South Lambeth Street police station. Brown was coordinating the unloading of computers, filing cabinets, desks, chairs and pin boards from the AMIP pantechnicon and moving them up into the Incident Room. By nine o'clock the whole station was buzzing with tension and an undeniable excitement as the glamour boys themselves rolled in.

Murder, above all else, is the rationale of AMIP. It is the Met's movable team of experts in the investigation of extreme crimes, and murder is the most extreme. As soon as it had been confirmed that the body found on the waste ground was a murder victim, their deployment was rapid. Within a couple of hours the murder squad consisted of three detective sergeants, sixteen hand-picked detective constables and six civilian office staff. Arriving singly and in groups, they greeted each other noisily, argued with the duty sergeant about car parking, sampled the canteen's bacon sarnies and criticised the coffee. Then they went upstairs and got the juggernaut of their murder inquiry rolling.

Also coopted into the AMIP team was Pat North. She discovered with a small jolt of pleasure – the kind of secret thrill she thought she'd grown too old to feel – that the senior investigating officer, Detective Superintendent Michael Walker, had put in a particular request for her when, late the previous night, he'd been over to see the South Lambeth Divisional Commander and arrange for the reception of his officers. She remembered Walker's words to her when she had last spoken to him, at the end of the Michael Dunn case the previous year: 'I look forward to working with you again.'

Walker was a driven man, a workaholic. Some people would say he wasn't the right stuff to head an AMIP team because he was too hands-on. Other SIOs confined themselves to strategic thinking, handling the deployment of officers, the media and the inquiry budget. But Walker was not a desk jockey; he liked to be out in the field, interviewing suspects, sniffing the evidence. He was a maverick, with a passion for justice and an untidy, competitive, intuitive mind. After the Dunn inquiry, Pat North had seen him a couple of times, but not really to speak to. At odd moments she had remembered things he had said, facial expressions, the way he had smoked. She wondered if he still tore off the tips of his Marlboros before lighting up.

In the Incident Room the list of the victim's clothes was being discussed. It was a pathetically short list.

'We got an ID on her yet?' North asked Brown.

Brown knew perfectly well what she was thinking. After their joint visit to Pinkers, they both realised it was odds on the body was that of the Harrow girl. She was the right physical type and age, and her boyfriend worked at the Snake Pit. And hadn't he made a point of not being there when they found the body? If it was Harrow, Walker's first move would have to be to question Nicky Burton.

'Nothing yet,' said Brown. 'No purse, nothing on the body. Of course, the raincoat fits the description of the type worn by Susie Harrow and the victim wore a wig the same as Susie Harrow's.'

'But it may *not* be her . . .'

Brown shook his head.

'Come on – you were there. You saw her!'

North perused the list, pulling at her lip.

'They found two hundred quid inside her shoe. A lot of toms stuff their earnings there if they're working the streets. But Susie Harrow isn't a hard-bitten slag. She's got a really nice kid and everything . . . Oh, God, I hope it isn't her.'

Brown tried to appreciate the detective inspector's train of thought. But, to be honest, a body had to be someone, didn't it? Why not Susie Harrow?

'Well, maybe it isn't her at all,' said Brown. 'Dr Smith says she thought the body had been dumped a long time.'

They were interrupted by a gruff Glaswegian voice immediately behind him.

'Wrong!'

Brown started and turned, and as his body moved out of the way North saw Walker's face for the first time since the Dunn case. He was looking at her narrow-eyed, intensely. But there was an edge of grim humour in his look.

'The body had severe mutilations,' he went on, 'and the unusually warm weather last week advanced its decomposition.'

Brown mumbled some sort of abashed greeting, but Walker ignored him, nodding at North.

'Sorry to miss you last night.'

Pat North looked at him and smiled.

'Am I staying then?'

'If your guvnor gives you the OK.'

She knew damn well he had. But she wanted to hear it from Walker's own lips. But now he seemed embarrassed, fumbling in his pocket for a smoke, drawing one out and snapping off the filter tip with that familiar, impatient gesture. Brown looked from Walker to North, then moved away to the other side of the room, where he was erecting a large white board. Walker's eyes narrowed even further as he squinted through the smoke.

'Reckon we worked well together on the last one, and besides—'

He ignited the ragged bush of tobacco that protruded from the end of his now unfiltered cigarette.

'I need someone already familiar with the case.'

North nodded.

'Thanks.'

Walker's smile broadened.

'Better the devil you know . . .'

Briefly their eyes met and a flicker of something – but what? – passed between them. Walker seemed almost taken by surprise. Then he looked at his watch. The body would have reached the mortuary by now.

'Right, let's get down to the post-mortem. She's being ID'd now so we've got to get moving. That Delia Smith seemed to know—'

'Delia?' interrupted North. 'You mean Deirdre. Delia's the cordon bleu cook.'

'What?'

Walker hesitated, wondering if Detective Inspector North was taking the piss. He decided not.

'Well, all I know is Delia's pretty meticulous. Whether she can *cook* or not's immaterial to me! You got some photographs of Susan Harrow?'

'Yes.'

'Good. Bring them. And I hope you have a strong stomach.'

Pat North followed him from the Incident Room thoughtfully. They'd been together on a child sex killing; didn't he *know* she had plenty of bottle?

* * *

At the mortuary, Bibi Harrow stood in a small windowless waiting room. She felt that she was at some deep level of the earth, far removed from normal time and space, as if in some kind of a burial chamber beneath the pyramids. The atmosphere was humming almost imperceptibly, and it felt hot. Or was it that she was hot? In the next room, through that anonymous-looking door, was a body, and they were going to take her in there to ask if this was her Susie. Bibi shut her eyes.

'Please, God, let it not be her.'

Almost from the first, Bibi had convinced herself that Susie must have decided she needed a break. Gone off for a small holiday. Maybe she'd met somebody nice at last and *he'd* taken her. She *must* have. Anything else was too painful.

A white-coated assistant came in with Detective Constable Jill Ashton. This was the policewoman who'd come to bring her down and been so kind, the family liaison officer. Bibi said she was ready, steeled herself and then followed them through the door.

There was a narrow table with a shapeless form lying on it, covered by a sheet. Beyond it was a vivid blue stained-glass window or picture, lit from the back but surely not by natural light. Bibi was so disoriented she no longer knew.

With a touch on Bibi's elbow, Ashton indicated that she should stand near one end of the table. The mortuary assistant stood opposite her and reached for the sheet. She glanced towards Bibi, signalling with a lift of her eyebrows: 'Ready?'

Bibi repeated her prayer for it to be someone else and nodded. The girl raised the end of the sheet. Bibi looked.

How could she describe that expression? This was not obviously the face of someone startled, angry, grieved, hurting. It seemed superficially in repose. But underneath, Bibi could see, the face was not peaceful at all but that of someone troubled and in pain. No, no, no. She found herself shaking her head – and then remembered what she was here to do.

Jill whispered, 'Bibi?'

'Yes,' said Bibi, nodding her head now. 'She's my daughter.'

*　*　*

North drove and Walker sat beside her, programming his phone with some of the numbers he would need during the case. For a while they were crawling in traffic, then they were released into a fast stretch before finding themselves back in traffic again. Walker looked at his watch and keyed the code for one of the stored numbers.

'Walker here,' he said crisply. 'I'm on my way with Detective Inspector North . . . OK, what's the result? . . . Uh-huh . . . Right, we'll be there in about fifteen minutes.'

He disconnected the call.

'ID's positive. It's Susan Harrow.'

North kept her eyes on the road. Her heart plunged.

'Where's the little girl? Justine?'

'Don't know.'

'Do you know if Jill Ashton contacted social services?'

Walker shook his head. He was looking out of the window, thinking.

He said, 'What do you think about the boyfriend, Nicky Burton?'

'Well, he's been done for pimping, served time for drug dealing and she's his girlfriend – or was. But is he that stupid? The body was dumped right beside the club he works at.'

Walker shook his head.

'Right little scumbag like that, though. Who knows, he might be clever. Might have been playing the double-bluff: you don't think I'd ever be daft enough to dump her body right where I work, so I'll dump her body right where I work.'

When they arrived at the mortuary, Walker led the way unerringly along a series of corridors and showed her the gowning room. Then, dressed in overalls and overshoes, they went through a door marked MORTUARY, where preparations for the post-mortem examination were well advanced. The room was brightly strip-lit and severely functional. In its centre, on one of the trolleys, lay the subject, covered by a white plastic sheet. Two pathology assistants were busy laying the surgical instruments onto trays with a busy clatter. Standing to one side were Dave Palmer, Tony Jenetta and another officer holding a camcorder.

'Want to see why we have to work fast?' asked Walker.

He moved towards the trolley and beckoned severely to the nearest assistant.

'Lift the sheet away.'

The assistant looked at his colleague and back at Walker. He seemed peeved but you did not argue with Walker in this mood. He leaned across the body and peeled back the sheet. But before North could move forward, there was a flurry of activity around the door and the pathologist, Dr John Foster, swept in. The assistant who had been caught holding the sheet tried to cover his tracks.

'No one's supposed to have access to the subject—'

Foster looked across and cut through the words. He was not in the best of moods himself.

'This one's going to take all day. With the amount of mutilation and decomposition, I'll need time. Dr Smith had her on site long enough, I'd say. Let's get on with it!'

Walker beckoned again, this time to Pat North.

'Like to know why we have no time to waste?'

Walker was studying the trolley's burden. Hesitantly, North moved to his side and tried to look with equal steadiness at

Susie Harrow's body. The sight made her gorge rise. Her voice would not operate louder than a whisper.

'What kind of madness does this?'

Walker was still looking almost ferociously, as if trying to imprint the horrifying sight on his mind. His voice was a growl.

'The kind that's going to do it again.'

It is usual nowadays for the senior investigating officer, and deputy, to attend the post-mortem of a murder victim. Accordingly, Walker and North stayed until fully eight o'clock, at which point, with Foster finished at last, Walker whispered a suggestion that they go for a drink. But on the way to the pub his mobile rang and he moved aside to answer it. Although he was obviously making an effort to keep his voice low, she could hear the strain in it. There was some crisis at home and Walker was not very happy. He closed the phone.

'Sorry, Pat. I've got to go. Really sorry. I can tell you, I needed that drink, after what we went through back there. Want a lift anywhere?'

'No, no. I'm fine. I'll get the Tube home. Need an early night anyway.'

'See you at the factory tomorrow then. Briefing's at eight.'

'Goodnight, guv.'

As she walked to the Underground station, she thought about him. There had been something in his face, a tension and almost a pain, which she found fascinating. Walker usually showed nothing.

And as she let herself into her flat half an hour later – an empty flat in which she had been living alone since Graham had gone off with his dental hygienist – she was still thinking about him.

CHAPTER 6

FRIDAY 24 APRIL. MORNING

'The victim has now been identified as the prostitute Susan Harrow,' said Walker, standing in front of a large board on which were displayed photographs of the victim both in life and in death. 'She was reported missing last Friday and DI North here investigated the victim's original disappearance exactly one week ago. DI North will be staying with us for the duration of the inquiry.'

He nodded at North and she noted again that half-smile and his narrowing eyes before he swivelled back towards the board. Some of the images displayed were hard to look at for very long. One or two of the fresher members of the team – not least the locally coopted pair, Phelps and Henshaw – simply found it difficult to look.

'This one is the worst I've seen in my entire career. I won't have the preliminary report from the post-mortem until this afternoon, but, having seen the victim, it's obvious she's been tortured.'

He looked slowly around, trying to meet the eyes of every officer in the room, as if to impress on them the full horror of this case.

'We don't have much to go on – just two lines of inquiry worth a damn. First, I want the witness Shiree Moyer reinterviewed. In her statement she says she last saw the victim talking to a possible punter, driving some kind of white van. The van is our first and most important lead. You got anything on it, Dave?'

He looked towards Detective Sergeant David Satchell, his closest professional partner. Satchell was a handsome, confident, capable detective and had been Walker's right-hand man for the past three years. As both of them knew, since the Bishopsgate and Canary Wharf bombings, the movements of vans around the capital had been of particular interest to the police and the detective sergeant had been in touch with the Divisional Intelligence Unit about possible vehicle checks.

'DIU are checking Crimint for recent vehicle stops which might fit the description. All divisions have been notified that we're looking for a white van.'

'Good,' said Walker. 'Now the second starting point for the inquiry has to be the boyfriend and what she did on the day she went missing. We're going to go back and talk to Nicky Burton. We've got to find out if she was in the club that night. We will also go back to the pub she worked in *and* the massage parlour. We will start again and turn her life over.'

A buzz of conversation arose which Walker quelled with a raised hand.

'One thing I want you all to remember. Susie Harrow was a prostitute, yes. That's an important fact for us because it determines how we proceed with the inquiry. But all of you bear in mind . . .'

He gestured again towards the exhibition of gruesome photographs behind him.

'. . . we have no private feelings about the importance or otherwise of this victim. Whether it's a brass or baroness is the same to us. This was a young person who had a mother of her own and also a child of her own. Just imagine what that mother's feeling today – and that child. So don't let me catch any of you treating this like the death of another worn-out old tom, OK? Now, let's get moving.'

* * *

Walker had to attend court in the morning, but first he asked North to drive him over to the waste ground where the body had been found. He wanted a look at the site again and to have a talk with Deirdre Smith. On arrival, Jenetta, the crime scene coordinator, was the first to greet them.

'Dr Smith here?' asked Walker, striding towards Jenetta.

'Yes, sir. Just there.'

They found her, a small figure in overalls, concealed by a heap of rusty once-white goods, a couple of fridges and a tumble dryer. She was crouching over something on the ground. Nearby a couple of scene of crime officers were combing the ground and DC Palmer, the exhibits officer, was taking Polaroids, while a third SOCO crouched a few yards away, bagging some find.

Walker approached Dr Smith, who greeted him cheerily.

'Morning. We've more or less finished here. We've not found much for you, I'm afraid.'

'Oh?'

'No. I'd say without doubt she was dumped, not killed in the area.'

Walker nodded. He hadn't worked with Deirdre Smith before. She looked like nothing so much as a housewife. But Dr Smith had a reputation for being incisive and she was a priceless asset in court: barristers were wrong-footed and juries thought she was Hetty Wainthropp.

'What kind of weapon should we be looking for, would you say?'

Dr Smith stood up, smoothing the rucked-up overall down over her plump form.

'Well, judging from the cuts to the clothing and body, I'd say a knife. I've got some loose fibres taken off that barbed-wire fence over there. Could be to do with her. Or the perpetrator. But I understand the area was frequented by local prostitutes.'

They stood with the taped outline of the body, as it had been found lying the previous night, between them. Walker looked at it.

'Her name was Susan Harrow.'

'Ah, good. She's been identified.'

Smith sounded as pleased as if Detective Superintendent Walker had discovered a new recipe for ice cream.

'I'd like access to her home, please.'

Pat North, who had stopped to talk with DS Jenetta, joined them just in time to hear the request and Walker's look of annoyance. She cut in.

'We've already been. There's nothing there.'

Dr Smith smiled.

'Oh, yes, there is. No offence, but there always is. The difference being, I know what I'm looking for.'

* * *

Brown returned to Pinkers, this time with Dave Satchell. Monica Fuller greeted them as if they were punters, with a wide, white smile – until she recognised Brown.

'Mrs Fuller, you'll remember me,' he said, showing her his warrant card. 'DS Brown. And this is DS Satchell. We're investigating—'

Mrs Fuller's face froze, then her smile drained slowly away.

'Look, as I told your colleague, I haven't seen Susie for days – well, it's a week now. If she's in some kind of trouble, it's nothing to do with me. I—'

Brown broke in, a warning tone in his voice.

'Mrs Fuller, Susan's body was found dumped on waste ground on Wednesday night.'

Mrs Fuller faltered, her mouth dropping open.

'I'm sorry? What did you . . .'

'Susie's dead. We believe murdered. I'm sorry, but would you mind answering a few questions?'

'Oh, my God! I had no . . . I mean, I never . . .'

'Yes, well. We need to trace all her clients. Ones from here – you know, maybe the private ones?'

Monica Fuller shook her head. She was struggling to understand.

'What? You think I've got their addresses listed?'

'Haven't you?'

'Well, if I did, you think they'd give their real names?'

Brown leaned across the reception desk, speaking gently.

'This is very important. Can you just give us a little list?'

The manageress sat without moving for a moment. She had got over the worst of the shock and her mind was beginning to function again. She said nothing.

'Well, did she have any particular friends among the girls?' asked Satchell. 'Anyone we can speak to?'

'Well, Shiree's here. Shiree Moyer. She and Susie were close.'

Satchell and Brown exchanged a glance.

Brown said, 'And the clients list?'

'All right, all right! I'll take you in to talk to Shiree. And I'll try to give you a list of her regulars – the ones I know of!'

* * *

Shiree took the news badly. For days she had been trying out in her mind all the possible reasons why Susie might have dropped out of sight. She'd finally settled on the one that gave her most comfort. Sooze must have done a runner with a wealthy punter – to Barbados most likely. That's what she, Shiree, would do given half a chance, so why not Susie? The two of them had fantasised about it often enough. But now she was facing the reality of that darker alternative which she had previously pushed firmly into the recesses of her mind.

For the first minute she sat without speaking, her face blank. For the next three minutes she howled, her face grotesquely distorted, tears and mucus all over her face until Satchell gave her a tissue. Then for another minute she was silent, calming herself, breathing deeply and then shakily lighting a cigarette. When Satchell asked her to go over the events of the evening on which she had last seen Susie, she was ready.

It had been a normal session, nothing unusual at all. They had both seen quite a few clients. She herself had had one man with terrible BO, but Susie hadn't as far as she could remember discussed any of her clients. They'd left the place almost together, Susie saying she didn't want to go for a drink. And then there was Shiree's taxi and Susie's white van.

'We want to know what make of van it was,' Satchell told her. 'I've got some pictures here of various types.'

He passed a small sheaf of photographs to Shiree, who blankly thumbed through them.

'Please think hard, Miss Moyer. Because this is very important.'

'I'm trying to, sod you! But I don't know. I only saw it for a few seconds and to be honest they all look alike to me. It was quite big though, not like a delivery van if you know what I mean. I . . . I . . .'

She ground to a halt, handing the photographs back. Satchell tried to get her to take them again.

'Just take your time. We'll go through them once more. Just try and remember everything you can.'

Shiree sighed deeply and lit another cigarette.

'I am. But like I said, I got this taxi. It stopped and I opened the door and I sort of turned, just to wave goodbye. I didn't think . . . I mean you wouldn't, would you? I just got in and we drove off.'

She was crying again now.

Satchell said, 'Did she get into the van? Did you see her get in?'

Shiree shook her head.

'No. Last I saw she was talking to the driver. That's it.'

Satchell held out the bundle of photographs and spoke very gently.

'Just look at the vans again, Shiree. It's the one thing you can do to help Susie, eh?'

So Shiree took hold of the pictures and began slowly to go through them one more time.

*   *   *

As they left Pinkers, Monica Fuller passed Brown a handwritten list of names, some with telephone numbers. There were no addresses. Back at the station, he gave the list to one of the clerical staff to put onto the system, along with the information, such as it was, that they'd got from Shiree Moyer. Meanwhile, Satchell collected DC Jack Hutchens and they drove to Nicky Burton's place.

The reception they received was predictably hostile.

'You still on about Susie?'

Walker had asked Bibi Harrow not to have any contact with her daughter's boyfriend until the police could see him again. Walker wanted it to be Satchell who gave Nicky the news that he no longer had a girlfriend. His initial reaction would be crucial to how he was treated in future – as a suspect or a grieving relative – and no one was better than Dave Satchell when it came to gauging the weight and quality of human reactions.

Now Nicky seemed tired, hungover. His scowl slackened as if he couldn't be bothered to maintain it. He even invited them in.

'Look, I already told you,' he said as they went through into a dark, overfurnished living room. 'Susie don't live here or nothing.'

Nicky switched off the electronically enhanced, digitally remixed derivative of reggae that was pulsing from the speakers of a powerful Swedish hi-fi. Then he turned to face the police. He was certainly nervous.

'I've said this over and over, right? I last saw her on that Wednesday night and that's it. She's not called. She's not come round for more than a week now.'

He picked up a gold chain which lay on the low glass-topped coffee table and tossed it up and down in his hand as he glared at Satchell. Suddenly a measure of his anger returned.

'Why don't you bastards come clean? If you're trying to lay living off immoral earnings on me, then screw you!'

So that's what he thought was going on. It didn't preclude the chance that Burton had killed Susie. Perhaps he had pimped for her a bit, on the side. Not so much now, maybe, because Pinkers didn't look at all Nicky Burton's sort of scene. But what if he had wanted to get her back on the game for him and she'd refused?

Satchell looked steadily into Nicky's eyes, which were flicking between the two policemen. Then he said in a soft voice, 'Mr Burton, I'm sorry to have to tell you, but Susan Harrow is dead.'

Nicky's face went blank. He had heard the words but it was as if they wouldn't compute.

'What? Say that again.'

'She was found late on Wednesday night behind the Snake Pit Club. You work there, I believe.'

'You mean . . . that woman found out back of the club? That was never . . . You mean that was *Susie*?'

He was staring, eyes very wide. Satchell noted every change in his expression, every twitch and blink.

'I'm sorry.'

'No! That was some junkie, wasn't it? Someone who OD'd!'

'No, and it wasn't drugs, sir. She was murdered. And we're trying to find out who did it to her.'

Suddenly Burton looked young and bewildered. His eyes were staring.

'But that was just some woman. It wasn't Susie! Not Susie! That couldn't be Susie!'

'Mrs Harrow identified her yesterday evening. There isn't any doubt.'

Nicky sank down onto the leather sofa, letting drop the gold chain. He lay back and closed his eyes, but not in repose. The muscles of his face were squeezed tight in pain and denial. Satchell continued to watch him shrewdly, but he already knew he was looking at an innocent man. There was no question in his mind. Nicky Burton was not acting. He was hearing this news for the first time.

CHAPTER 7

FRIDAY 24 APRIL. AFTERNOON

Walker was back in South Lambeth in time to grab a sandwich from the canteen, which he ate while North drove. They were due at the pathology labs at two for a recap of the post-mortem's findings. After rapidly devouring his meal he called Dr Smith. She was not available. He then called Detective Sergeant Satchell.

'Dave, you get anything from the massage place?'

Satchell passed on a full account of the Pinkers visit. As he listened, Walker grunted occasionally but said nothing. He shut off the phone, just as North was sliding the car into an empty space in the pathology labs' car park. On their way towards the main entrance, Walker gave her the gist.

'No joy on the tart who saw the white van, but they have got a list of Harrow's clients – ones that used the massage parlour.'

'Anything come in from the pub she worked at?'

'Not yet. She worked hard and was well liked. That's all we got so far. The client list looks like a priority, but it'll take well into next week to find everyone. Brown's running the names through the computer now, see if there's anyone screaming for our attention.'

Dr Foster was waiting for them in his office.

'Right, if you want a recap I'll have to try and work all this newfangled equipment. It's supposed to reduce the length of time spent over the cadavers but, quite frankly, fathoming it has been nerve-racking.'

His reluctance was really a blind. Delighted at this chance to show off the new computerised system for post-mortem photographs and results, he sat down in front of the terminal and, using a mouse, clicked the screen. A menu came up. He clicked again and the image of Susan Harrow's body, laid out on the operating trolley, filled it. More clicks brought a series of close-ups showing the injuries to the body.

'Right, she's been dead for less time than I first thought. The open wounds and the unusually warm weather last week speeded up decomposition.'

'When do you think she was killed?' Walker wanted to know. It was what all policemen always, and above all, wanted and needed to know.

'Obviously I can't give an exact time. But as you know, the contents of her stomach can be a guide and let's see . . . She ate a substantial meal, a curry, which has been there just over a week.'

He clicked through a few more images and pages of text and found one he wanted the two detectives to look at. It showed Susie Harrow's hands, with their long red nail extensions.

'Now look here. No sign of skin or human blood beneath the nails – they're all intact and exceptionally long. No nail varnish chipped either, so she didn't claw her attacker.'

Another image showed the victim's wrists.

'She has distinctive clamp-like markings here, on her left wrist. Looks like she'd been handcuffed.'

'And on the right wrist too?' asked Walker.

Foster shook his head.

'No, just the one wrist. But there are heavy bruises caused by finger grips on both forearms. In addition, both knees were grazed, maybe carpet burns. And she had bruising on the backs of both thighs. I'd say she was forced into a kneeling position – forensics might have some fibres for you.'

More clicks and they were suddenly looking at the gashed and bloody remains of Susie's breasts.

'OK, now . . . quite terrible as you can see. The victim is minus her left breast, with the right one severely slashed . . . She also had severe bruising around the neck and she has a 25-centimetre-long slice almost from ear to ear, right to left. It was probably done by an exceptionally sharp knife, thin-bladed. It must have been long too. The cuts are quite clean. Below and around the ribcage there are heavy bruises about the size of a toecap, and several ribs are broken.'

'In other words, she was kicked.' said Walker.

Foster did not reply but clicked again.

'Now, this is the worst part – although you can't see it fully on screen. Her vagina was assaulted by some kind of very sharp instrument. It's a deeply incised wound and it has almost sliced through the abdominal wall from the vagina upwards.'

He clicked again, showing a view of the body cavity opened up.

'A general examination of the vital organs shows they are pale, which suggests she bled to death. But interestingly enough . . .'

With another click he brought up a shot of Susie's face.

'Here, on the face, she was untouched. Except, you can just see, above the right ear – a largish clump of hair has been torn out by the roots. Has it been found anywhere?'

Walker shook his head.

'I didn't think it would be. It's been done deliberately anyway.'

'Why?' asked North.

'I wouldn't know,' said Foster. 'And I never speculate.'

'What about semen?' asked Walker. 'Any sign?'

Foster clicked through to a checklist of samples sent for analysis.

'Can't tell yet. All swabs and samples are still with forensics, they might know by now. We also removed small splinters of wood from the vagina and intestine which are with them also.'

Rather deliberately, Foster took off his glasses and twisted around to look at Walker.

'All in all – and this is not speculation – whoever did this is about as sick as they come, Mike.'

'Yeah,' Walker grunted. 'Tell me about it.'

And then his phone rang. It was Dr Smith to say she could see him now.

* * *

For a woman who had spent at least twenty hours over the past two days combing the waste ground and Susie Harrow's flat, Dr Smith looked as cheerful as Pollyanna and as fresh as morning flowers.

'Detective Superintendent Walker, Detective Inspector North, I welcome you to my lair.'

She led them through to her office, past benches where white-coated assistants peered into comparison microscopes and took spectrometer readings. She picked up a pile of computer print-outs.

'I can give you a strictly interim report. There's still quite a lot of biochemical analysis and especially DNA profiling to be done.'

'You got a lot of samples to test from the flat?'

'No. As I said this morning, there was little enough at the waste-ground site and, disappointingly, the victim's flat was the same. Did you see the place?'

North nodded.

'Then you'll remember it was very clean and well maintained.'

Walker wanted to know about the traces found on the body. Dr Smith puffed out her cheeks.

'The fibres taken from the girl's knees don't match any of the carpet at her flat. They're from a different type of coarse, heavy-duty, commercial-quality carpet. It's the kind often used inside vehicles.'

'Was there anything on the clothes? The ones she was wearing?'

Smith beamed at him.

'Yes, good news! We found semen on the clothes!'

'And?'

She shrugged.

'It's just semen. I can't tell you anything more yet. I've sub-mitted it for DNA testing. We also found these on her skirt.'

She pointed to a microscope slide on her desk.

'Several strands of a fibre in three colours: red, green and blue. They could well have come from the clothing of her attacker, but I won't continue with this fibre examination until I have something to compare it with. No point.'

'Could she have been killed at the flat?'

Smith shook her head.

'In my opinion it's highly unlikely. There are no traces of blood whatsoever and, believe me, there would have been. She would have bled extensively. Now what else?'

She thumbed through the sheaf of documents.

'Ah, yes, I'm also looking at some slivers of wood sent here following the PM. They were found inside the victim. We're looking to see what type of wood they are. We're also looking for any semen on the internal swabs. Nothing so far.'

'Any ideas about these wood splinters?'

Smith shrugged. 'The preliminary PM report indicated that the injuries may have been caused by a weapon shaped like an arrowhead. It was pushed into her, twisted and pulled out. Very unpleasant. The wood may have come from the shaft, which means it was rough wood. He's good, Foster. Doesn't miss much. Oh! By the way, we found this at the site this morning.'

She gave Walker an exhibits bag containing a battered woman's watch.

'You might like to find out if it belonged to the victim. If so, it seems likely it stopped after it was smashed in the attack, in which case you have a possible time of death . . .'

She looked at the watch face through the transparent plastic.

'Not to mention a date – 16th April, eleven forty p.m. How's that for a result?'

CHAPTER 8

SATURDAY 25 APRIL

Going over to see Bibi Harrow at ten the next morning, Walker and North took with them Detective Constable Jill Ashton. As family liaison officer Ashton was skilled in bereavement support and at softening the seemingly hard demands made by officers pursuing a murder inquiry. But she also had a crucial role to play in building up a picture of the victim's family and relationships: the police are always aware of the statistics which show that a high percentage of murderers are known by their victims. She sat next to Bibi on the sofa and gently explained what they hoped this morning's interview would achieve. Bibi, crying, smoking and sipping her tea, agreed that all she wanted was for the man, whoever he was, to be caught.

'Before it happened, everything was OK. Now this man has not just destroyed my Susie's life, he's ruined Justine's life too. I don't know what's worse. He will be caught, won't he, Mr Walker?'

Walker nodded several times. From somewhere in the flat – a bedroom? – he caught the unmistakable sound of television, of American cartoons.

'Oh, yes, Mrs Harrow. Don't doubt it. Could you just take us over the last evening you saw your daughter alive? The Thursday evening?'

Bibi squared her shoulders and lit another cigarette.

'OK. Well, I don't get in from work until about a quarter to six. Susie came round with Justine at about six. Maybe a little later. She had some clothes for Justine and some fruit and stuff, you know . . .'

Her voice trembled. Thinking of the ordinary, unremarkable things her daughter had done in the last hours of her life – that was the hardest. She took a deep breath.

'Anyway . . . she left her overnight bag. She said she'd stay over, you see, so I made up this . . .'

She touched the cushion she was sitting on.

'It's a sofa-bed.'

'May I see her overnight bag, please, Mrs Harrow?'

'It's there.'

She pointed to a small grip which had been placed discreetly by the wall. Walker rose and fetched it. He held it in his fingers delicately.

'May I open it?'

Bibi nodded. Walker slipped the bag open and felt inside. He pulled out a skirt, a nightdress, a set of clean underwear. It was at this point that Walker realised it would have been more delicate to have let Detective Inspector North search the bag, but there was no going back now. A pair of tights, a blouse, a wash-bag. In a little zip-up case was Susie Harrow's make-up. In the washbag were toothbrush, toothpaste, dental floss, shampoo, condoms. That was all. He carefully put everything back.

'Did Susie say where she was going for the evening?' he asked.

Bibi sniffed.

'To work of course. Sometimes she had to stay late, evening shift . . .'

She was staring over at the sideboard, on which were a small selection of framed photographs – Susie as a schoolgirl in her uniform, Susie posing on a seaside pier, Susie holding up a diploma.

'I know what they're saying about her, but I don't believe it. She was a good girl – a good mother! She always was good and it's not true, not true, that she was a – a pro. She wasn't. I mean, I'm her mother. I'd have known.'

Very gently, North put her hand on Bibi's forearm.

'We'll need a list of all her friends – that you know of.'

The woman gave a tiny snort.

'Friends? She hardly had time to socialise! She was always working. She got no child support, you know. She paid for everything herself. Always so *nicely* turned out too . . .'

She started crying again, snuffling and groaning as she tried to stop herself.

'I don't know what I'm going to do – about Justine. I don't know what I'm going to do!'

'Mrs Harrow – Bibi,' said North. 'I'm so sorry, there's one more thing about Susie. Do you know what kind of handbag she was carrying that night? Only we've not found one.'

'I don't know . . .'

Bibi thought for a moment.

'I think it was black, a shoulder strap one . . . I don't know, but I *think* so.'

Suddenly the door swung open and Justine walked in. She was still wearing a nightdress.

'Nana, when's Mummy coming home?'

Bibi did not answer but she held out her arms and Justine snuggled into her grandmother's lap.

North said, 'Bibi, will you allow one of the Child Protection Team to talk to Justine?'

'Child Protection? What, are you taking her away from me?'

'No, no. Nothing like that. We should ask her some questions, but we ourselves are not allowed to interview her.'

'What about you, Jill? Can't you do it?'

Jill shook her head.

North said, 'Afraid she can't. Her job is family liaison but not specifically children. CPT are there for that, specially trained.'

Walker smiled, as reassuringly as he could.

'And don't worry. We'll be close by and she'll come to no harm. Sometimes the procedures we're forced to follow make our job very complicated but—'

North intercepted the moment of hesitation.

'There's a good reason for them, Bibi. And Justine'll be very well looked after.'

Bibi looked down at her hands. There was a hideous crashing sound from the distant television as she nodded her head.

'All right then. When do you want to do it?'

They wanted to do it that very afternoon, before Justine's young memory banks were permanently wiped.

*　*　*

A plethora of violent assaults, sexual abuse, alleged Satanism and murder by so-called (but ill-named) paedophiles over the past decade has obliged the Metropolitan Police to take children more seriously, and treat them more carefully, than ever before. There is a climate of sympathy towards children, but this is not the whole story. Their evidence is subject to intense scrutiny in court because it can so easily be contaminated by clumsy questioning: many children spend their lives trying to supply whatever answer they believe is wanted – not the same thing at all as the truth.

This is why there are now twenty-seven Child Protection Teams in the Metropolitan Police area, each led by a detective inspector. For many police officers a two-year stint in a CPT will be seen as useful on their CV, but many applicants are surprised to find themselves refused. Aggressive thief-taking, Cracker-style mind-gaming, brilliant hot-pursuit driving – these are achievements to make a hero of an officer. But not in Child Protection. There the emphasis is on sensitivity and patience. A video camera ensures that the child's expression and body language are also recorded.

The interview of Justine Harrow took place at one of the houses specially equipped for the purpose. In a video control room with a one-way window, DC Ashton sat with the recording technician. They listened to Justine talking to a member of the CPT, a sympathetic woman calculated to look as ordinary as possible. The child was kneeling on the floor in front of a low table on which paper, paints and brushes were laid out. She was painting a landscape with a prominent tree. A social worker sat silently to one side.

'Mummy never come to me at school and I got a taxi all by myself,' said Justine, as she rubbed her brush in the paint and applied it to the big red tree.

'Did you? So you remember that day, do you?'

'Yes. Mrs Hully come to the school gate. She said where's your mummy?'

'On the day before your mother didn't collect you,' said the policewoman, 'can you tell me if anyone was at home in the morning before you left for school with your mummy?'

Carefully, and with her tongue sticking out, Justine was painting green dots all over the tree.

'Nicky gave me my Game Boy.'

'Nicky? Who's that then?'

'Mummy's friend. He give me a Game Boy and spilled all the orange juice at breakfast. Mum got angry and they had a big fight.'

'So how come Nicky was having breakfast with you?'

'He stayed over.'

She put down her brush, looking around her. There were two plates of biscuits in the middle of the table.

'Can I have a chocolate one? I don't like the custardy ones.'

'Yes, of course. Take one. What were you saying about Nicky?'

'He stays lots.'

She bit her biscuit and chewed. 'He works late at night and he wakes me up when he comes in . . .'

She stopped eating for a moment, concentrating. You could see that the scene was in the front of her mind: Nicky creaking past her room in his leathers, calling for her mummy, who comes out of the bathroom shushing him up, saying, 'You'll wake the *kid*!'

Justine knit her brow. It was a long time since she had seen Mummy. Why? She looked at the CPT officer. 'Do *you* know the answer?' she asked 'Where *is* my mummy?'

* * *

Walker called a meeting that evening to review progress and exchange the day's information. North thought he was edgy, impatient. Walker had once confided to her that, for him, the early stages of an investigation could be the most interesting. He was still faced with the unknown, all things were possible. But if suppressed excitement usually stoked up Walker's work rate, the effect was missing tonight. He was tired, thought North. Something extracurricular was bugging him.

'Now, I'll keep this brief and I'll start with the most important thing,' he said to the assembled team in the Incident Room.

'We've got confirmation that the watch found at the site was Susan Harrow's. So now we know she died around eleven forty p.m. on Thursday 16th April.'

He looked around. Several of the officers were jotting notes.

'The second thing is, the last sighting of the victim we have is eleven ten that night, looking as if she was picking up a punter in a white van.'

On the wall behind him was an array of vans. Walker tapped them.

'The witness Shiree Moyer can't say much more, but thinks it might be one or other of these. OK, third. We're checking out her regular clients from the massage parlour. Those she'd seen that night. One had a nail extension, another, a Mr Smith, was in for massage and hand-relief. He's a regular who they all know about – every Thursday. We're following up the rest of them. OK – anything else?'

He looked around.

North said, 'We've got a bit of a development on the boyfriend, Nicky Burton. According to his statement, he didn't see the victim after Wednesday night. But the little girl, the daughter Justine, told the CPT he stayed overnight and left on Thursday morning.'

Walker didn't think much of it.

'That's not much use. How old is she – five?'

'Why would the child lie? Or Nicky Burton?'

Walker sighed. He knew that Satchell didn't fancy the boyfriend as a murderer, but would have to admit there was a discrepancy.

'Bring him in and let's find out. Right . . .'

He looked at his watch.

'That's me done for tonight! Pat?'

He gave way to Pat North, wandering over to the display boards and the grim story they told of Susie Harrow's last forty minutes of life. North raised her voice to quell the buzz of conversation as the team began to think of the pub.

'Look, one more thing for you all to ponder on. We need to find her handbag. I've got only an approximate description but it could be black with a shoulder strap.'

She shrugged.

'OK, I know – there's a million like that out there, but it's all we have. Now, that's it, everyone. Get yourselves home and tucked up next to him and her indoors. We all need our sleep!'

She squared her sheet of paper and then walked over to her desk, passing Walker, whose back was still turned to the room.

She said, 'You still here? I was just wondering . . .'

He swung round and she could see how tired he was – but it was too early in the inquiry for that. What was the matter with him? She plugged on.

'Have you spoken to the press office? Only we do need to put something out to trace this van.'

Walker snapped his fingers. He had forgotten.

'Deal with it for me, would you? Only I've got a terrible headache just now.'

He was looking around the room, hardly attending to her. He raised his hand.

'Oi, Satchell! Fancy a pint?'

She saw Dave Satchell give the thumbs-up as he shrugged into his coat. The two men set off on a converging path towards the door.

North said, 'Which pub are you going to?'

She must have spoken too gently, too hesitantly. At any rate, they seemed not to hear as they passed out through the swing doors.

She shut her eyes in frustration and opened them again. She saw Henshaw.

'Henshaw! Can you get on to the press office. See if we can do a *Crimewatch* – you know, "Have you seen a white van?" etc.'

Brown walked past.

'Now, it was a busy street,' he said, intoning in the singsong manner of a television presenter. 'And *not* very late at night. So if *you* walked down that road and saw anything suspicious, *or* out of the ordinary, please give us a call . . .'

'Oh, God, give us a break!' said Palmer, balling up a computer print-out and hurling it at Brown. 'Has no one told you yet? It's a lousy impersonation.'

Brown headed the paper onto the photocopier and leapt in the air, celebrating. Henshaw was on the phone to a press officer as the room gradually emptied, leaving Pat North sitting alone and wondering which reports she should take home.

CHAPTER 9

MONDAY 27 APRIL. MORNING

Bibi's employer had given her compassionate leave. She didn't know how long they would indulge her – a week at most, she thought – but in the meantime she had many things to do, the sad, tidying-up things that on these occasions are left to a mother. She asked Jill Ashton if she would be allowed to go over to Susie's place and start to pack up some of her possessions.

'Yes, the police and various scientists have been all over it now. Would you like me to come over with you?'

'Oh would you, dear? It would be so helpful. You know, I'm not sure I'm brave enough to go alone.'

'Well, there is something we can do while we're there as a matter of fact,' said Ashton. 'That's have a look through Susie's various handbags. We need a description of the one she was using on that last day. It might help jog your memory to look through her other bags.'

'Oh dear. Well, if you like . . .'

The flat had the dusty quietness of all uninhabited dwellings. There was a pile of junk mail on the hall floor and an unopened copy of Saturday's *Express* – the only edition Susie used to have delivered. Bibi had not bothered to look at any of the papers' coverage of the case, so it came as a shock to read the enormous headline: PROSTITUTE FOUND BRUTALLY MURDERED. In slightly smaller type it read BODY OF SUSAN HARROW DUMPED IN WASTE LAND.

She let the pile of letters fall as she read the article, her face contorting with anger and grief.

'They got no right, no right! Calling my daughter a *tart*.'

Ashton moved to take the paper gently from Bibi's trembling hands.

'I'm sorry, Bibi. I really am. Come on, let's go and sit down for a bit, eh? Would you like a cup of coffee? Tea?'

Bibi allowed herself to be led to the sofa.

'I'll bloody sue them. They got *no* right!'

* * *

Nicky Burton had gone to the police station voluntarily, wearing his dark glasses, jogging-pants and a torn T-shirt. He was making a good job of appearing to be only half interested in what Walker was putting to him, lolling in his chair, fiddling with his gold neck chain and jiggling his knees.

'We just need to clarify some details from your previous statement, Mr Burton. You said you had not seen Miss Harrow since the Wednesday night. But Justine told us you were there on the Thursday morning.'

Nicky showed a lot of teeth when he smiled. He was suddenly cooperative.

'Look, I was just pissed off when I said that, right? I didn't know she was dead! I just thought you were coming after me, like you's always doing.'

Walker studied him and spoke very deliberately.

'So are you now saying that you were lying? That you *did* see Miss Harrow on Thursday?'

'Morning, yeah. I stayed over at her place Wednesday night.'

'And what time did you leave Miss Harrow's flat?'

Nicky shrugged and opened his hands out, miming a certain amount of latitude for himself.

'Breakfast time. When she took the kid to school.'

'And did she tell you her plans for the day?'

'No.'

'Did you part on good terms?'

Nicky looked down. He was jiggling his knees again.

'Did you?' repeated Walker.

'Look, man. We had a stupid argument because I spilled some orange juice. She was like that. She hated for anyone to mess up her beautiful neat flat . . . Yeah, that was the last time . . . that was the last time I saw her, OK?'

And Walker could have sworn he saw a glint of a tear through the dark lenses of Nicky's shades.

* * *

By Monday morning, as well as the massage client 'Mr Smith' already located by Satchell on Saturday, another of the massage customers seen by Susie Harrow on the day she died had been found and interviewed. He was quickly eliminated from the inquiry which left one remaining, a Mr Slater, who had given Pinkers a daytime contact number. It was a direct office line which, over the weekend, was unattended except by voicemail. This gave the information: *You have reached the voicemail of Thomas Slater. Please press the star button for special sending options.* Unfortunately none of these options included connection to Thomas Slater's home address, but a reverse directory check showed that the number was registered to a solicitors' practice, Smith, Brown and Asquith. At ten thirty on Monday morning, Satchell and Brown paid Mr Slater's office a visit.

The receptionist sat them down in comfortable sofas and offered them coffee. She was a blonde with the kind of looks that earn fortunes in fashion magazines.

'Mr Slater's in a meeting but he'll be with you shortly,' she said, flashing them an orthodontically brilliant smile.

She clipped back to her desk on platform shoes. While her back was turned, Brown gave Satchell a theatrical nudge.

For the next twenty minutes they just listened to her. The job seemed to consist almost entirely of typing at her computer keyboard in between putting on an artificially cheerful voice in response to her constantly chirruping phone.

'Hello, Smith, Brown and Asquith? . . . Certainly, I'll put you through . . . Smith, Brown and Asquith? . . . Yes, putting you through . . .'

'Will we have to wait much longer?' asked Satchell, when he'd heard enough of this tinkling litany.

'Mr Slater has another appointment, I'm afraid.'

She had not seemed put off by the fact that they were police officers, but nor had she seemed interested until this moment. Now, in a pause between chirrups, she asked, 'Is this to do with parking tickets?'

Satchell got up and fixed her with a severe look.

'No, it isn't anything to do with parking tickets. Look, we've been very patient so far, but we'd like to see Mr Slater – now!'

There was a click from the inner door and, as if on cue, a dapper man in a business suit appeared, ushering out a client. As the client was holding out his hand to shake goodbye, Satchell said, a shade aggressively, 'Mr Slater? Detective Sergeant Satchell, and this is Detective Sergeant Brown, South Lambeth Street police station.'

'Er, yes?'

'We are investigating the murder of Susan Harrow. You may have seen something about it on the weekend news.'

The client lowered his proffered hand and stared. Slater looked uncomprehending. The receptionist did not stop typing, but Brown noticed her looking sharply across at Slater, who had turned white. Then the client was already halfway to the door, moving almost at a scuttle. The murder squad! Wait till he told the chaps at his office.

Slater looked shifty. He waited until the client had gone and then said, 'What on earth has that got to do with me?'

Satchell did not spare him in front of his employee.

'I understand you were a regular client of hers.'

'Oh, I . . . well, er, you'd better come straight in. You see, this is perfectly easy to explain, so won't you just come through to my office, where we can talk in comfort?'

* * *

They had taken most of the bags out of the wardrobe and laid them on the bed. There were loop-handled bags, shoulder-strap bags, evening bags in a variety of sizes, colours and styles.

'I remember,' Bibi was saying, staring at the display.

'It was a black leather shoulder bag she had, with a gold clasp in the shape of a tiger, a kind of leaping tiger. I remember it now. It was leather-lined as well. There were gold links on the strap.'

Ashton snapped open a PVC evening bag, squinting at the manufacturer's label.

'Do you know the make? Did Susie ever mention it?'

Bibi thought briefly and shook her head.

'No. It might have been Italian. But they all sound Italian, don't they, even if they're not? But it was expensive, I do know that. She was always well turned out.'

'What would she have had in the bag, Bibi?' asked Ashton.

Bibi went back to the wardrobe and from the back of the wardrobe fished out a rather larger PVC bag, a case really.

'She would have had a make-up kit in there. And a purse and a picture of Justine, a small version of that one.'

She nodded towards the framed photograph of her grand-daughter which stood on the bedside table next to an open Japanese fan displayed on its stand. As Ashton looked at the snapshot, Bibi pulled out the contents of the bag she was holding. At first she didn't understand what she had found. She opened it out. It too was in black PVC, like a corset, with wide strengthening 'bones' sewn into it, a half-cup bra in the top and laces up the front. But Susie didn't need . . . Suddenly Bibi twigged. Her mouth fell open and she hastily stuffed it back before Ashton could get a glimpse. She talked hard to cover her confusion.

'And, well, I think, I mean I'm *sure*, she would have had her, um, her Filofax in it. Yes. She once said to me, "God help me if I ever lost this, Mum. It's got my life in it."'

Bibi shut her eyes briefly, visualising the scene. Susie had been sitting at the kitchen table in Bibi's flat, writing something in the organiser's diary section. A bright, sunny morning. Springtime.

In one movement she turned back to the wardrobe and pushed the PVC bag down and out of sight behind the shoe rack.

CHAPTER 10

MONDAY 27 APRIL. AFTERNOON

In the Incident Room, Satchell and Brown were telling Hutchens about the interview with Thomas Slater.

'They're a firm specialising in libel apparently. Bit ironic, really. It was when I told him in front of the receptionist that we knew he was one of her regular clients! Bloody wetting himself, he was!'

Satchell laughed.

'Anyway he's in the clear. Mr Hand-Relief went back to the office after his massage, worked late and was having a sandwich about eleven at his club with that geezer who runs, you know, the magazine that exposes all the ministers. Pity – it would have been a laugh to give him a spin.'

The door of the Incident Room crashed open. It was Palmer, out of breath having hurtled up the stairs.

'Where's the guv?'

Satchell could immediately tell that Palmer had something sensational to impart. His face had that tell-tale wide-eyed expression.

'What is it?'

'It's King's Cross CID. Urgent.'

Pat North walked in with a copy of Jill Ashton's memo about the shoulder bag with the tiger-shaped clasp. Palmer turned to her.

'There's a Detective Inspector Batchley from King's Cross wanting a word. Line two.'

As North reached for a phone and punched for the correct line, Palmer pointed to the board where Susie's mutilations remained on view.

'They got one too.'

'One what?' asked Brown.

'One of *those*! Same mutilations.'

'Jesus!'

Within a minute of taking down a summary of Batchley's details, North was almost running along the interviews corridor, looking for Walker. She called out to Henshaw, who was carrying some files towards the Incident Room,

'You seen Walker?'

Henshaw twitched his head towards one of the interview rooms and North looked through the open door. Walker was sitting with his back to her, talking quietly into the phone.

'*Don't* lay this on me now, Lynn. It's not a good time ... Yes, I know. And I *do* take my responsibilities seriously, very seriously. I'm just not— Hello? Hello? Shit!'

He looked at his phone and switched it off. North took a step back and paused behind the wall. He hadn't seen her. She took a deep breath and then stepped back into the doorway, rapping gently.

'Guv!'

Walker was sitting with his head bowed, rubbing the bridge of his nose between finger and thumb. Hearing North, he swivelled round, flustered.

'Yes?'

'We just got a call from a DI Batchley. The murder index at Scotland Yard have contacted him re our job.'

The murder index is an information comparison and exchange programme which matches similarities between crimes committed in different parts of the capital. The idea is to avoid having two units chasing the same criminal.

'What?' said Walker. 'Who's this Batchley?'

'King's Cross CID. There's another one. Woman attacked, similar mutilations. They found her last night.'

Walker sprang to his feet.

'Shit, shit, SHIT! I knew it! I bloody *knew* he'd do it again.'

North held up her hand.

'Hang on, hang on. It's different. She's still alive. Though they don't know for how long.'

'Come on then!'

The chair behind Walker's legs crashed to the ground as he pushed it back and strode from the room.

* * *

North and Walker met Batchley at the Middlesex Hospital – a very tall, assured and stylishly dressed officer, not fazed by his brush with the glamour boys of AMIP. He also looked formidably fit: a man who worked out. North liked the look of him.

'God only knows how she's still alive.' he was saying. 'They're about to operate on her now. She's got terrible slash wounds to her neck and horrific breast and stomach injuries. That's just for starters.'

'And she's a known prostitute?' asked Walker.

Batchley nodded.

'Yeah, been around longer than I've been stationed at King's Cross. Tough, quite old.'

'Like, how old?' North wanted to know.

'Oh, late thirties. We've had her in for soliciting more times than I could shake a stick at.'

They heard a door bang behind them as a nurse left the operating theatre. Walker stopped her.

'How's she doing?'

The nurse looked startled at Walker's intensity.

'Are you a relative?' she asked.

Walker snapped open his warrant card and bore down on her.

'No. Police. Is she going to live?'

The nurse stood her ground. She looked at him unblinking.

'It's been touch-and-go, but she's a fighter.'

* * *

The doctors ruled out any chance of an interview in the foreseeable future. In the interim, with the help of DI Batchley, Pat North went down to King's Cross, looked at police records, talked to other toms on the street and built up a detailed profile of this new victim. The name was Marilyn Spark and she had been on the game most of her adult life, initially to make money, then to fuel the heroin habit she'd picked up along the way and finally, after she'd detoxed and stayed off the smack in a hostel for several months, to get a roof over her head. Now she had a flat and a modicum of self-respect. But she was still doing tricks for thirty quid a time in cars and sleazy hotels around King's Cross.

More than twenty years of sexual wear and tear had coarsened Marilyn's heart and mind so that now, little enamoured of the softer things in life, she confronted the world uncompromisingly. But her body, in its way, had fared better. It was her best asset and she had looked after it, exercising and eating sensibly and keeping it in such good physical shape that, except around the face and eyes, she might have passed for a woman ten years younger. But all that, thought North, had gone now. Battered and mutilated, would Marilyn's body never again have the power to fool a punter into thinking, even for a moment, that she was an athletic twenty-something?

The interim medical report on Marilyn Spark by her surgeon, Dr Imram Jaffre, arrived at the Incident Room in the early evening. The damage it described closely paralleled what had been done to Susie Harrow. The knees had identical carpet burns, the torso had similarly savage kick marks, the left wrist had the same abrasions. As in the case of Susie, Marilyn's left breast had been sliced away, her upper body slashed with a razor-sharp knife, her sexual organs gouged and gashed from the inside and her throat cut. Both women had been found on waste ground, partially clothed and lying in a pool of blood.

As Walker read the report, his interest shifted away from these similarities. He was already taking it as read that the attacks were the work of the same man. So now he began to think about the differences, for in both the detail and the severity of the injuries there were significant variations. The body's bruising and internal injuries were less extensive in Marilyn's case, her throat having been less efficiently slit and the only instance of more serious injury was in the right hand. Susie's had been cut and grazed but in Marilyn's case the fingers all had fractures too. But these were all nuances compared to the one gross discrepancy, which was, of course, that Marilyn Spark had been found to have a pulse.

Walker put his mind hard to the problem. He knew that concealed in these details there might be a hidden key. Was there a reason why Marilyn's overall injuries had been lighter than Susie's? What prevented her being finished off? And why was she not carefully hidden after being dumped? The obvious answer was that the killer had been interrupted. But how? And by whom?

* * *

But events were still outrunning Walker. At about nine o'clock at a small run-down factory in Stockwell, nightwatchman Ahmed Al-Said was on his shift, just about to carry out his hourly perimeter-fence check. The night was warm enough and he was trotting along beside his German Shepherd, Bruce, when they were both startled by a sound. It came from the end of the alleyway on the other side of the fence which Al-Said was patrolling. There was a large construction site down there, idle because the work had been suspended several months previously. What *was* the sound? A sort of moaning, or sobbing. Must be a couple of cats, thought Al-Said. He craned his neck to see through the chain-link fence and along the alley. Of the building site he could see only a rusty Portakabin and the outline of a vehicle parked in front of it. They sounded almost human sometimes – cats.

He went back to his patrol. It ended in his little caretaker's office, where he made himself some strong, brackish tea with two spoons of sugar. He drank it and dozed in front of the fuzzy image on the screen of a portable television set, whose sound did not work properly. But half an hour later he was awoken by Bruce pawing at the door, ears pricked. Al-Said heard a shriek and a woman crying. There were flats a hundred yards away, full of families living in poverty. Also the half-finished concrete caverns on the building site were used by groups of down-and-outs to get together and drink. Al-Said was a devout Muslim and hated alcohol. He shook his head and tutted. Drunken women were the worst.

An hour later when he went out he could hear the crying and yelling again, muffled but unmistakable. Al-Said let Bruce off his chain to roam the perimeter on his own as he went back into the office. After ten minutes he called the dog in again. Al-Said was annoyed, distracted by the disturbance. He shut the window of his office with a bang. He did not hear the woman's voice again but, around eleven o'clock, he heard those cats starting up once more, until they too fell silent. Shortly after that, looking out and up the alley again, he saw the door of a parked van open and shut. Figures were getting in. Then it started up and, executing a neat U-turn, drove back down the alley to the main road.

* * *

At about this time a man called Colin Lennox contacted Tooting police to tell them that his wife had left her job at eight thirty and had still not come home. None of her friends had seen her and, with three little girls indoors, one of them running a temperature, he had absolutely no idea where she was. The police told him to call back in an hour if Mrs Lennox had not returned. Holding his feverish youngest daughter, Janey, in the crook of his arm, Colin called back at midnight. This time the police agreed to send a car round to the Lennox house and take his wife's particulars. By the time the two officers had returned to base from this foray, the station's CAD officer already knew that a mutilated woman's body had been found by a wandering alcoholic three miles away on a Stockwell building site. It was the work of less than a minute to take the estimated age and physical description provided in the CAD message and compare these with the smiling snapshot of Carol Lennox which Colin had given the police.

'Better get on the trumpet and have the guvnor out of bed,' said the duty sergeant, as he pointed at the photograph over the CAD sergeant's shoulder. 'He won't like it at all, but then again, *that* looks a match.'

CHAPTER 11
TUESDAY 28 APRIL. AFTERNOON

A successful news blackout on the attacked prostitute Marilyn Spark had been maintained by the police ever since Sunday night. But the horrible murder of a young teacher was quite another matter. News of it had begun to filter out around breakfast time, too late for the morning papers, but the *Evening Standard* splashed it all over the front page of its own early edition. So the officers already knew much of what Detective Inspector North had to tell them at their two o'clock briefing, though they still listened in tense silence.

'Now, the body was found just after midnight. It was that of Carol Lennox, not a prostitute but a middle-class married woman with three kids. She was, in fact, a teacher at an adult education college – evening classes. The husband contacted his local station when she didn't arrive home. Her car was found at the college where she taught. It had broken down, flat battery apparently, and she'd abandoned it to get a taxi. After that we can't find anyone who saw her alive.'

Satchell had his head in his hands. Now he looked up.

'Dear God, tell us this is not the same type of attack!'

The paper had not published all the details of the victim's physical state when she was found and she was, after all, a different type of woman. This could still be unrelated to the Harrow–Spark cases – just.

North quashed his hopes by holding up a Polaroid.

'Afraid it is, only worse, if it possibly could be.'

She handed round the pictures.

'This was how they found her. The guvnor's been at the scene this morning, should be on his way back. The heat's really on us now.'

When Walker arrived, he had a typed witness statement in his hand. His mood was building up to storm force.

'Have you read this?' he roared at North. 'This guy – this *git* – heard her screaming for *two hours*! We have to talk to Marilyn Spark. Those doctors have got to agree now!'

Brown had been on the phone. He called out to Walker.

'Guv! DI Batchley on the phone. Wants a word. Says the National Crime Faculty's analysing the data on the three attacks. Looking for links between them.'

The National Crime Faculty is a special criminology unit based at the National Police Training Centre at Bramshill. It is where comparative case analysis on serious crimes – rapes, murders and terrorist attacks in the main – is carried out by psychologists and crime statisticians, with a view to uncovering interconnecting patterns. But Walker didn't care to talk to Batchley. He was already on his way out of the room.

'Tell Batchley I'll see him at the hospital.'

With the door still swinging behind Walker, North spoke quietly to Brown.

'Put Batchley through to my desk, will you?'

Noting Satchell's raised eyebrows as she passed him on her way back to her desk, she thought, to hell with Satchell! If she wanted to talk to Jeff Batchley, talk to him she would.

'Hello, Jeff, it's Pat.'

'Hi, Pat. It's about Marilyn. She's conscious all right, but she can't talk, her vocal cords are fucked. But she can move her hand, so we've got a system of red and green lights which she presses for yes and no answers. It's all ready to go.'

'That sounds good.'

'Should be better than nothing anyway. Well, look. There's something else I wanted to ask . . . How about you and me going out some time? I don't know . . . dinner, movie, whatever. I was thinking tonight. You free?'

North glanced around the room. The other officers present were ostensibly hunched over their various tasks, but she wouldn't mind betting that some at least were earwigging her end of the conversation. Trying to put as much warmth into her voice as was possible without letting her colleagues know that she fancied DI Batchley, she said, 'OK. Why not? But give me your mobile number in case something comes up.'

Walker was back in the room now, stirring a soluble aspirin into a glass of water. The mixture fizzed as he drank it swiftly, like a shot of schnapps.

As North wrote down Batchley's number, she heard Walker say, 'Can we see Marilyn, then?'

Satchell jerked a thumb towards North.

'I don't know yet. She's getting an update . . . or a date.'

Walker stopped and looked at North, who hung up.

'What?'

Pat North was blushing as she said, 'Batchley says we should get over there fast.'

Walker did not move. He continued to look straight at North as she tidied up the file she'd been working on. Finally, when she hoped the blush had subsided, she looked up again and met his glance.

'He's worked out a way we can interview Marilyn Spark even though she can't actually talk.'

Walker was suddenly back in action. He crossed to his own desk and snapped his fingers in the air for the attention of Dave Satchell.

'Right, good! Dave, I'm not satisfied with this pathetic statement by the nightwatchman.'

He handed the statement to the detective sergeant. 'There's got to be more he can tell us. I mean, two *hours*, for Christ's sake! So get down there and talk to him again, take him through this piece of shit word by miserable word. Pat! You and me, the Middlesex. Let's go.'

* * *

In the car North tried to explain Batchley's red and green lights.

'She can't speak because of injuries to the voice box and larynx. And she's got four broken fingers. But Batchley thinks she can press the buttons, green for yes, red for no.'

'Batchley's an idiot.'

Walker was staring ahead, his face set. The murder of Carol Lennox had hit him hard. It had come too soon, too soon after Marilyn Spark. Things were quickening up unbearably. Their killer was cutting a swathe of destruction. The AMIP area manager had been on the phone, chasing Walker's progress. The media and the public, not to mention the Home Secretary, were baying for an arrest.

They were going round Parliament Square and into Whitehall when Walker's mobile phone trilled. It was Satchell, talking fast.

'Thought I'd let you know straight away – the nightwatchman reckons there was a van parked on the building site.'

'He does? Shit!' exclaimed Walker, gripping the phone between ear and shoulder and breaking the filter off a cigarette.

'So are you thinking what I'm thinking?' asked Satchell.

'You bet. Get him to see if he can identify the make. Call me back!'

Batchley was waiting, standing just outside the hospital entrance smoking.

'Is she still able to see us?' asked North as they crossed reception.

Walker's phone sounded again.

Batchley nodded.

'Yes, but the docs are very wobbly. Truth is, they really don't know how she's still hanging in there at all. It's kind of tense . . . You look nice.'

'Thank you.'

They banged through a pair of double doors on their way to intensive care while Walker stopped in reception to take the call. When he caught them up they were chatting in the IC waiting area. Walker's face was lit by renewed optimism.

'Satchell's witness, the Iranian bloke, reckons we're looking for a white Sherpa van. I've sent Brown over to talk to that Shiree girl at the massage parlour and show her the picture of the van, see if it jogs her memory.'

Lagging a little behind, Walker fished out his mobile again, switched it on and keyed in another number. Batchley continued his interrupted conversation.

'We could see a movie first, eat late, yeah?'

'Fine by me,' said North.

Walker passed a large sign telling him not to use his mobile phone inside the hospital. He looked around and noticed a payphone on the wall.

He said to North, 'Got any change?'

She trawled a few twenty-pence pieces from her purse and handed them to him. As he was dialling, he heard Batchley say,

'Do you like Chinese? Only there's a very good one where I know the owner in Audley Street.'

North would have agreed to a burger, a vegetarian milk bar, anything.

'Sounds great.'

Dr Jaffre, a stocky man with a large stethoscope dangling from the pocket of his white coat, put his head through the door of intensive care and beckoned to Batchley, who went through with him. Walker cradled the payphone and returned to North.

'Chinese?' he said, mock suspiciously. 'Are you pulling him, Detective Inspector?'

North smiled. 'Hey! Piss off, will you?'

Walker gave her back her coins and jabbed his forefinger at the payphone.

'That's out of order.'

'And so are you, guv.'

* * *

It was the first time either North or Walker had seen Marilyn Spark. Through the observation window they could see her where she lay densely surrounded by high-tech equipment. Her gaunt face below the cropped and bleached hair was heavily marked by bruises and cuts. A tracheotomy tube was taped to her neck and hooked up to a ventilator. An intravenous drip from a bag on a stand was inserted in her left arm, feeding her a colourless liquid. An oxygen saturation monitor was attached by tube to her left ear.

Marilyn's throat, chest and belly were covered with dressings and her right hand was bandaged, as was her left wrist. But she was awake. They saw her eyes open and blink and her left hand move.

Dr Jaffre was explaining the ground rules.

'You can have ten minutes. But I shall intervene and stop the interview if I think it is adversely affecting her. She is still in a critical condition.'

Walker said, 'Have you given her something to keep her awake? We're taking important evidence which may have to stand up in court, especially if she's unable to go in the witness box. If she makes a statement on heavy medication, a good defence lawyer will be able to drive a logging truck through it.'

Jaffre nodded at Batchley.

'The detective inspector here has already mentioned this. We put it to her and she has agreed to have no painkillers. Personally I advised her against this, as her doctor, but she insisted. So the point is, she's in a great deal of pain until you've finished with her – understood?'

'How did she do that? I mean, refuse drugs if she can't talk.'

Jaffre smiled.

'Of course she can't talk, Detective Superintendent. Nor would you be able to after major surgery and with a tracheotomy tube in. She's got a laryngeal fracture and her larynx is as swollen as a balloon. Hurts like hell, but she can just manage to shake her head.'

The three police officers moved into the room quietly. Walker sat down beside Marilyn's head, as near as he could get without disturbing her monitoring machinery. North sat next to him and pulled out a notepad and pen while Batchley produced a small unit with red and green indicators mounted on it. The ventilator puffed evenly and, in the background, a pulse monitor lightly beeped. A nurse joined them, sitting opposite Walker and keeping a watchful eye on Marilyn and her monitors.

Walker spoke in a soft voice, a completely different tone from his usual growl.

'Marilyn, I'm Michael. This here is Pat.'

Batchley handed the unit to Walker who placed it on the bed, lifted Marilyn's left hand onto it so that she could feel both the red and green buttons. Her hand was shaking.

'Look, I know you're in a great deal of pain. But we need you to help us catch the man who did this to you. So we would really appreciate it if we could ask you some questions.'

Marilyn's fingers tightened on the switch. Batchley leaned forward.

'You only have to press lightly,' he said. 'Green – this one – for yes; red – this one – for no. Do you understand, Marilyn?'

They waited, watching her left hand. It tensed and the fingers searched about. Then the green light came on.

'*Good* girl,' said Walker, while North smiled and nodded encouragingly.

'Right,' Walker said. 'We'll make this as short as possible.'

He shut his eyes briefly, cleared his mind and then continued.

'Did you know the man who attacked you?'

They waited again but this time Marilyn was quicker. She pressed the red button.

'No,' said Walker. 'I'll do that every time you answer, OK? I'll confirm what I understand to be your answer. Was he white?'

She pressed green.

'Yes. Dark-haired?'

She pressed red.

'No. Blond? Yes. Very blond?'

Marilyn thought for a moment, then grimaced before pressing red.

'No. Blond mousy? Yes. I see. Short-haired? Yes. Any facial hair? No. Good. Very good.'

He looked up at North and again she smiled.

'Now, let's go for the age. Was he between sixteen and twenty?'

Marilyn pressed red.

'No. Twenty and twenty-five? No. Twenty-five and thirty? Yes, good! Was he tall?'

Marilyn did not answer but she frowned.

Walker said, 'I mean *especially* tall?'

She pressed red.

'No. Between five foot eight and six foot? Yes. Good! Was he medium build? No. So was he thin? Yes. Great, Marilyn, you're doing really well. Did he have an accent?'

Marilyn had to think about this one before finally pressing the green button.

'Yes. Foreign? No. English? Yes. London? Yes. You're doing great, Marilyn, sweetheart. Keep going. Did you pick him up like a punter? Yes. Had you ever seen him in the area before? No. Did he drive a car? No. What about a van?'

They waited. Marilyn seemed to be experiencing a spasm of pain. It subsided and she pressed green. Walker beamed.

'Yes! OK, we need to find this van, so I'll run through some colours. Just press "yes" when I say the right one. Blue . . . green . . . yellow . . . red . . . er, maroon . . . white . . .'

The green light came on.

'Yes!' exclaimed Walker, hardly able to keep the excitement out of his voice. 'So it was a white van? . . . Yes.'

Walker tucked a finger into the collar of his shirt above his tie, tugging at it. It was warm in the room and he wanted a smoke.

He said, 'Marilyn, if we ran some makes of vans past you, can we do the same thing?'

Marilyn's face was tense from pain, sweating. She pressed on the green button, making it flash on and off.

'Wait,' warned North, leaning forward. 'She's trying to tell you something. What is it, Marilyn? Is it about the last question?'

Marilyn was wheezing, a thin noise from somewhere inside her damaged throat. She looked in the direction of her hand and pressed green.

'The van,' said Walker. 'Something about the van, yes?'

Marilyn pressed green.

'Yes. But what?'

The victim raised her left hand from the switch and gestured towards the door.

'The door?' said Walker. 'The van door?'

She pressed green.

'Yes. Front door? No. Back doors of the van? Yes. Hmm.'

He looked at the other two and Batchley said, 'Something *on* the back door?'

Marilyn's face began to contort. She coughed, reacting to a fresh wave of pain. She continued pressing the green button as she writhed slightly from side to side.

Batchley whispered to North, 'Do you think we should give her a rest—?'

Walker heard and growled, 'Stay *out* of this!'

North said, 'Writing. Is it some kind of writing? A company name?'

Marilyn pressed red.

'No, but there is something on the back doors of the van?'

Green.

It was noticeable that the pulse monitor's bleeping had increased. The nurse stood and looked into Marilyn's eyes.

'I'm sorry,' she said, speaking rapidly. 'She can't do any more. Her pulse has weakened . . .'

The nurse moved rapidly away from the bed and picked up the house phone as the machine's bleeping became more urgent.

'Dr Jaffre please.'

North squatted down beside Walker. Any second Jaffre would be among them, terminating the interview. But she sensed they were on the edge of some breakthrough information.

'You are trying to tell us something was on the back doors of the van?'

Green.

'Dr Jaffre,' the nurse was saying, 'Marilyn Spark's respiratory rate is rapid and shallow, up to thirty-two per minute. She's fighting the ventilator . . .'

'Was it a picture?' asked North.

Red.

'Was it a . . . you want my pen?'

Marilyn's hand had moved to North's biro and was tapping it as they heard the nurse saying, 'She's in a cold sweat and her oxygen saturation has dropped to eighty-eight per cent. I think you'd better come in here immediately.'

North fitted the biro into Marilyn's fingers and she moved it to the bedclothes. Slowly, trying desperately to control her shaking, Marilyn began to draw a line. Suddenly the line went up, then down.

'Is she trying to write?' asked North.

'This should stop,' said Batchley.

He picked up the switch from beside Marilyn's hand, which had started moving again with a new line, again showing the distinctive up-and-down squiggle. Walker jumped in.

'Was there a zigzag on the back of the van? Give her the switch!'

Batchley gave Marilyn back the unit and she pressed green – then immediately red. North frowned, but Walker was tuned into the interviewee wavelength now.

'A *red* zigzag?'

Marilyn pressed green just as Dr Jaffre walked in, hurrying over to look at his patient.

'Right!' he said. 'That's it, I'm sorry.'

They looked at the bulb unit. The red light was flashing on and off furiously.

North said, 'Another minute, please, doctor. Please! She's trying to say something else – is that right, Marilyn?'

Marilyn had raised her hand again and was pointing at North, apparently at her coat.

'My coat?'

Red.

'My sweater?'

Green.

Marilyn now pointed to the red and green buttons without pressing them, then searched around the room with her eyes. She raised her hand again and touched the nurse's dress. A blue dress.

North nodded. 'I've got it – a red, green and blue sweater, yes?'

Green. But Marilyn's eyes were moving around again, jerking from side to side.

'She's still trying to tell us something,' said Walker.

Marilyn was looking at North again. She was looking at her head and shoulders, trying to nod her head towards it, fighting the pain. Walker looked too. North was wearing a parka coat with a hood. Jaffre came and tried to stand between Walker and the bed.

'That's it! Out now! Nurse, set up an adrenalin nebuliser.'

The doctor was checking the pulse on the oxygen saturation monitor.

Walker leaned past him and grasped the hood on North's coat. 'She's got a hood on her coat, Marilyn. Is that it? The coloured jumper had a hood?'

Marilyn's face contorted. She couldn't move her mouth except to grimace. She gave out a shuddering, guttural sigh as her finger pressed the green button.

'Yes! Brilliant!' said Walker.

He stood up and leaned over her, almost whispering.

'Thanks, Marilyn, you've been more help than you can imagine. We'll find him now. You just get better.'

CHAPTER 12
TUESDAY 28 APRIL. EVENING

This had been the day of a major breakthrough and everybody in the Incident Room knew it even before Walker returned from the hospital to summarise the main points of Marilyn's unconventionally communicated statement.

'The thing is we now have a description of both the man who attacked her and the vehicle,' he told them. 'That's gold dust. He's white, slim build, mousy-blond hair, about five foot ten. And he drives a fucking white *van*, for Christ's sake, with a red zigzag on the rear doors. And the nightwatchman saw a van in Stockwell, where Carol Lennox was found – a Sherpa, so he says. You don't need the National Crime Faculty to point out the link there!'

He tapped the ash off his Marlboro.

'Now, the other thing. Marilyn also says this man wore a hooded sweater in a mixture of colours, red, green and blue.' He glared around the room. 'And, since you've *all* read the forensics reports with the utmost care, you will be aware that this is not the first we've heard of these three colours. They were the colour of fibres found on the skirt of Susan Harrow. Now look, someone, *someone*, has got to *know* this bastard! Find that someone, for Christ's sake. I don't want ever to see a woman left in that state again – *ever*!'

* * *

'Word is,' said Satchell, as he sat in his car with Walker beside him, 'she's maybe getting the leg over with *Blotchley*!'

They had just watched Pat North walk across the car park to her own car. Even though it was now dusk they could see she had changed and carefully applied make-up. Normally, Detective Inspector North's face was a more-or-less cosmetics-free zone. Walker grunted.

'Batchley's a seven-foot prat.'

'He's a great prop forward – plays for the Met's rugby team.'

Walker sighed, fiddling with the end of his tie.

'I could do with a bloody prop. Lynn's having a go at me morning, noon and night. How's *your* wife?'

'Moved in with her sister,' said Satchell cheerily as he started the engine and backed the car out of its bay.

Walker looked across at him sharply. Last time he'd checked Dave Satchell was married in a nice semi in Enfield. But he couldn't remember how long ago that was.

'I'm really sorry, Dave. I had no idea. You should have *told* me! You think . . . you think you'll get back?'

Satchell laughed.

'I sincerely hope not, guv. Angie wouldn't like it.'

'Angie? Who's Angie?'

'Well, you remember that case we were on last July? Old guy found on waste ground near Shepherd's Bush? I met her then – social worker.'

Walker frowned, thinking for a moment as the car sped out onto Wandsworth Road. Then he remembered. Angie!

'You bastard! You mean that redhead?'

'That's the one. She's a right little cracker and you know what's nice? She's easy, I mean easy to be with. She understands about the job and that. I don't get GBH of the earhole every time

I'm late. There's no, *I had your dinner on the table and it was your favourite bleat, bleat, bleat!*'

Through traffic, Satchell was an enviably skilful driver, the kind who seems to find the gaps opening up in adjacent lanes as if just for his use. Now he wove his way around a couple of slow lorries and settled in behind a soft-topped MG. But it was the vehicle in front of the MG that was riveting Mike Walker's attention. He furiously dug his elbow into Satchell's ribs.

'Shut up and look. Do you see what I see?'

Satchell glanced sideways at the detective superintendent and followed the direction of his eyes, over the top of the MG and towards . . . a white van.

Walker grabbed the car radio as Satchell said, 'Oh, my God. Look what's on the rear doors.'

A distinctive red line – starting horizontally, then zigzagging in the middle – ran across the centre of the van's doors.

Walker said, 'One area HQ from Walker. Receiving?'

The radio operator told him to go ahead.

'Urgent PNC check, please . . .'

On cue, Satchell slid out beside the MG and went past it, moving up close to the van so that Walker could read the number plate.

'Delta 3-1-8 Foxtrot Yankee Foxtrot.'

'Stand by, guv,' said the radio operator.

They continued to shadow the van, which was moving fast but legally towards Lavender Hill. Within a minute the radio fizzed again.

'Walker, receiving?'

'Receiving.'

'Re your car check: Delta 3-1-8 Foxtrot Yankee Foxtrot. Last registered keeper shown as a Mr Brian Andrew Morton,

Morton's Electrics, 24 Penn Hill, SW8. Should be a white Sherpa van.'

'Message received,' said Walker, shutting off the radio and scribbling down the details. He looked at Satchell.

'OK, go for it. Pull him over. *Do it!*'

Like all CID vehicles, Satchell's car had a detachable domed blue light which could be positioned to cling magnetically to the roof. This could even be done while driving, simply by opening the window and putting the light in place. This is what Satchell now did, setting it to flash before powering alongside the van.

Walker indicated to the driver to pull over. The driver indicated left, eventually coming to a stop outside a row of shops. Satchell's car slipped in front and the two policemen got out, approaching the van, one on each side. Standing beside the driver's door, Walker reached for his warrant card.

'Detective Superintendent Walker,' he said. 'Please can you step out of the van?'

It was almost, but not quite, dark. Walker stared into the driver's eyes, coldly and implacably. He watched them change from irritation to surprise and then to fear. His own ice-blue eyes narrowed and he reached for the handle, jerking the door open.

'Get out!'

*   *   *

He said his name was Jimmy Garrett and the first disappointment was that he was nothing like Marilyn's description of her assailant. He was six foot three or four, with a thick mop of curly red hair and bottle-end glasses. He weighed a good twenty stone.

Walker's instant assessment was that here was a great big, inadequate, overgrown schoolboy. He wore a large woollen shirt, flapping open over a red T-shirt, and his enormous belly spilled out, forcing the waistband of his jeans down to his hip-bones. He jiggled about nervously as he gave Satchell the details of the van, breathing heavily and speaking too fast.

'It's Damon's, Damon Morton's. I work for him. It's OK, it's not stolen. What's this about? It's not about me jumping the lights back at the crossroads?'

He looked at Walker appealingly, but the detective superintendent took no notice. He had been on the phone, trying to hurry up the vehicle removal team. Walker had already decided that the van would have to be impounded for the attention of Dr Smith and her forensic colleagues. Now he spoke quietly to Satchell.

'Check the back. I'll look after this one.'

Satchell went to the rear and opened the doors. He shone his torch inside. The whole interior of the van was clean and neat, with a range of second-hand electrical goods – television monitors, video recorders, music systems, washing machines. Satchell noted the carpet tiles covering the floor, the toolboxes and work clothes, the coils of flex.

He shut the doors and returned to Walker and the boy.

'How long are they going to be, guv?'

'On their way,' said Walker, turning to Garrett. 'We are seizing this vehicle because we have reason to believe it has been used in a series of criminal offences.'

Garrett stared. His back was to Satchell's parked car. With his mouth open, he looked as if he would like to run. He blinked instead.

'Ah, shit! I was just picking some stuff up for Damon. How am I going to get back to the yard?'

Walker said, 'We might just be able to give you a lift.'

Walker had noted the way Garrett always spoke the name of his boss. Damon. He seemed to get it in almost every time he opened his mouth, pronounced it with pride. Suddenly Walker wanted to meet this Damon Morton very much indeed.

'What does Damon look like, Mr Garrett?'

Garrett looked at him, blinking.

'Damon? He's got sort of fair hair, and he's just normal size.' He laughed with a nervous snort. 'Damon's thin, not fat like me.'

He turned as two squad cars, with sirens wailing and lights flashing, carved their way through the traffic in the darkness. Behind, crawling through the traffic towards them, would be the police low-loader, which would pick up the van and take it away to the forensic labs. Walker escorted Garrett to Satchell's car.

* * *

It was only a few minutes' drive to Penn Hill and, at about nine o'clock, Satchell's car drew up outside a pair of wooden gates on which was a sign: MORTON'S ELECTRICS. On the way over, Walker had called Phelps and Henshaw at the Incident Room, telling them to meet him there ASAP.

They waited a minute or two for the back-up. Garrett had fallen silent. His chatter about the legendary Damon Morton had dried up and he now sat withdrawn and pale in the back seat, his pudgy hands resting on his knees. Suddenly Walker's patience ran out. He grabbed a torch and jerked open the car door.

'Come on, I can't wait any longer. Let's get in there.'

Inside the gates was a cobbled yard, across which they saw the rear entrance to a house whose facing windows were in darkness and whose front must give onto the parallel Wycliffe Road. To the right of the gates as they entered the shadowy yard, was an old wooden hut raised on wooden supports, entered by means of an outside staircase. Under it, where lengths of timber had once perhaps been laid to season, there were stacks of electrical machinery and other household detritus. Walker scanned the raised hut. Some of the windows were boarded and others were patched with both clear and frosted glass, but there was light coming from these and the sound of moody rock music. The figure of a man dancing hypnotically in front of the light source cast a shadow on the window glass. Walker nudged Garrett.

'Damon?'

Garrett nodded.

'You call him out, eh?' said Walker. 'Shout up to him.'

Garrett looked flustered. 'What shall I say?'

'Tell him anything. Tell him there's a problem with the van. Just call him down.'

With a push, he urged Garrett into the centre of the yard, where the faint light from the streetlamp shining over the gate picked him out. From the shadows, Walker and Satchell watched. Fat and ungainly, Garrett looked like a clown in the circus ring, a figure at the same time pathetic and ludicrous. He raised a hand to his mouth, to direct the sound.

'Hey! Damon! You there? It's me, Jimmy.'

There was no response. The shadow had ceased to pass across the window but the music was still playing. Garrett turned to Walker who hissed, 'Call again.'

'Damon! Damon!' This time Jimmy was yelling. He was terrified. In the lamplight, Walker could see the beads of sweat on his forehead.

They listened and heard a squeak, which turned into a creak, and the song, 'Silver Tongued Devil', increased in volume as the door of the hut swung open. Damon Morton was coming out.

Walker looked around and noticed a pair of arc lights mounted on the yard wall. There was a weatherproof light switch on one of the legs which supported the hut. He motioned Satchell over towards it, murmuring, 'Put the lights on when I say.'

Morton began to saunter down the steps, a slim figure dressed stylishly in jeans and a cotton shirt. Walker could see that his hair was a very light brown – 'mousy blond'.

'Christ, it's him!' he whispered, half to himself.

'You took your time, Jimmy. What kept you?'

The voice was identifiably that of a Londoner, the tone was confident and mocking. Garrett was openly shaking now and this did not escape Morton. He looked keenly at the young man standing in the middle of his yard, who suddenly started to stammer.

'I . . . I guh-got something tuh-terribly wrong with the vuh-vuh-van, Damon.'

Morton reached the ground and stood leaning on the hand-rail, perfectly at ease. Walker heard car doors slam just outside the gates and gave the signal to Satchell, who suddenly pulled down the switch. Instantly the yard was flooded with light, shining into the eyes of Morton, whose arms went up to shield his eyes.

'Hey! What's all the drama? You're blinding me.'

They could see that his clothes and footwear – leather cowboy boots – were entirely black. At his neck a large silver medallion glinted.

Phelps and Henshaw had moved through the gates and Walker stepped forward in front of them.

'Damon Morton, I am Detective Superintendent Walker.'

He motioned the two constables forward. They seized his arms and cuffed his hands in front of his body.

'For Christ's sake, what's this?' Morton said.

Walker continued, 'I am arresting you on suspicion of the attempted murder of Marilyn Spark. You do not have to say anything, but . . .'

He read him his rights as Morton held up his cuffed hands once more to shade his eyes. Then, with Phelps and Henshaw flanking him, he was led towards the gates as soon as Walker had finished advising him of his position. Jimmy Garrett was still standing there, his mouth gaping open.

Morton stopped beside him and looked at Garrett rather as a market inspector might look at a rotten piece of meat.

'You dumb piece of shit!' he said, curling his lip.

Garrett flinched. A look of outright terror had possessed his face.

CHAPTER 13

TUESDAY 28 APRIL. NIGHT

At South Lambert Street police station, with the news that suspects for the two murders and the attack on Marilyn Spark were on their way in, the atmosphere was charged. Everywhere it was busy. Computers were booted up, interview rooms prepared, forensic scientists contacted. All officers of the AMIP team not on duty were plucked from their pubs, clubs, couches and beds by pagers and mobile phone. The place was like a warship preparing for action.

Pat North was paged at the Lucky Legend Beijing Duck House. She and Batchley had seen the new Bruce Willis movie in Leicester Square and were now exchanging desert island movies as they started on a selection of dim sum dishes. Abandoning the food and the getting-to-know-you confidences, they had paused awkwardly to say goodbye on the pavement in Audley Street before she hurried back to South Lambeth Street and he went home. On her way to the 'factory', tuning her radio to the news station, North might have regretted not even getting to the hand-holding, let alone to the kissing, stage. But she was too full of curiosity and purpose about what lay ahead. The only thing she knew for certain was that this would be a long night. Walker didn't pull in a suspect for fun.

Satchell greeted her in high spirits.

'It was amazing. We were just on our way for a drink when we saw the van. It was just in the bloody street, driving along!

Driver was a fat kid – a few nut truffles short of the Milk Tray, if you ask me. But his boss is another matter.'

'His boss? That the other one we've arrested?'

'Yes, and it's *him*. I mean, it's the exact description Marilyn Spark gave: slim, not too tall, right-coloured hair. Brian Andrew Morton, calls himself Damon. He's got a poxy little electrical business. The bloke driving his van was a huge fat kid and he was absolutely bloody terrified of Morton.'

He pointed across the room, to where Brown was mousing his way through a computerised search of criminal records.

'Brown's seeing what we have on him – receiving stolen goods is not impossible in my opinion. Meantime, guv wants you in with him and Morton in Interview Room One. I'm in Five with the butterball. Name's Jimmy Garrett. Forensics are at Morton's yard and Palmer and Hutchens are giving his gaff a spin. It's the same location as the workshop.'

'What about the van?'

'Ah, the van! It's gone to the lab. Bloody great red stripe right across the back doors. We've got him, Detective Inspector! Worth ruining your date for, eh?'

* * *

Satchell returned to Interview Room Five, where he and Brown were taking a witness statement from a nervous, twitchy Jimmy Garrett.

'How long have you been working for Brian Morton?' asked Satchell.

'You mean Damon?'

Satchell nodded.

'Oh, about eighteen months.'

'Do you often have to work late?'

'No.'

'You were tonight, though, weren't you?'

Garrett looked at the table, his eyes moving from side to side as if searching for something to prompt him. Then he looked across at Brown, writing in a notepad. The boy was completely adrift.

'I, er, had to finish something.'

'What type of work do you do?'

'Fixing things – electrical things.'

Satchell detached a photograph from the file in front of him and slid it face up under Garrett's eyes. It was Marilyn Spark.

'Have you ever done any work for this woman?'

He searched Garrett's face as he examined the photograph blankly.

'No.'

'OK – how about her?'

He replaced Marilyn Spark with a shot of Susie Harrow. Garrett looked at the picture intently but didn't say anything.

'Mr Garrett?'

When Garrett still didn't speak, Satchell took a photograph of Carol Lennox and slid it into place alongside that of Harrow.

'Well, do you recognise this woman at all?'

As he looked at the photographs of the two murdered women, lying side by side on the table; a drop of sweat fell with a slight splash on the vinyl between them. Satchell, closely studying his reaction, saw that Garrett was trembling violently.

*　*　*

North had found Walker waiting for her outside Interview Room One. For once he seemed in no tearing hurry.

'We'll just tread gently. Morton's not asked for a brief yet, so we'll leave it at that for now.'

'What's he like?' asked North.

'A cocky bastard, very relaxed, laughing and joking all the way in. He's married, two kids. They live next to the yard. He'll be a tricky one, and there's no knowing how long it could take. You ready?'

North nodded.

'Let's go then.'

On arrival at South Lambeth Street, Damon Morton had been processed by the duty sergeant. His clothes and belongings had been logged, he had been given a custody number and a white paper police-issue jumpsuit, and assigned to a holding cell, where he had been kept until they escorted him to the interview room. None of this appeared to disturb him in the slightest. He lounged in his chair at the interview table in his paper suit and greeted the police officers with a mocking smile. He chose to reverse the expected scenario by acting the part of a man relaxing in his own living room.

'Detective Superintendent Walker! Ah, I see you've brought your friend.'

He rolled his eyes at North.

'And ve-ry nice too – you have good taste. Sorry I couldn't receive you both in more formal attire.'

Walker and North first looked up, identifying themselves to the small video camera whose lens captured all the action in the room. Walker then nodded at Form 987, the statutory notice to anyone whose interview is being recorded concerning their right of access to the tapes. It lay on the table in front of Morton.

'Mr Morton, you understand that this interview between you, myself and my colleague Detective Inspector North is being video-recorded?'

Morton nodded.

'Yes.'

Walker cleared his throat.

'Mr Morton, you have been arrested on suspicion of the attempted murder of Marilyn Spark, which occurred on Sunday 26th April. Do you understand?'

Morton nodded. The mockery had gone for the moment. He was serious now, ready to engage in conversation with the police in what was obviously a weighty matter.

'Did you drive your white van at all on Sunday? That would be 26th April.'

Morton frowned and tapped the table, as if wanting to take the question seriously but finding it somehow problematic.

'Sunday? You mean at *any* point or do you want to give me specific times?'

'Between nine fifteen and midnight.'

'Ah, Sunday evening. No, I spent the night with Cheryl. Clapham.'

The answer had been decisive and now it was Walker's turn to frown.

'Cheryl?'

'Goodall. My girlfriend. Fourteen Ridbelow Road.'

'Clapham, right?'

'Right.'

'Does anyone else have access to the van?'

'Yes, of course. My employees do. They—'

There was a knock on the door and Hutchens appeared, fresh from searching the Morton house. He signalled to Walker that he wanted a word. It looked important.

Walker nodded to Morton.

'Excuse me.'

North looked at her watch and said for the tape, 'Twenty-one fifty. Detective Superintendent Walker leaving the room.'

Morton lit a cigarette and looked at North. She met his gaze but could not sustain the contact, opening her notebook and studying a blank page while she thought about Morton's performance so far. He was certainly close to the physical description given by Marilyn. He was also clean and extremely confident and his voice approached being what used to be called 'well spoken', that is, he didn't excessively elongate his vowels or clip his consonants and he didn't compulsively swear. His eyes were clear and blue and they were not afraid of making contact. On the contrary, they seemed to seek it. This was, she realised, a man who could command considerable reserves of charm and, if he chose, intimidation.

But it is hard to assess a person wearing a paper suit and shorn even of his rings and watch. There was just one thing about Morton that possibly gave the game away. The nails of his right ring finger and pinkie had been varnished deep black. But who . . .? And why?

She glanced at his face again. He was still staring at her, a faint half-smile haunting his thin lips. She looked away, drumming her fingers on the table. It was a relief when, seconds later, Walker swept back into the room, with Hutchens close behind. They identified themselves to the recording equipment and Walker, his eyes hard, showed Morton a clear plastic exhibit bag with something woollen and brightly coloured inside. The colours of the wool were clearly visible: green, red and blue.

'Mr Morton, do you own this sweater?'

He held it up to the camera.

'Exhibit number DP/10.'

Morton leaned forward and flicked his eyes over the bag. Then he relaxed back again.

'No,' he said languidly.

'We've just found it at your house.'

'It's Jimmy's – the guy you've got in there.'

He jerked his head to indicate one of the other rooms.

'How did it come to be in your house?'

'He must have left it.'

'In your sitting room?'

Walker held Morton's gaze for two, three seconds, then handed the exhibits bag back to Hutchens.

'Check with Garrett,' he said. 'Detective Constable Hutchens leaving the room.'

As the door closed behind Hutchens, Walker kept his eyes in contact with Morton's.

'Right, Mr Morton, where were we? Ah yes, the van.'

He could not sit, so he paced.

'How long have you owned the white Sherpa van, registration number D318 FYF?'

Morton considered.

'About five years, I think.'

'Does anybody else drive it?'

'Yes, Jimmy does – as you know. And sometimes I lend it to Antonio Bellini. Family are Italian. He and his brother were brought up here. Antonio Bellini – sounds like some kind of ice cream, yeah?'

He grinned. Walker smiled back, coaxingly.

'Or circus act?'

Morton liked that.

'Yes,' he said. 'Or circus act. Too right.'

'How do you know this Bellini?'

'I employ Antonio. He's good with televisions – fixing them.'

'Full-time employment? Cards and everything?'

Morton shook his head.

'No, no, no. I can't be bothered with all that. Casual labour, that's him. Jimmy too. Strictly casual.'

'But you lend them your van?'

'Yes.'

Walker sat quietly for a moment, looking down. He shook a Marlboro from its packet, ripped off the filter and lit up. He still didn't look at Morton.

'Now, Mr Morton, this next question is not in connection with this offence but could you also recall please what you were doing on the night of 16th April. That was a Thursday evening.'

Morton rubbed his chin.

'I was . . . I was at home with my wife and kids. Watching television.'

Walker raised his eyebrows.

'You have an impressive memory, Mr Morton. That was twelve days ago. What about last night?'

'At home again.'

'With your wife and kids?'

'Yes.'

'We'll have to check your alibi, Mr Morton, to see if it matches up with what your wife and your friend Mr Garrett tell us.'

'Him? He's a mental retard. He can't remember what he had for lunch half the time.'

Walker's questioning became a few degrees more forceful.

'But *you're* not a retard, are you, Mr Morton? You have a clear memory of exactly where you were on three separate nights. You didn't even have to think twice, did you?'

Morton shrugged, holding his hands wide.

'It's not too much of a mental strain. You see, I hardly go out in the evening. I prefer to spend my time with my wife and kids.'

'Except when you're spending it with Cheryl?'

Morton was not in the slightest embarrassed. It was clear there was nothing clandestine about Cheryl.

'Yes, and Cheryl.'

Walker reached into the file and drew out a photograph of Marilyn Spark. He placed it square on the table in Morton's sightline.

'Will you look at this photo, please?'

Morton leaned forward and looked. His eyes remained on it for perhaps three seconds before he drew back.

'I have never seen her before in my life. I am very sorry I can't help you, Detective Superintendent. I mean, it's obvious something terrible must have happened to her, or else why would you be arresting me?'

He looked again at the picture.

'And as you were with Jimmy Garrett when you picked me up, I can only presume he must have said something, or implicated me in some way . . .'

His eyes were very wide, innocent-wide. Then very slowly he blinked.

'Otherwise, why would you bother with me?'

Walker shook his head carefully. He waited a single beat, then, looking hard into Morton's eyes, said, 'She gave us a very good description of the man who attacked her.'

North thought she saw a flicker of a reaction cross Morton's face. Dismay, it might even have been, or surprise that Marilyn was alive and able to talk. But the impression was so fleeting that, as soon as it had gone, she found herself doubting whether it had been there at all. It was not something that would have registered on the video. Walker retrieved the photograph and slid it into the file, which he flipped shut.

'Would you be prepared to take part in an identity parade, Mr Morton?'

'Yes.'

'Good. But I'm afraid you will also have to be held overnight, to assist us in our inquiries.'

Walker stood and stretched his back. Morton tapped the table again, his single nervous tic.

'Will you please contact my wife? Tell her I won't be home – she gets worried.'

Walker took no notice. He swung round and looked at the video camera on its wall mounting.

'Interview terminated at twenty-two twenty-three.'

When Sergeant Morris, the duty sergeant, came in, Walker said curtly, 'Take him down to the cells.'

Damon remained sitting, one arm slung at ease over the back of his chair. As North moved towards the door, she took a last look at him and his incredible assurance.

He said, 'Goodnight, Detective Inspector North.'

'Goodnight.'

North didn't know why she did it – a reflex of some kind – but her mouth twitched into a half-smile. Morton's face immediately lit up.

'Ah, I knew it!' he said, with a full smile back. 'You're so pretty when you smile.'

* * *

In Interview Room Five, Satchell and Brown had shown the coloured sweater – red, blue and green – to Jimmy Garrett. When he saw it his face dropped. He nodded his head.

'Yeah, it's mine.'

The exhibits bag with its potentially incriminating contents lay on the table between Satchell and Garrett. The boy, looking young and lost in his sweaty, obese body, kept taking off his glasses and wiping them.

Satchell, driven mad watching this performance, asked, 'You want to know where we found it?'

'Where?'

Garrett's mouth had dropped open. He'd sounded as if he genuinely wanted to know.

'In your mate Damon Morton's house. How do you think it got there?'

Garrett licked his lips, pulled off his glasses and began to wipe them yet again on the sleeve of his shirt. Satchell was trying to work out if the routine with the spectacles was random or could be correlated to Garrett's lies.

'I must have left it there this morning. It's mine, anyway.'

'Does Damon ever wear it?'

'No,' Garrett whined. 'It's *mine*! All right?'

Satchell shut his eyes. This was not what he wanted to hear. When he opened them, Garrett was replacing his glasses.

'Let's get back to the photographs, OK?'

Satchell removed the exhibits bag and again dealt out the photographs of the three victims one by one: Susie Harrow, Marilyn Spark, Carol Lennox. By the time Garrett had dropped his hands from his face, the images of the slasher's three victims were there in his direct line of sight. When he saw them he gave a squeak, as if he had been punctured. He immediately covered his face with his pudgy hands.

Satchell sighed.

'OK, Jimmy. Look at the photographs, please. Look at them!'

Garrett lowered his hands once more, although he held them in readiness just below his chin, like a bespectacled hamster. He blinked as he looked at the three images. Then his shoulders started to twitch and his hands trembled as they dropped towards his knees. Seconds later tears were welling into his eyes and he had started to sob, shaking his head from side to side.

'I just don't want to . . . to suh-see their faces.'

Satchell tapped on the photographs.

'These or just any faces? I can't follow what you're saying, Jimmy.'

Garrett had his head averted now and he pointed to the table.

'Them, please. I don't want to look at them.'

'Why, Jimmy? Why don't you want to look at them?'

Garrett was snivelling now, his upper lip snotty and his chin wobbling.

'Damon didn't have nothing to do with it. Never, right? Please tell him – it wasn't my fault.'

Satchell hit the table with the flat of his hand.

'Wait! Wait just a second here, Jimmy. I still don't get you. First, you said Damon—'

'Didn't do anything!' Garrett interrupted him. He paused and sniffed heavily. He nodded once. 'I did it!'

Satchell looked at Brown. What the hell was going on?

'What exactly did you do, Jimmy?'

Garrett was sobbing freely now.

'I'm so sorry, I'm so sorry . . .'

'You're going to have to help me out here, Jimmy. Come on now. Look at these photographs. Start with this one here. It's a photograph of Marilyn Spark.'

Garrett looked and shut his eyes immediately. Tears squeezed out between the lids.

'Yeah, I did her. She's a tart, works the King's Cross patch. I got her.'

'What do you mean, you "got her"?'

'Picked her up, like the others. Got her into the back of the van and did it to her . . .'

He saw Satchell frowning and tried to elaborate.

'You know, *cuffed* her and that . . .'

'Can you give me more details?' asked Satchell. 'Do you mean you *hand*cuffed her?'

Suddenly he raised his arm, the left arm, to just above head height.

'Like this!'

*   *   *

Walker knew he hadn't finished with Morton, but he wanted to know what Jimmy Garrett was saying before he returned to his prime suspect. So he hung around outside Interview Room Five, smoking, tapping his foot, waiting for the Garrett interview to finish.

'Bit of a result,' said Satchell, emerging at last, his hands miming a dusting-off gesture. 'The fat boy's admitted doing every single one of them.'

Satchell lit a cigarette as Walker let his body sag back against the corridor wall, his face slack with surprise. 'He admitted *what*?'

This was *not* the avenue he would have chosen to go down.

'Susie Harrow, Carol Lennox, Marilyn Spark, all of them. He's given details of how he handcuffed them first. He says he did them all and Lord of the Flies in there' – he nodded towards the custody cells – 'is as pure as the driven snow.'

'Which he certainly isn't,' said Walker. 'I *know*, I just spent the last hour getting to know him.'

'Fat boy doesn't want a brief, or doesn't care rather. All he wants is that I get the message that he did everything and his Damon's got to be released. Those were his words, not mine. You have to release Damon.'

Walker dropped his cigarette butt and stood on it.

'Get Garrett to repeat it a second time on tape now. We'll do a more in-depth interview tomorrow, when he's got a brief.'

Satchell was shaking his head.

'It's weird. He's right on target with Lennox and Harrow. But with Marilyn Spark something's not quite right. He's . . .'

'Lying?'

Satchell looked at his boss and shook his head.

'I just don't know. He certainly doesn't appreciate the fact that Marilyn Spark is still alive.'

Walker snapped his fingers, frustrated.

'Damon Morton's got an alibi for all three nights, so he says.'

Satchell frowned, thinking.

'Damon? That's the devil's name, isn't it? Or was that Damian?'

*　　*　　*

Half an hour after both suspects had been banged up in their night-time accommodation, no one in the Incident Room had gone home. When Walker came in with a coffee and slumped in his chair, the room grew quiet. He looked around at the circle of detectives, all of them closely watching him.

'Houston, we have a problem,' he joked feebly. 'Damon fits Marilyn's description of her attacker but the Garrett kid's put his hands up, says he did all three. I think he's lying, about Marilyn Spark at least, and I think Morton's lying as well.'

He pointed to Satchell.

'Dave, tomorrow you go for Jimmy Garrett's family and do his drum over with a nit comb.'

'We still looking for the weapon, guv?'

It was Henshaw who had asked. Walker grunted.

'Of course. Weapons, plural. But remember also, the women all had a breast removed. So, maybe the killer collects trophies.'

He allowed a beat while the group took this in, then said, 'Yes, Detective Inspector?'

'The sweater, guv. The one found at Morton's house. It's been sent to forensics, so it'll be a while before we get anything. When we get the DNA results from the semen found on Susan Harrow's clothing we'll be able to see if they match up with Jimmy and Damon.'

Walker sipped his coffee.

'I'll go and interview the friend, Antonio Bellini,' he said, grimacing at the cold insipidity of the drink. 'And then we'll have another go at *Mr* Morton.'

He checked his watch.

'That's it. Get some shut-eye, because we've got a long haul ahead of us. We'll have another full briefing at eight tomorrow evening.'

CHAPTER 14
WEDNESDAY 29 APRIL. MORNING

'I had your lot in here till four o'clock this morning.'

Through the frosted glass of the front-door panels, Cindy Morton looked a fair, slim and ethereal figure as she questioned the need for Pat North and Detective Constable Matthew Baxter to disturb her family yet again. But North insisted and Cindy opened the door at last, turning immediately to lead the way into the open-plan kitchen-living room, a quite bright but very untidy room after the previous night's search. There was a curious, unexpected range of objects decorating the place. An oriental fertility goddess stood on a low table. A witch-doctor mask, with straw to represent a straggly mop of hair, hung on one wall. A portrait of Napoleon had been placed opposite.

'This won't take long,' said North, studying their suspect's wife. She was a pale, skinny, high-cheekboned blonde in jeans and a T-shirt, still under thirty but looking older. She had hollow eyes and there was something haunted and distant about her manner. Is she being abused? wondered North. Or is it just the drugs?

'I've not been well,' said Cindy, as if responding to North's thoughts. She shrugged and folded her bare thin arms. There were no visible track marks but, then again, with 'brown' being smoked all over the place these days, she didn't have to be an injector. 'What is it now?'

'Wouldn't you like to sit down?'

Cindy took no notice. As she lit a cigarette, her hand had a distinct tremor. 'What's he been arrested for?'

She stood near the wall, leaning against a low unit of drawers. Behind her right shoulder was a child's splodgy painting, a purple angel flying upwards between blue and yellow trees.

North said, 'Your children here?'

Cindy smiled sardonically.

'Charmaine's at school. Karl's asleep. You'd better not wake him! So come on then; why have you taken Damon in?'

'Your husband's been arrested on suspicion of the attempted murder of a woman called Marilyn Spark. You recognise the name?'

'No.'

'Could you tell me where your husband was on Sunday night, last Sunday that is?'

Cindy was about to reply when, from the room above, there came a series of convulsive yelps, followed by a continuous, not very musical howl.

'Oh, shit,' said Cindy, closing her eyes in despair. 'Now he's woken up.'

* * *

Over at the Garrett house, Jimmy's mother greeted Satchell and Henshaw with a yellow duster in her hand. She must have been in her early sixties, a well-dyed redhead with watery eyes. She led them into the living room and said, with a weight of sorrow in her voice, 'When he didn't come home last night I did wonder if he'd got himself back in trouble. What is it? Not shoplifting? I'd hoped he'd grown out of that.'

Satchell had looked around. It was a well-kept home, the furniture carefully matched. There were horse-brasses and a picture of white stallions cantering in the surf above a gas-coal fireplace. Antimacassars lay over the backs of the armchairs. The place convinced Satchell that there was no way its inhabitant could comprehend her son's current situation.

'What – is it stolen cars?' she asked in a resigned voice.

'No, I'm sorry to tell you it's more serious. Jimmy's admitted to – but won't you sit down, Mrs Garrett?'

She shook her head. She was looking steadily at him.

'Go on. Admitted to what?'

'Well, Jimmy's admitted to killing two women and attempting to kill a third.'

Mrs Garrett's hand went to her mouth. 'Oh, dear God! There must be some mistake.'

Mrs Garrett lurched against the sideboard. Satchell softened. 'Mrs Garrett, I'm sorry . . . But we need to know if Jimmy was at home on any of these evenings . . .' He opened his notebook but Mrs Garrett was already moving across the room, utterly dazed. 'You'd better . . . you'd better come through into the kitchen. I'll look at the kitchen calendar – I'm, er, not good with dates, you see.'

* * *

At the Morton house, Cindy was insistent. 'Damon was here, with me and the kids. On Monday night too.'

While she'd been upstairs, Baxter had had a discreet look around, opening a few of the kitchen drawers. There were plenty of knives there, and several very sharp ones. He had shut the drawers by the time Cindy came back down after settling

Karl. Before sitting down next to North on the sofa, she picked up a photograph album and now, as she talked, she idly turned the pages.

North wrote Cindy's reply down and asked her to confirm it.

'So you're saying your husband was definitely at home on all three evenings I have asked you about?'

'Yeah. We spend a lot of time at home. Saves on babysitters.'

North nodded and flipped a page of her notebook.

'You know someone called Cheryl?'

Cindy, who had seemed calmer since she'd put Karl back – courtesy of the Valium bottle, who knows? – suddenly snorted aggressively.

'That little slag! Yeah, I know her. A right tart, all of sixteen. They start ever so young, nowadays, don't they? It's the drugs they're on. They're all at it, at it, at it! Me – I never touch them.'

Like hell you don't, thought North.

* * *

The sideboard in the Garrett house was loaded with photographs in stand-up frames, all of them featuring young Jimmy Garrett in various guises – as a primary school kid, a Cub Scout, a candy-floss eater, a roller-skater, a uniformed comprehensive boy. His mother stood beside it now, with the kitchen calendar in her hand.

'Well, on Monday night he was out, but Sunday he was definitely here,' Mrs Garrett was saying. Her voice was flat. She had still not taken in the reality of her son's situation. 'It was my wedding anniversary, you see, and since my husband died it's been a terribly sad night for me. Jimmy's a good son and he understands I don't like to be on my own. He sent out for a

Chinese . . . more for him than me. I'd have cooked, but he likes Chinese.'

While Henshaw wrote this down, Satchell was at the sideboard, looking at the Jimmy Garrett gallery of photographs. He picked up one of Jimmy at four months in a Baby-gro. Give or take a pair of glasses, he didn't look very different now.

Mrs Garrett smiled when she saw which picture Satchell had focused on.

'I'd wanted a baby for so many years, but I'd given up. Eric said it never mattered to him. Eric was my husband. Then I found out I was expecting Jimmy. I was a bit old you know. Anyway, he's always been odd and we had a very difficult time with him growing up. Sometimes he could be so nasty, bad-tempered. And then he'd be ever so pleasant and placid, he'd do anything for you.'

Satchell wandered back to the fireplace and sat down.

'Do you know his employer, Damon Morton, Mrs Garrett?'

Suddenly she looked alarmed, followed by a touch of anger. The mention of Damon clearly made some of the things Satchell had been telling her fall into place in her mind. There was suppressed anger in her voice as she said, 'I won't let *him* in the house.'

* * *

The Mangia 'a Mamma restaurant was a popular cheap hangout and eating place for the young couples of the surrounding area. They liked the odd mixture of styles in the decor – flamenco pictures, Elvis memorabilia, trailing pot-plants – and the relaxed atmosphere of a slightly down-at-heel diner, with plastic-veneered tables and chairs and a counter from which the Bellini family dished out the plentiful and delicious – if plain – southern Italian meals. Salvatore Bellini, the proprietor, had been to the bakery and was unloading his van when he spotted Walker and Hutchens.

'What's it mean?' asked Walker, looking up at the restaurant sign. Back home in Glasgow there was a large indigenous Italian community and Walker had eaten in many an Alfredo's and Franco's. But this was a new one on him.

'It's dialect – from where I come from. Means "Eat up for Mamma". It's what my wife was always saying to me and my boys, see?' He patted his considerable pasta-paunch with a chuckle. 'And look, I did what Mamma told me! How can I help you?'

'Mr Bellini, I'm Detective Superintendent Walker. This is Detective Constable Hutchens. We'd like a word with your son Antonio. Is he at home?'

'Was when I left. Here, *you* open up, I got the fresh rolls.'

He tossed Walker a bunch of keys.

'I don't know, but they used to deliver. Now nobody does nothing for nothing. I say, "Look, you want to charge extra for delivery – I'll pick the bread up myself!"'

Walker had opened the restaurant door and followed Bellini, with his tray of bread, inside. There was a sullen-looking but slim and strikingly handsome youth standing playing a pinball machine. Bellini strode past him, dumping the bread behind the counter.

'Hey, Roberto, *cosa fai*? I thought I told you to open up.'

He bustled through a door which led to an inner hallway and a flight of stairs. Walker and Hutchens stood waiting.

'He's coming down,' said Bellini, breathing hard as he rejoined them. 'Why you want to see him? Fighting, is it?'

'No, sir, he's not been fighting,' said Walker. 'Tell me, do you know a Damon Morton?'

Salvatore didn't reply at first, but his action was sufficiently eloquent. He walked to a bin beside the service counter and spat into it.

'He's dirt. A madman. Thinks he can eat here and not pay. I say to him, "What you think I am, a charity?" He's bad. Got bad feelings, I think.'

On the counter were various packets of meat. Bellini began unpacking the cuts and wiping them before placing them on Pyrex dishes for transfer to the refrigerator.

'What's my Tony done? Serious? Is it serious? Because, you know, he's a good boy – only a bit crazy.'

While Hutchens jotted down notes, Walker was warming to the old man. Indulgently, he let him ramble on.

'Tony, he's not like his brother.'

The proud father tipped his head towards the pinballer.

'I got one with a brain, anyway – Roberto's going to university, he got four A levels! *Hey, Tony!* You coming down?'

He had stopped by the inner door. They heard a muffled voice from above.

'Get down here!' shouted his father.

Antonio Bellini looked only two or three years past twenty, with short cropped black hair and deep brown eyes. Yawning and half asleep, he wore a T-shirt and tracksuit bottoms, with no shoes.

'What d'you want, Papa?'

Before Bellini could answer, Walker stepped up to him.

'I am Detective Superintendent Walker of South Lambeth Street police station. You want to sit down, son? I need to ask you some questions in connection with an investigation into the attempted murder of a woman called Marilyn Spark.'

Antonio had not been looking at Walker as he reached for the chair. But he looked now and, in his shock, stumbled sideways, making the chair screech as it moved under his weight. Hanging on to the chair back, he looked in agony across at his father, who read the look, and what it imported, instantly.

'What you mean?' he asked. 'What you saying?'

Walker ignored him, keeping his eyes fixed on Antonio's face.

'I understand you work for a Damon Morton, Antonio. That right?'

'Yes.' Antonio Bellini's voice was still dull, but his face had begun to change, to twitch awake.

'Now Mr Morton tells us that he sometimes lends you his van. Is that right?'

Antonio was gripping the chairback. He was probably not aware how tightly, but his knuckles were white.

'Yes,' he said, very quietly, almost in a whisper. 'That's right.'

Walker became aware that the pinball had ceased to buzz and ping. Roberto Bellini had turned and was looking towards his brother.

'What's going on?' he asked.

Without warning, Antonio let go of the chair, wrenching his hand away so that it ricocheted from him, turning over and bouncing before coming to rest. Antonio covered his face with his hands. He was crying.

'I'm sorry! I'm sorry! Papa – I'm so sorry. I did it. I did it. I killed them!'

CHAPTER 15

WEDNESDAY 29 APRIL. AFTERNOON

They took Antonio Bellini back to the station and charged him. They now had two men admitting to these murders, neither of whom remotely fitted the description provided by their one and only witness. The previous evening, when he'd seen Morton descending the stairs of the hutted office, Walker had felt as certain as he had ever felt in his whole career. 'It's him,' he had said, and with these two words his imagination had begun to construct a case as strong as Fort Knox. But now the complications had come along and Walker was beginning to wonder, for the first time since he'd heard the name of Damon Morton, if the man could possibly be innocent.

Once Antonio Bellini had been delivered safely into the care of the duty sergeant, Walker and North drove to the pathology labs, where Foster was waiting. Walker had asked him to brief them about the similarities between the attacks on Carol Lennox and Susie Harrow.

'Well, this is very pressured, isn't it?' remarked Foster as he led them through to his office. 'The forensic labs are working overtime as well.'

The lugubrious pathologist sat himself in front of his computer terminal and clicked through images of Carol's body juxtaposed with parallel ones of Susie.

'Ah, right. Your last victim had similar wounds. More aggressive this time but similar breast mutilation . . . Large clumps of hair torn out by the roots in both instances ... And the latest victim was also penetrated by a similar object, pointed like an arrowhead – a sort of multi-barbed arrowhead, if you see what I mean. We found the tissue was torn but also cut inside the vagina and intestines . . .'

'And again there was no semen in the body, just on the clothes, right?'

'Yes. Apparently forensics are rushing through the DNA tests, so you should get both sets of results by the end of the week.'

He looked at the screen, contemplating the frightful images he saw there. He pointed.

'You can see by the amount of bleeding around the lacer- ations that she was alive when they were done.'

'Would you say the same person . . .'

'I'd say the same person committed the attacks – or if not, some- one with close access to that same person was "copy-catting", as I believe the expression is. DNA will tell us a lot. But one of the reasons I asked you to come over . . .'

He moved the pointer around on the screen, dragging down various menus and clicking to bring up a series of images.

'This picture, no – this one! See? It's a picture of Carol Lennox's abdomen and it shows marks, heavy marks which indicate she probably *was* conscious for some of the time and had to be held down. That means to inflict these wounds would have required more than one person – at least two.'

Walker felt the hairs on the back of his neck stand up.

'Two? Did you know we are at the present moment holding three men?'

'Really?'

Foster did not seem particularly interested. He scrolled down a file of pictures and clicked one which opened an image of Carol Lennox's arm.

'But now look here. These marks are slightly abraded and we found fibres embedded in the abrasions. They could be from a glove, where she was gripped between finger and thumb. If you ever find that glove, forensics will be only too happy to assist.'

He did not take his eyes off the screen, speaking in a level, quiet but very deliberate tone.

'This was a very sadistic, almost, one might say, but don't quote me, satanic killing. The perpetrator must have taken great pleasure in the agony of his victim.'

He found a new picture file and opened it. A double image side by side of some greatly enlarged splinters of wood.

'Now this is the other thing I particularly wanted to show you. Remember the slivers of wood inside Susan Harrow? Those are the ones on the left, removed from her abdominal wall. And Carol Lennox also had the same splinters inside her – almost identical in type and location. It looks to me like the same weapon was used on both victims.'

* * *

Much had happened since the briefing late on the previous night. Indeed, events were moving so fast that Walker had brought forward the day's briefing to two o'clock – six hours ahead of schedule. But facing the whole AMIP team he now felt tired and depressed. After he'd got home last night – late yet again – Lynn had simply refused to speak to him. So he'd told her what he considered to be a few home truths and, as a result, he'd passed the night in the spare room. What was more, with last night's bullish feeling about Morton giving way to the unbearable thought that he may be cheated of his prey, he felt frustrated, inclined to question his very judgement and instincts. He didn't even feel like speaking to the team, but asked Pat North to update them instead.

'OK, so this is what's been going down,' she announced. 'Guv brought in Antonio Bellini, who also admits to all three attacks. This guy does odd jobs for Morton, drives the van and so forth. He's been crying non-stop since we brought him in.'

Dave Satchell raised his hand.

'According to Jimmy Garrett's mother,' he said, 'Jimmy was at home on the night he's admitted to being in on Marilyn Spark's abduction and assault.'

Walker nodded his head grimly. Satchell went on.

'Mrs Garrett's pretty adamant about it. Says it was her wedding anniversary night, 26th April. It was ringed in her calendar and all.'

'So what the hell's he playing at?' muttered Walker, looking again at Pat North and nodding to her. She went on.

'Morton's wife is still not giving way on any of our dates. Says he was with her. But Morton himself disagrees. He's said he was not at home on the Sunday night, but with his girlfriend, and ex-babysitter, Cheryl Goodall. So it does look as if the wife's lying and could well be telling porkies for all the dates.'

Walker looked at his watch.

'Anything else, Pat?'

North smiled, not to be hurried.

'Cindy Morton also hates the girlfriend. Not surprisingly. But I think we should concentrate on pushing it with Cindy and with Cheryl – I've not interviewed Cheryl yet.'

Walker stood up.

'OK, do it. Shame Morton's not got a previous record. Anything come up from the search of his yard? Palmer?'

'No, sir,' said Palmer. 'I mean, he has a lot of unpaid bills and he's very far from up to speed on tax and VAT as far as I can see. As for the missing body parts you mentioned earlier—'

Walker cut in, almost savagely.

'You *can* say the word "breasts", you know, Palmer!'

Palmer was stopped in his tracks for a moment. He looked abashed.

'I'm sure I can, sir, I'm sure I can. But we found no severed *breasts* at all. We—'

'What about the eyewitness on the Carol Lennox killing?' broke in Walker again. The exchange with Palmer had got him going. 'The bloke from the factory? Has anybody gone back to him? If not, why not?'

Satchell waved a piece of paper: Ahmed Al-Said's statement.

'He was all over the shop, guv. Says he saw the white van, then he says he didn't, then he said he heard voices, then only one voice. He's really edgy.'

North wanted to know, 'What about the van then, guv? Any joy there?'

'Not yet,' said Walker. 'Forensics are still working on it. In the meantime, there's interviewing to do. I want to get my teeth into young Jimmy Garrett. He got a brief yet, by the way?'

'Yes, guv,' said Satchell. 'Fellow called Cookham. He's young – looks harmless enough.'

* * *

Walker and Satchell sat opposite Garrett and his solicitor, Stephen Cookham, in the interview room. Garrett, his flesh bulging under the white paper suit he was now required to wear, was sitting with his hands between his knees, his lips moving silently. Walker fished out the photograph of Marilyn Spark and spoke for the tape.

'I am showing the suspect a picture of Marilyn Spark.'

Satchell cleared his throat.

'You don't have to say that now, sir.'

He nodded towards the camera mounted on the wall. 'It's on video.'

Garrett was already nodding childishly.

'Yes, I did it,' he said.

Cookham cleared his throat and leaned forward.

'Jimmy, just wait until they ask you a question, all right? Like we discussed.'

Satchell said, 'There's one tiny problem with what you just said, Jimmy. We had a word with your mum. She says you were with her that night.'

Garrett blinked, looking from Satchell to Walker and back again. Walker was the next to speak, in his gentlest, most persuasive voice.

'So let's get this straight, shall we, Jimmy? Where were you on that Sunday night? That was the 26th.'

Garrett's eyes were still flicking around. He glanced sideways at Cookham, who raised his eyebrows in encouragement.

'Er, 26th April? Oh yes, home with my mum. It's her wedding anniversary – well, not really, because my dad's dead, but . . .'

'Were you at home *all* evening?' asked Satchell.

'Er . . .'

Garrett's face was a picture of confusion. At some level in his brain the truth was vying with another set of instructions and he seemed quite unsure where the priority lay.

'Nuh-nuh-not after,' he said, at last.

'After what?'

'Er, after dinner,' said Garrett. 'After dinner I went out, didn't I? I did her then.'

'What time was that?'

'Half-eleven?' asked Garrett. 'Yeah, half-eleven. I duh-duh-did her then.'

His eyes rested blankly on the photograph of Marilyn Spark.

* * *

Cheryl Goodall lived in a flat with her mother in Clapham. When North and Phelps rang the doorbell, they were greeted by the mother, a thin woman of about forty, her hair in rollers.

'Oh, I'm sorry,' she said in a strong Liverpool accent. She had noted the warrant card but did not seem particularly alarmed. 'I've just washed my hair. Got an interview for a job in a bit.'

She ushered them into her living room, where the curtains were still partially drawn. Apart from its scruffiness, the room was not strongly marked by the personalities of those who lived in it.

North said, 'I really wanted to speak to your daughter, Cheryl.'

Mrs Goodall shook her head.

'She's not here. She's gone to the clinic, works there part-time as a receptionist.'

'What time would she be home?'

'After four, I should think. What's all this about?'

'Can you remember at all what you did last Sunday night?'

'Me? Yes, I can. I work Saturdays and Sundays in a wine bar, the Blue Canary, down the High Street.'

'Evenings?'

'Yes, from seven. Get home about midnight if I'm lucky. So that's where I was.'

'What about Cheryl?'

Mrs Goodall was puzzled and looked considerably more cagey now.

'Cheryl? I don't know. Now what's this all about?'

'Do you know Damon Morton?'

The fog cleared from Mrs Goodall's brain. She nodded her head. As soon as Damon's name was mentioned her tone turned icy.

'Yes, I most certainly do. I loathe him. And I've tried to keep Cheryl away from him. That's why we moved here, as a matter of fact. We used to live two doors away from them – the Mortons. Cheryl babysat for them, because he's got two kids – as well as quite a few others dotted around the place, I shouldn't wonder. She was only fifteen when it started.'

'What started?'

'You know!'

'No, I don't, Mrs Goodall. What started?'

'Is this why you're here? Well, thank God somebody's doing something about him. I told him myself he's a lucky beggar that I didn't get the police onto him.'

Pat North nodded, glancing at Phelps, who was writing furiously.

'Well, if your daughter was underage, why *didn't* you report him?' she asked.

Mrs Goodall sighed.

'Because Cheryl was hysterical. Said she loved him and if I did anything against him she'd run away with him.'

'But that was a while ago?'

'A few months.'

'Is she still seeing him?'

'I hope to God she isn't. She swore she wouldn't.'

'So you don't know if he was here on Sunday night?'

There was a movement by the door. A girl was standing there in a short, blue skirt and blue denim jacket, chewing gum. How long had she been listening? Long enough, obviously.

'What do you want to know about Damon for?' asked Cheryl Goodall as she marched into the centre of the room. Centre stage, thought North. This was a young woman used to getting attention and also used to getting exactly what she wanted. Mrs Goodall spoke, her voice betraying incipient anguish.

'*Has* he been here, Cheryl?'

Her daughter paused, weighing something in her mind. Then she turned sharply to her mother. Her voice was full of contempt.

'Yes,' she said. 'He has been here. Every Saturday and Sunday, as a matter of fact.'

Mrs Goodall moved towards her daughter with her hand raised and, before North could stop her, she slapped Cheryl's face. The slap resounded and the girl's cheek glowed red.

'Feel better now, do we?' the daughter retorted.

* * *

Even before the news arrived that Cheryl had confirmed Damon Morton's alibi, the team were gloomy about news from the hospital.

'Marilyn Spark's not going to be fit to ID anyone for at least a week,' Hutchens reported. 'We're going to have to let Damon go!'

Pat North's news simply underlined the unpalatable prospect. She told Walker, 'Cheryl Goodall insists Damon was with her on Sunday. Sorry, guv.'

Walker took it badly. He closed his eyes.

'Bugger! Cheryl, Cindy, one of them must be lying, for fuck's sake. But we've got sod all on Morton and he's the one who's behind all this. I'm convinced.'

He said the words, but they were not solidly spoken. Some of the conviction, at least, had leaked away. Yet the truth remained, if Morton *was* responsible, it was going to be an act of criminal folly to release him into the community.

Hutchens, standing next to North, was looking puzzled.

'What about Jimmy and this Antonio? You saying you think they're innocent?'

Walker shook his head slowly, looking at the floor.

'No. They're not innocent by any means. But Morton is the key to all this, not them. And *we've* got to let him go!'

CHAPTER 16
WEDNESDAY 29 APRIL. EVENING

And let him go they did. By five o'clock, Damon Morton had walked out of South Lambeth Street police station in plenty of time to satisfy the requirement of PACE, the Police and Criminal Evidence Act, which stipulates that a suspect cannot be held for more than twenty-four hours without there being quantifiable reasons to extend his detention. The fact that Detective Superintendent Walker considered Damon Morton a lying, conniving and perverted serial killer was unfortunately not quantifiable enough. They needed hard evidence.

Walker was concentrating on the most recent outrage now, the Carol Lennox murder. He sent Palmer back to the witness Ahmed Al-Said, in the hope of extracting further information. But his main hope was to break down one or both of the admitted killers. As Morton was looking for a taxi to take him home, Satchell had Garrett brought back into the interview room.

As soon as he looked at the stern face of the detective sergeant, the boy started crying again.

Satchell said in a soft, persuasive voice, 'Did you kill Carol Lennox?'

Garrett heaved his shoulders. His solicitor, Cookham, sat beside him. He raised his pen, as if to warn his client, then dropped it again. All his attempts to counsel Garrett had proved futile.

'Yes I did, yes. It was me. There wasn't anyone else.'

'Hey!' Satchell spoke sharply. 'What if I was to tell you we have a witness who swears there *was* someone else with you?'

Garrett shook his head. 'We were on our own.'

The tone of voice was a miserable, pleading one. He was desperate to be believed. But why was it so important to him?

'Wait a minute,' said Satchell. 'You just said, "We were on our own." What do you mean by that "we", Jimmy? It sounds to me very much as if you were with someone else.'

Garrett was snivelling and rolling his eyes.

'Oh, God, I'm all confused. I don't know what I'm saying.'

'Well, our witness knows what he's saying, and he says—'

Garrett interrupted him, his voice brimming with anxiety.

'What witness? No one came into the alley. They couldn't have seen us. They're lying.'

Satchell shook his head.

'No, *you* are. You just did it again. If you were, as you say, alone in that alley, why did you say "us" just now?'

'I didn't.'

'You did, Jimmy.'

He pointed to the wall-mounted camera.

'It'll even be on video. So come clean, how many were with you when you killed Carol Lennox?'

Garrett mumbled something into his chest.

'What was that, Jimmy? Say it again!'

'Three of us.'

Satchell smiled. Three of them – got him!

'Go on then, let's have the names, Jimmy.'

'It was me, Tony and Bob.'

Satchell's jaw dropped. *Bob?* Garrett noticed his confusion. He nodded.

'You know – the two Bellini brothers.'

* * *

In the adjoining interview room, Walker and Brown faced Antonio Bellini, who had now acquired a solicitor of his own, Crispin Oxley. Throughout the interview, Oxley confined himself to taking notes and tapping his teeth with the end of his ballpoint.

'You understand the interview's being video-taped?' asked Walker.

'Yes, sir,' whispered the suspect. He was not looking at Walker but sat bowed forward in his chair as if in supplication.

'All right. Now, let's go through the night of 27th April again. You have admitted your involvement in the murder of Carol Lennox. Were you alone?'

'Yes, sir.'

Walker took a deep breath.

'We are holding in custody a James Garrett – Jimmy. Do you know this man?'

'Yes. Yes, sir, I do.'

'And how do you know him?'

'I work with him sometimes.'

'Were you with him on 27th April?'

For the first time Antonio looked up.

'Er, yes. Has he said anything?'

'So in other words you were not, as you have stated, alone?'

Silence. Antonio had resumed his penitential pose. Walker glanced at Brown in frustration and shook his head.

'Mr Bellini, are you now saying you were *not* alone? That Mr Garrett was with you?'

Antonio took a long time replying and Walker let him stew. Finally, the young man spoke.

'I don't remember.'

Walker sighed.

'You now don't remember? Come on, Antonio, who are you trying to protect?'

He opened his file and searched through it until he came to the item he wanted – a photograph. He held it up for the camera.

'I am now showing Antonio Bellini a photograph of the victim, Carol Lennox. Take a good look, Mr Bellini. This is the woman you have admitted to killing brutally. You have also stated you acted alone, that you *alone . . .*'

He put the photograph down and tapped hard with his finger on the bloody mess of Carol Lennox's body.

'. . . did this!'

Antonio had bowed his head and started to weep again, a desperate mewing sound.

'Unfortunately for your credibility, we have a reliable witness who states there was more than one man with Carol Lennox in the van. So come on, Mr Bellini. Who else was with you?'

Antonio was heaving and snivelling now, rocking in his chair. Walker pressed on.

'You didn't kill her alone, did you? *Did you?*'

Suddenly Antonia was shaking his head.

'No. No. I was with Jimmy – Jimmy and my brother.'

'Your brother?'

Walker glanced again at Brown, frowning.

'Please, could you state your brother's name.'

'Roberto Bellini. We did them all together.'

'All? Are you saying there were other victims?'

'Yes – there was a prostitute, she worked around King's Cross. We did her too. We enticed her into the van, and hand-cuffed her to the rail inside.'

* * *

As soon as Walker had talked to Satchell, and heard that Garrett too was implicating Roberto Bellini, he knew he would have to arrest the boy. Christ! And he was only, what, eighteen?

He thought of the father, Salvatore Bellini. When they'd met, Walker had instinctively liked the man – hard-working, humorous, human. And son Roberto – 'the one with a brain' – was obviously the light of his life. This was a disaster that would come close to putting that light out for ever.

He shut his eyes, wondering if he was losing his grip. This case was close to the edge for everybody. The papers, the Commissioner, the politicians, the bloody newsagent he bought his paper from in the morning – they were all nagging on obsessively about the possibility of a serial killer on the loose. It was a madness that infected everybody.

It even seemed to have got to Palmer, who arrived back in the Incident Room breathless, his eyes staring. But the news he brought was very far from insanity.

'Hey, everybody! Our nightwatchman's changed his statement!'

He produced his notes.

'He now says he saw the men.'

Walker strode across the room.

'Saw them?'

'Yes, four men, he now says.'

'Four men. I knew it!'

Palmer nodded vigorously.

'He even came up with descriptions, believe it or not. Said he didn't want to get involved before but now he's overcome by a citizen's sense of duty. Says he saw them getting into the van under a streetlamp apparently.'

'Let's have a look,' said Walker. He grabbed Palmer's notebook and began scrutinising it, but, able to make nothing of Palmer's handwriting, he handed it back. 'Well, any of them Morton?'

'Not exactly, sir. But one of them was wearing a hood, though he never saw his face.'

'Has to be Morton.'

'The guy's got a hell of a clear view of the alleyway. I made him take me over it. Showed me the spot where the van was, where he was. Trouble is, the area's not well lit. Kids have smashed the streetlamps. But there is one left working at the end.'

Walker was pacing now, mashing a fist into the palm of his other hand.

'Wait, wait. Let's go back. He saw four men – right? Is he sure?'

Palmer nodded.

Walker said, 'Four men did this *together*?'

His mouth was tight, the lips drawn back in disgust.

'And they all planned it, worked out the details, allocated the roles. They all *wanted* to do this?'

Palmer looked at the guvnor, a little taken aback. What was he on about?

'Yes, sir,' he said. 'It seems so. His description of the white van fits Damon Morton's.'

'Yeah, well, this is good,' said Walker, relaxing a little.

His mood suddenly brightened visibly.

'Anyway, something tells me we'll get him now. We'll get all four of them, the bastards.'

'So, what *about* Morton?' Satchell mused. 'What do we do with him?'

Walker was patting his pockets for cigarettes. Quickly Satchell fed him one.

'Hmm. Well, we're walking into a minefield, of course. Maybe Damon Morton is our very own Charlie Manson, or maybe he isn't. But we can't take the chance. Let's bring him back in.'

He ripped the filter off his detective sergeant's offering of a cigarette and lit up. As he inhaled, he looked sideways at Satchell through the cloud of smoke and jabbed his thumb towards the door.

'Go on, Dave. Arrest Morton on suspicion of the murder of Carol Lennox. And, Pat, you go down to the Mangia 'a Mamma and pull Roberto. Let's move this case along.'

* * *

'I was with Jimmy Garrett,' said Roberto, after taking his turn in the interview room opposite Walker. On the table between them lay the photograph of Carol Lennox.

'And—'

He swallowed hard.

'And also my brother, Antonio.'

Sitting beside him was Archie Wilson, his solicitor. Roberto took no notice of Wilson because he was completely turned inwards, his face white, tense, his forehead beaded with sweat.

'*Only* the three of you?' asked Walker.

'Yes, sir. The three of us did it.'

'So there was just *three* – not four?'

Roberto shook his head.

'No. Damon Morton was not with us.'

'Morton?' said Walker sharply, glancing at North. 'Why did you mention Morton's name? I didn't mention Morton, did I?'

Roberto froze. Then he shook his head again, but it was a different shake, like someone trying to clear their head.

'I don't know. I don't know.'

Walker shuffled the papers in his file.

'Mr Bellini, I am going to show you two more photographs. I will identify the persons by name as I place them in front of you. Susan Harrow.'

Roberto looked, then turned instantly away.

'Yes. We killed her.'

'How did you kill her?'

'With a knife.'

'Where is this knife?'

'I don't know.'

'What did you do with it?'

'I don't remember.'

Walker waited a moment, then dealt the second photograph.

'Marilyn Spark. Do you know this woman?'

Again, Roberto looked at the picture momentarily.

'Yes.'

Suddenly his head bobbed down and he half retched into his cupped hand. He was shaking.

'She's a prostitute,' he went on when the impulse to vomit had left him. Now, his voice barely audible, 'She works around the King's Cross area. I . . . enticed her into the van and I, er, handcuffed her to the rail inside. I forced her onto the floor, made her lie down and . . .'

His voice tailed away.

'And *what*?'

But Roberto could sustain his calm no longer. He broke down spectacularly, sobbing like a six-year-old, with great heaving gulps of tears.

'I'm . . . I'm sorry,' he managed eventually.

He sat sniffing as he brought himself under control again.

'You were saying,' Walker supplied. 'You forced her to lie down – and *then* what?'

Roberto's account of the horrifying things he had done was given almost in a whisper. Once or twice Walker had to ask him to speak up. But when it was done all the speaking up in the world would not have brought him closer to getting any mud to stick to Damon Morton.

CHAPTER 17

THURSDAY 30 APRIL

'It's unbelievable,' said Walker to the entire Incident Room first thing the next morning. 'The three of them have all confessed to all three attacks. Like parrots, they've insisted that Damon Morton wasn't there.'

'So maybe he wasn't,' said Pat North, voicing a thought that had occurred reluctantly to every officer in the room. 'Cheryl Goodall insists Damon Morton was with her on the Sunday night.'

Walker scoffed at this.

'Odd, as his wife says he was with her.'

It was Satchell who provided clarification on this point.

'Not any more she doesn't. When we picked him up, she went out of her way to talk to us. Said she'd been mistaken about that night.'

Walker laughed incredulously.

'What? That instead of being home with his wife and kiddies Damon was with his girlfriend, Cheryl?'

Satchell checked the air with his finger.

'Correct.'

Pat North had a computer print-out which, as the other officers drifted away to their duties, she handed to Walker.

'One other thing, sir. Damon Morton's not asked for a brief. This is the list of duty solicitors. We should get him represented.'

Walker took the list without comment and glanced at it. He grunted and put it on his desk.

'Where are you off to?' he enquired casually as she put on her coat.

'The Middlesex. Marilyn's out of intensive care . . . just. Thought I'd see how she was progressing.'

'Is he going to be there?' Walker looked up. 'The rugby prop?'

'No. But if it's all right with you, I'm meeting him later for a drink.'

North flashed him a forced, fuck-you smile.

'Do you want the name of the wine bar?'

'No need to get tetchy.'

Walker turned and set off for his own desk, still carrying the list of lawyers. North made a face to his back.

'I'm not the tetchy one.'

After she'd gone, Satchell appeared at Walker's desk with two coffees, giving one to the detective superintendent, who told him about his conversation with North.

'Told you she's getting the leg over,' Satchell said, sipping his coffee. 'This one's sugared – you've got mine.'

They swapped coffees and Walker cocked a thumb at the police photographs of the four men, taken when they'd been arrested and now on the nearby display board.

'They're playing around with us, Dave. Why the hell are they covering up for him? They're going down for life anyway. So what have they got to gain?'

He tapped the desk.

'Pat's right.'

'She usually is.'

Walker shot Satchell a mock-murderous look.

'I *mean*, we should get Morton a solicitor. Here's the list.'

Satchell picked it up and studied it. 'That's a name I don't know – Corinna Maddox. You seen her?'

Walker shook his head.

'And hey, look who else is here – the fragrant Belinda Sinclair.'

Walker laughed. They both had mixed memories of Sinclair from the Michael Dunn case.

'Christ, I hope he doesn't pick her. What a pain in the arse.'

'Got a nice one herself, though,' said Satchell.

Walker's reply, if he had one, went unheard because at this point Phelps burst into the room.

'Guv! There's a Salvatore Bellini downstairs, asking for you.'

'Another brother?' asked Satchell.

'No,' said Walker curtly, hurrying towards the stairs. 'The father. And I have a feeling I should see him.'

*　*　*

The amazing thing about Salvatore Bellini's manner, amazing enough to give Walker much food for thought in the night during his long hours of spare-bedroom insomnia, was the man's old-world courtesy. He sat in the waiting room, revolving his hat between his knees, his face a mask of gravity. What was going on behind the facade was difficult to guess.

'Thank you for seeing me, sir. I am sorry if this is inconvenient.'

Walker felt sympathy for the elderly restaurateur. His troubles were so bad – could they be worse? – yet here he was, speaking the language of politeness and concern for Walker's convenience. Walker could think of nothing to say. He nodded his head in a way that, he hoped, would communicate his feelings. The old man continued, 'It's just that I know my sons would not get into bad trouble. Not *murder*.'

Walker's heart felt heavy.

'I'm afraid they are *in* bad trouble, Mr Bellini. They have already confessed.'

'*Vero?* I don't understand, sir. I don't understand nothing no more.'

Walker leaned forward.

'I wonder, would you mind answering some questions, Mr Bellini? I need to find out – it's difficult for you I know, but I want to determine if either of your sons was at home on Sunday night – last Sunday, the 26th. Or if not, if you know where they were.'

Bellini brightened. 'Sunday was Antonio's *compleanno* – his birthday.'

'The 26th?'

'Yes, I make a cake. We have a little family party.'

'Both your sons were there?'

'Of course – me and my sons.'

Bellini's face showed that he understood the importance of this information. He beamed. He had given an alibi for his sons.

'I knew this was a mistake. I knew this was all confusion.'

*　*　*

Finding himself short-staffed at a week's notice, the senior partner of Clarence Clough, solicitors, Derek Waugh, had activated a well-tried locum arrangement. These days his wife devoted herself largely to bridge, golf, the three Waugh teenagers and an extensive Wimbledon social life. But once, as Corinna Maddox, she had been a hot-shot solicitor in her own right and when her husband offered her the chance to represent Damon Morton, she wasn't going to turn it down.

'I've put all Belinda Sinclair's belongings in that cardboard box over by the bookshelf, in case she deigns to come back to collect them,' Maddox told her husband, who was absorbed in his newspaper. 'I only wish someone would head-hunt me. When are you going to replace her?'

Waugh was not listening. He was riveted to his *Telegraph*, which, with its usual thorough reporting of crime, had given a half-page feature to the 'slasher' murders, as they were becoming known.

'Quite extraordinary,' he said, tut-tutting over the gory details. 'This serial murder case, most unusual.'

'Oxley's a bit fresh, isn't he?' remarked his wife, stacking a pile of old memos addressed to Belinda and depositing them in the wastepaper basket. 'I'm sure you wouldn't have let him take the case – nor Cookham, come to mention it. They're both doing rather well since they left us.'

Waugh laughed briefly and uncomfortably at this concealed criticism.

'It's an open and shut case. Their clients are pleading guilty.'

'An interesting scenario, though, isn't it? I mean, how will the trial be conducted? All in the dock together or what, Derek?'

Waugh folded his *Telegraph* impatiently and tucked it under his arm.

'Good God, Corinna, I don't know! What I do know is that the unpleasant Detective Superintendent Walker's heading the investigation. We had run-ins with him last time, on the Michael Dunn fiasco. That was Belinda Sinclair's case, as you may remember.'

The telephone on his wife's desk buzzed. Waugh grabbed it before she could turn round.

'Hello, Derek Waugh. Yes, Sue . . .'

He held out the receiver dramatically.

'It's for you, dear. Mr Damon Morton.'

*　　*　　*

With Marilyn Spark out of intensive care, Pat North had at once gone down and taken a more detailed statement about the attack at King's Cross. But there were still a few anomalies to iron out. She decided to take Jill Ashton, the family liaison officer, down to the hospital and introduce her. Ashton's training in victim support would help to reassure the victim that, having extracted her tortuous statement, the police had not abandoned her. It might be a valuable relationship for the police too. A family liaison officer frequently gleaned information that turned out to be crucial to a case.

The two officers sat beside the woman's bed. She still wore the tracheotomy tube taped to her neck and connected to a ventilator.

'She can't talk at all yet,' the nurse had told them. 'But she can move her head a little now.'

So North started gently, confining herself to questions that could be answered with a shake or a nod of the head.

'Marilyn, I'm really sorry, but we want to take you back over the night when you were attacked. Can you manage it?'

Staring at the ceiling, Marilyn jerked her head decisively up and down.

'Good. That's really brave of you. So let's get it over with, eh? You described one man – mousy-blond hair, five foot eight or nine, jeans, white shirt, sweater and hood in red, green and blue and trainers. You stated that this man stopped in a white van and approached you. All right so far?'

Marilyn nodded. Her face still looked haggard, bloodless. Her lips worked, mouthing words which North and Ashton couldn't read.

'It's all right,' said North, touching her arm. 'I know this is difficult. But I also know you want us to catch this man, right? So – when you agreed to go with him, you went to the back of the van freely, yes?'

Marilyn nodded again.

'And at this point he became violent and handcuffed you to a rail inside the van. He then abused you sexually.'

Marilyn was moving her head from side to side, not shaking her head to say 'no', but maybe looking for something.

'You OK, Marilyn?'

She nodded. She nodded towards her hands, lying on the coverlet, and mimed a fist holding a knife, slashing at the bedclothes.

'You mean, your clothes? He cut some of your clothes? OK. This man proceeded to threaten you with a long, thin-bladed knife.'

North had a slim folder of photocopied drawings showing various knives. She showed these to Marilyn to remind her.

'You picked out a knife from the pictures we showed you. It had a black ebony handle, or maybe good-quality plastic, with silver or steel. He forced you to take the knife with your right hand, yes? And, while your left remained handcuffed to the rail, he told you to cut yourself. Said he would kill you if you didn't.'

Marilyn's eyes were shut, her face contorted. She was reliving it as she nodded again. North looked at Ashton and leaned forward.

'OK, now this is important. Did you at any time see any other man inside the van?'

Marilyn shook her head.

'Not even in the front – in the driving or passenger seats?'

Marilyn shook her head even more emphatically.

'So this man was *alone* with you at all times?'

Marilyn nodded, a weaker movement this time. She was already drained and North decided that was enough questions for now. But there was one more she had to ask. She needed to prepare the ground for the day when Marilyn would be fit enough to make the journey up to one of the Met's special ID suites at Kilburn police station for that vital identification parade. She had to know if Marilyn was up for it.

'You're a very brave lady, Marilyn. But if we're going to catch this man we need to see if you can pick him out in an identity parade. It means you may have to see the man again. Would you be prepared to help us?'

Marilyn's eyes were open again, staring at the ceiling. North saw fear but also determination in them and she knew, even before Marilyn's head moved, that she would give a weary but emphatic nod in answer.

* * *

When Roberto Bellini's solicitor, Archie Wilson, arrived to speak further to his client Roberto had cried throughout their interview, and asked for his father. Wilson could hardly believe the way his client had volunteered such a simple confession to these horrendous crimes, without attempting to offer a shred of mitigation in his own defence. But nothing Wilson could say would divert Roberto from his chosen path.

'Please,' Roberto repeated. 'I want to speak to my brother, and call my father. I am worried about my father.'

'Mr Bellini,' said Wilson patiently. 'The police have a taped confession where you admit to carrying out two murders and—'

Roberto was nodding, making tears splash on the table between them.

'Yes, that's right. But please, I want to call my father!'

'So are you saying, Mr Bellini, that everything you have said in this statement is the truth?'

'Yes. Yes. Now please, I got to speak to my father.'

* * *

'Sarge,' whispered the constable on the desk, phoning Satchell in the Incident Room a few minutes later. 'Morton's brief's here, Corinna Maddox.'

'Maddox?'

'Yes. If you don't know her, think one half of the Two Fat Ladies.'

It was indeed an eccentric figure who faced Satchell when he came down to greet her – a large lady in a cape, plentifully made-up (especially in the use of the black eye-pencil) and jangling with big earrings and bracelets.

'Ms Maddox, I'm Detective Sergeant—'

'Satchell, isn't it?'

'That's right – you have a good memory.'

'And I believe Detective Superintendent Walker's heading the inquiry. Yes, Detective Sergeant Satchell, I've been reading the statements. I'm representing Brian Morton and I'd like to see my client.'

Satchell stepped aside and made a sweeping gesture with his arm.

'This way, Ms Maddox. He's waiting for you.'

They found the suspect in a meditative pose, resting his elbows on the interview table, with his fingertips propped against his temples. Satchell made the introductions and left the lawyer alone with her client. She sat herself down.

'How do you do, Mr Morton?'

Morton raised his head and smiled thinly.

'I'll feel a lot better when you get me out of here. May I call you Corinna?'

'No, you may not.'

Briskly she opened the case file.

'Now, Mr Morton, you have been arrested but no charges have yet been brought. Would you like to tell me in your own words why you are here?'

Morton settled himself back in his chair.

'OK. Initially I was arrested for the attempted murder of a prostitute. I've been accused of kidnapping her, handcuffing her inside my van and forcing her to perform sexual acts, then torturing her and mutilating her, before kicking her out in the street. Now it seems I'm accused of murdering someone else, called Carol Lennox.'

Maddox remained impassive. She jotted down his words on her notepad while thinking, *Very articulate, intelligent. Has presence.*

'And did you?' she asked, looking up.

Morton stared icily into her eyes.

'On the night the prostitute got it, I was with my girlfriend. On the other night, I was with my wife and kids. I didn't do it. Three men that work for me and drive my van have been arrested, by the way. They are James Garrett, Antonio Bellini and Roberto Bellini. They have all admitted to doing it.'

Maddox arched her well-pencilled eyebrows.

'How do you know that, Mr Morton? Have you spoken to these men since they were arrested?'

'No,' said Morton simply. 'I don't need to. I know.'

She saw that thin, confident smile again.

Cocky. Provocative, she thought.

She considered for a moment, a forefinger against her lip. She had read the case notes and she had already made up her mind about the police case against Damon Morton. Unless they could come up with considerably more than they had at the moment, he was going to go free.

* * *

'That was Kilburn ID suite,' said Satchell, dropping his handset into its cradle. 'No sign of Al-bloody-Said yet. If he's still going to show for the ID parade he's cutting it a bit fine.'

Marilyn Spark was in no shape for an identity parade just yet, but Walker decided, shaky though he may prove to be, Al-Said's evidence – that he had caught sight of the men in the van under the one functioning streetlamp in the alley – was enough to warrant a visit to Kilburn in the hope that he would pick Morton out. The witness had been due at the identification suite twenty minutes ago.

Satchell expected Walker to agree. His impatient nature tended to feel everything was being cut a bit fine when the heat was on. But today the guvnor was oddly relaxed, just for once.

'I wouldn't worry. Morton's not ready anyway – he's still with that Maddox woman.'

'Corinna Maddox.' Satchell pronounced the name sardonically. 'I remember her, now that I've seen her. Worked on a case in Fulham about five years ago and got nicknamed Batwoman because of the cape. Bloody nightmare she was too.'

Before Walker could reply, Pat North arrived back from the Middlesex.

'How's the patient?' asked Walker immediately.

North had moderately good news, but was in no hurry to impart it. She deliberately hung up her coat and sat down at her desk, firing up the computer. Walker hovered over her impatiently.

'Well? What did the doctor say?'

'She's made a remarkable recovery. She's a tough bird.'

'Good. So we can . . .'

North shook her head.

'No, we can't. Not yet. There's no way we're going to get her to the ID suite for a while. She's still bedridden, can't move around.'

Walker turned and walked smartly back to his own desk, where he picked up the phone.

'Get me the front desk.'

He tapped a pencil while he waited.

'Let's just hope Al-Said can ID Lord of the Flies then. I don't want him walking out of here again. Ah yes, is that the ID inspector? Detective Superintendent Walker here. Has Mr Al-Said come in yet? No? Give me a buzz as soon as he does, OK?'

The door of the Incident Room swung open and the legal profession's answer to the greatest of the comic-book super-heroines stood at the threshold.

'Detective Superintendent Walker, please,' Corinna Maddox called out in a commanding voice.

* * *

'I'd really rather you didn't smoke, Mr Walker!'

In the interview room Maddox wafted the air with her hand, sat down and waited for him to stub out his cigarette. She was treating him like a recalcitrant small boy.

'Mr Walker, you arrested my client on suspicion of the attempted murder of Marilyn Spark two days ago.'

Walker nodded.

'You subsequently released him after sixteen hours and then arrested him *again*, a few hours later, for the murder of Carol Lennox.'

These were not questions but assertions. Nevertheless, Walker felt compelled to answer.

'Yes,' he admitted.

Maddox opened her eyes wide.

'I *must* say, I'm surprised. Even after you'd searched his premises, you found no evidence to implicate my client in the murder of Marilyn Spark, either at his home or his office.'

'No, we found—'

'Marilyn Spark was the reason he was originally suspected, correct?'

Walker searched in his pockets and pulled out his packet of cigarettes.

'Yes. However, we did find a distinctive sweater at his home which matches perfectly the description of the clothing Marilyn Spark's assailant was wearing.'

'Uh-huh.'

Maddox was looking at her notes.

'But hasn't my client told you the sweater is not his?'

Walker stonewalled the question.

'It's with forensics now. We're checking.'

'And you have his company vehicle – a white Sherpa van – and it is being examined for forensic evidence?'

'Yes.'

'But so far, no results have been forthcoming on either the van or the sweater?'

Walker slid a cigarette out and played with it between his fingers. Maddox frowned.

'Not yet, no,' he said. 'However, an eyewitness to the murder of Carol Lennox has come forward and identified a distinctive hooded sweater worn by one of her attackers. This also matches the one found at Morton's house.'

Maddox was shaking her head now.

'But your eyewitness has not identified my client?'

'No.'

Maddox relaxed a little. She squinted at Walker.

'Mr Walker, is there a problem with this eyewitness? My client tells me he was supposed to be taking part in an identification parade this afternoon.'

Walker snapped the tip off the cigarette, put it between his lips and flourished a lighter.

'There's no problem, Ms Maddox,' he said and lit the cigarette. He inhaled deeply, watching her eyes narrow with disapproval.

'Or at least, none that I know of.'

Pat North tapped on the door and beckoned him out. In the corridor he had good news.

'Al-Said's just turned up at Kilburn, guv.'

Walker spun on his heel and confronted Maddox as she emerged from the interview room.

'You wished your client's ID parade to be expedited, Ms Maddox. Well, your wish has been granted. Are you familiar with the route to the ID suite at Kilburn?'

'I think I can manage to find it, Detective Superintendent.'

She swept past Walker and North towards the car park. Walker looked after her.

'What a lovely couple they make – Damon the Devil and Batwoman!'

North laughed. 'Batwoman? That's good.'

She held a file out for Walker to take.

'You're going to love these, guv.'

Walker pulled out the report forms, running his eyes rapidly over them.

North said, 'The slivers of wood found in both victims match each other and the DNA of the semen on both Lennox and Harrow is the same. We've got DNA matches for Garrett and both Bellini brothers.'

'And Morton?'

North shook her head.

'Shit!' said Walker. 'We'd better pray this Al-Said guy picks him out.'

*　　*　　*

At the Kilburn identification suite the viewing room has a one-way window through which witnesses are invited to pick out possible suspects from a parade of nine individuals. Ahmed Al-Said stood with the identification officer, whose job is to run the parade according to a set of rigid rules of procedure.

The lights inside the line-up room came on brightly and a green light shone in Al-Said's face. There were nine men in there, all around five foot ten and of similar build. They sat in a line, their hair of various shades from blond to brown, their clothes much of a muchness. The identification officer read out his text in a formal voice.

'On 27th April at about eleven p.m you saw four men in an alleyway near your place of work,' he was saying. 'One of these men may or may not be on this identification parade today. But I would ask you not to make any decision as to whether you can identify him before you have looked at each member of the parade.'

Al-Said nodded. He looked carefully up and down the line. He studied each man carefully, one after another, numbers one to five, six, and then seven and eight. He stared at each man. It was number six who gave him the most trouble. There was something about the man's eyes . . .

'It was very dark,' he murmured. 'Hard for me to see clearly. You understand?'

'Take your time.'

He did take his time. But after five minutes of dithering and getting increasingly anxious – he was finally almost in tears – Al-Said admitted that he did not know. He could not be entirely certain if any of the nine men had been present in the alleyway that night.

* * *

In the Incident Room Walker fumed at the news.

'We can't hold off any longer. Let's charge the other three for Harrow and Lennox and get them to the magistrates' court first thing. As for Damon Morton, he's in the clear.'

'We're not charging them for Marilyn Spark?'

'No.'

'But they've admitted it.'

Walker waved his hands palm down in front of her.

'I know they have admitted it. But Marilyn Spark insists only one man attacked her.'

North nodded her head.

'Damon Morton.'

'Who else? But it's not enough to hold him on. We've had to let him go – again!'

*　*　*

Next morning, at the magistrates' court, the Bellini brothers and Jimmy Garrett were remanded in custody. They stood in the dock like three dumb animals, penned and helpless. As they turned to be led away to the cells, they ritually cast their eyes up to the public gallery. There were Mrs Garrett and Salvatore Bellini, their eyes equally awash with tears. But the accused seemed hardly to notice their distraught relatives. They looked instead towards a slim figure in black, with a distinctive silver clasp on his leather bootlace tie. And Damon looked down on them, leaning on the rail, with a controlled smile on his face. Those three arseholes were going down, he was thinking. And everything was looking rosy. What was particularly gratifying was the way all of his three former employees had looked at him, the way sheep looked at their shepherd. There was not the slightest trace of resentment – and that was what he liked to see.

CHAPTER 18

MONDAY 11 MAY

For Walker and his team it now became an urgent priority to keep tabs on Morton. For one thing, there was the ever-present chance that their man would abscond, disappearing into the criminal underworld, from where it would be tedious, time-consuming and expensive to flush him out. But the other possibility was even worse. If Walker was right about Morton, what would there be to stop him murdering again?

Walker ordered a programme of twenty-four-hour surveillance. In the meantime, he wanted to know everything that could be known about the suspect. Some parts of Morton's background were deeply obscure. And the record had gaps where it was difficult to know his movements and activities with any certainty. But within seven days Walker had reasonably full information on Brian Andrew (alias Damon) Morton.

He was born in 1970 in Battersea, south London. His father, Declan Morton, who had been born in Ireland, had worked as a railwayman, though for most of the suspect's childhood was unemployed due to disablement. He may not, in fact, have been all that disabled, as there were eight little sisters in the family as well as young Brian.

It seemed that his mother may have engaged in casual prostitution, although this was difficult to confirm. There was no police record and while three of Morton's sisters were traced, none was willing to talk about the family. Brother Brian, in particular, seemed to have been excluded from their lives.

He attended Lavender School and Queen Henrietta Maria RC Comprehensive School, where records were consulted, showing a persistent pattern of truancy and disruption. The unruly child was placed in local authority care on two occasions (1979 and 1984) for periods of up to eighteen months when his mother could not cope with his behaviour. Social services were not prepared to release his care file but it was understood from Satchell's conversation with a retired caseworker (who requested her name to be withheld) that young Morton had caused considerable concern as a teenager, because of an apparent interest in Satanism and the occult, not to mention two unproved allegations of torturing and killing domestic pets.

He was already calling himself Damon when he left school at sixteen, at which point he ceased to live with his family and was taken in by his father's brother, Theodore Morton, who had an electrical repair business in South Lambeth. Damon Morton worked for his uncle, showing himself to be willing and quick to learn the trade. Uncle Theo, however, had his own police record, as it turned out. Once fined for gross indecency, twice cautioned for acts of indecency, he had been on an unofficial register of homosexuals known to police since the mid-1950s.

In November 1986 Theodore Morton was admitted to St Thomas's Hospital with severe lacerations, fractured ribs and skull and a broken arm. Damon Morton, sixteen at the time, was interviewed about these injuries but Theodore Morton had refused to press any charges. By 1988 Damon had left his uncle's house, and begun working as an unqualified electrician in various parts of the country. It could not be established for sure where he was living, but he almost certainly moved around – he was possibly in Liverpool and Scotland for a while, and US Immigration recorded that he entered America on a tourist visa through Newark, New Jersey, in 1991. He apparently stayed no more than two months.

In 1993 Theodore Morton died and left the house at Wycliffe Road and the adjoining business to Damon, who had by this time married Cindy. She had been born Cindy Taylor in 1975 and came from a south London background. Little else was known about Cindy. She may have been the same Cindy Taylor arrested for possession of a controlled drug (heroin) in 1992, for which she received an eighteen months' suspended sentence.

Since 1993, as Walker learned, Morton had become – outwardly at least – a model citizen. Although he was behind on the paperwork, there were no significant tax or VAT irregularities. He was unknown to social services, the benefit office and (until now) the police. On the face of it, then, this was the story of a man's rise from poverty and squalor to a degree of self-reliance and even, relatively speaking, respectability. But whenever Walker was tempted to believe that, he remembered Cheryl Goodall. The girl was now sixteen but, according to the mother, she had been underage when the affair started. That fact in itself was an antidote to any thoughts of Damon as an innocent man unwittingly drawn into the company of perverts.

Over the next ten days Morton couldn't have taken a roadside slash without Walker knowing about it. But in fact there had been nothing to disturb the suspect's set routine.

'Kisses wife . . . goes to work . . . screws teenage slag . . . kisses wife . . . goes to work . . . screws teenage slag,' complained Walker to Satchell, reviewing the day's surveillance report. 'It's the same thing every day.'

'Doesn't sound a bad old life to me,' remarked the detective sergeant.

'Shut it, David. You know how important this is,' warned Walker, slamming the reports down on his desk. 'That's what pisses me off – he's not put a foot wrong. Even Lolita here's the right side of sixteen now.'

'What about Marilyn Spark? If we can go ahead with the ID parade—'

'Pat's down at the hospital now. We're hoping the poor woman might be ready to ID the bastard tomorrow.'

As he spoke he turned, hearing the door swinging shut. It was North.

'Don't count on it, guv. She can't talk, just grunts and gurgles. And the way she looks – Christ, I've seen people in the mortuary looking fitter.'

* * *

At six Palmer and Hutchens took over from Brown and Baxter on observation duties.

'Anything new going down?' asked Palmer.

'Don't be funny,' said Brown. 'Just the old Cindy–Cheryl– Cindy shuffle, with a spot of carting around old tellies to liven things up.'

At seven fifteen Palmer's surveillance log recorded: '*Subject leaves the yard, driving black Fiesta hatchback, registration number C127 GWN, turns left into Flaxman Street . . .*'

'Off to cuddle Cheryl,' he said.

'As per usual,' said Hutchens.

They followed him along the first part of the route leading to Clapham. They had done this so often that Hutchens could have driven it with a sheet of brown paper pasted across his windscreen. At South Lambeth Road, anticipating Morton's normal left turn, Hutchens flipped his indicator down and moved into the nearside lane. It was Palmer who spotted the change: Morton was still in the offside lane and he was indicating right.

'Hey, *watch* him. He's going the other way!'

Extracting a long honk from the driver immediately behind them, Hutchens swerved abruptly back into line, four cars after Morton's Fiesta, and turned right behind him, heading north towards Vauxhall, the river and, beyond that, the West End. It was the first time their man had deviated from his routine. This had to be significant.

* * *

In the Incident Room Pat North watched Walker screwing up sheets of paper into balls and tossing them at the wastepaper basket. He was unusually tense, which – since tense was already his default condition – meant his nerves were now pulled taut as piano wires.

'So what *is* the earliest you think Marilyn'll be well enough to attend the ID parade, Pat?'

She had already told him that Dr Jaffre was refusing to be specific about Marilyn's prognosis. North shrugged. If the docs were hedging their bets, how would she know? Walker's face registered something between regret and a scowl.

'For God's sake, all we need her to do is sit in a wheelchair and take a look at nine blokes behind a glass screen. Not take them behind the bike sheds.'

The phone was ringing. Walker snatched it.

'Incident Room, Walker here. Hello? . . .'

Walker's face reacted graphically to the telephone. He usually seized the receiver full of energy, in the expectation of developments, movement, a *break*. But now his face dropped instantly and he momentarily held the phone away from his ear and looked at it sourly.

'Look, Lynn . . . yes, I know, but I can't . . . I can't talk now, OK? Yeah, I realise that, but—'

He rolled his eyes heavenwards in a mute appeal for strength. North got up and gestured to Satchell, miming a cup of coffee. As they left Walker, they heard him say, 'Lynn, God knows, if I could wave a magic wand I would. But I haven't got one.'

On the way down Satchell murmured, 'If he had one of those he could turn her back into the sweet and loving princess he married. That's what he really wants. But it's too late.'

'What's she like, Dave?'

'Don't know. Never met the woman.'

North could hardly believe it.

'What? You've been working with him just about every day for four, five years, and you never met his missis?'

Satchell shrugged.

'That's Mike Walker for you. Keeps his life in sealed compartments. He prefers it that way.'

* * *

Damon parked his car off Shaftesbury Avenue and plunged into the sex district of Soho. Dodging along behind him through the neon-and-spandex jungle of strip shows, sex video shops and table-dancing bars, Hutchens and Palmer were struck by how relaxed Morton was in this environment. Swapping remarks good-humouredly with the peep-show touts, he strolled at ease through the area.

He came to the door of a club with theatre lights around it and two heavyweights in bulging suits hovering inside. He had a few words with them and passed inside.

'That'll be twenty admission, gents,' said the first bouncer when Hutchens and Palmer arrived half a minute later.

Hutchens paid up with a sigh.

'Each,' said the other, holding out his hand to Palmer.

Inside the club there was a plethora of spangle and shine and an overwhelming sound system, powering out 1980s hits like they hadn't gone out of fashion. Various bored, kittenish hostesses sat around, their dresses extremely abbreviated, their lips glossed to a shine which matched their long, Lycra-shimmering legs. Morton was sitting on a chrome barstool, talking to one of the girls and drinking a beer. The police detail chose a table in the middle of the room. They were smiling together: this was what you could *call* duty!

Morton was now talking to the barman, who began mixing two drinks, poncy-looking cocktails, each with a paper umbrella spearing a cherry.

'Expecting company, is he?' said Hutchens.

'No, it's probably for the girls.'

The drinks were ready and duly shown to Morton, who nodded his approval and, clicking his fingers, summoned one of the hostesses. He spoke to her for a second, she put the two drinks on a tray and wiggled over to Hutchens and Palmer. She put the drinks down in front of them.

'What's this?' demanded Hutchens, who was a second row forward and a beer man.

'All taken care of,' she said in a little girl voice. 'Your friend at the bar.'

With a jerk of the head and a dazzling smile, she indicated Morton, still sitting at the bar.

'He says, do you want to party?'

They both looked simultaneously at Morton, who raised his glass and smiled.

* * *

Walker was not best pleased.

'Right, you dozy pillocks,' he said to Hutchens, Palmer, Brown and Baxter, 'as Mr Morton has gone some distance out of his way to let us know that, thanks to your screw-up, he is now surveillance-conscious . . .'

He looked around the chastened officers. He could see that Henshaw, Phelps and Brown seated nearby were enjoying their colleagues' discomfort. He went on, 'He is expecting us no doubt to get off his back. For that very reason we will not be doing so.'

Henshaw piped up, dubiously.

'You mean we maintain surveillance even though he knows we're on to him?'

Walker turned and fixed Henshaw with a withering look.

'You some kind of psychic, Henshaw? I could have sworn I just said that. But, if not, you must have read my mind.'

He glanced truculently around the room. There was complete silence except for the chatter of a fax machine.

'I also have to tell you all that the news from the hospital on our witness isn't great. We are *not* looking at an ID parade any time soon.'

'If she pulls through at all,' chipped in North.

Walker snapped his head round.

'What was that?'

Pat North shook her head. 'I saw her. But it's not all doom and gloom, guv. Forensics have positively identified the fibres found on the bodies of Susie Harrow and Carol Lennox and on the clothes of Marilyn Spark – they come from the jumper we found in Morton's house all right.'

'That doesn't help us if Jimmy Garrett claims the sweater's his and not Morton's.'

'Yeah, but we know Garrett,' said Satchell, 'he'll apparently admit to anything to keep Morton in the clear.'

Walker mashed his right fist into his left hand.

'Exactly, so if we're looking at losing our ID, I want two things. Any other evidence linking Damon to Marilyn Spark and any piece of evidence, apart from the flaming sweater, linking him to victims Harrow and Lennox.'

North said, 'We can link the van to the attacks. Dr Smith has found traces of blood from all three victims in it, even though it's been well cleaned out.'

'But not Damon Morton's blood. In fact, nothing from Morton at all. All we've got on the bastard is Marilyn's description. We need *more*! So I want everybody out there, I want you to go back over the ground again and if necessary again. There is something we've missed. There has to be!'

As he glared around the room, Satchell and North exchanged a glance. The guvnor was being a little heavy-handed tonight, wasn't he?

CHAPTER 19
MONDAY 18–TUESDAY 19 MAY

Over the next week the team revisited the ground they had already combed so carefully. Prostitutes at King's Cross, clients at Pinkers, dancers in the Snake Pit Club, residents in Stockwell, Carol Lennox's adult education students, all were reinterviewed. At one point North was on the track of a hooker who'd told another hooker that a man tried to lure her into a van, but it turned out that the man was fifty and the van was a lorry. At another point, Satchell thought he'd found Susie Harrow's still-missing bag.

'It was in Battersea Park. A similar type, but Susie's mother says it's not hers.'

'Pity,' said Walker. 'You actually seen the mother? She bearing up?'

'I don't know, guv. I do know old man Bellini's not doing too well. Had a stroke.'

Walker was concerned.

'You mean Salvatore? Will he be all right?'

Satchell nodded.

'He's OK, I think.'

Walker shook his head.

'I liked that old guy. He didn't deserve what happened to him. Bloody hell!'

Dull-eyed, Walker stalked out of the Incident Room in search of a coffee just as North was finishing the call she'd been on. She chased out after him.

'I was on to the hospital, guv. Marilyn's doing better. They say she's up for the identity parade. She's also able to talk a little.'

Walker had stopped in mid-stride. Now he turned, and his eyes were suddenly shining again. As the scales go down on one side they rise up on the other.

'Detective Inspector North, I was beginning to lose faith in women, but good news is never so welcome as when it comes from you!'

North was a little dumbfounded, not at all sure what to make of the remark. A compliment? A piece of sarcasm? A veiled confidence? Walker was rubbing his hands.

'Well, thank God something's happening anyway. Inform Ms Maddox, will you, that we'd like the pleasure of her client's company at an ID parade. I'm going for a coffee.'

North didn't want to let that 'faith in women' remark pass without some kind of response. It obviously betokened something new about Walker's domestic situation.

'Guv?' she asked, treading carefully. 'How *is* Lynn?'

Walker turned again.

'Lynn?'

His face was blank again and he spoke the name as if it was that of a stranger.

'How the hell should I know?'

Back in the Incident Room, Satchell told her the news of what had happened in the Walker household.

'He's renting a bedsit.'

North's jaw dropped.

'Did *he* tell you that?'

'Didn't have to. He was on the phone when I came in earlier, talking about "furnished" and "unfurnished". And he's underlined all these ads in today's *Loot*.'

Satchell was so know-it-all when it came to Walker, so sassy. She said, 'I see you're a detective after all, Satchell.'

'You still seeing that fat rugby player, then?'

Why did he ask that question? Probing to see if she was available to console Walker?

'Yes, as a matter of fact, and he's not fat. He's exceptionally fit, unlike some.'

'Oh, you go for the athletic type, do you?'

North snorted in derision.

'Be hard put to find one of those at this station, Dave. Get my drift?'

* * *

Walker asked Satchell to get over to the Morton house in the late afternoon. Ostensibly this was to ensure that Damon knew of the ID parade the next day, but Satchell's real purpose was to see how things stood in the Morton household. Were they confident or nervous? Calm or gouging each other's eyes out?

He found an outwardly cosy domestic scene. The table was littered with sauce bottles and dirty plates. Charmaine was colouring at the table. Karl, curled up in Damon Morton's arms, was toying with the silver medallion around his father's neck. And Cindy, sitting apart from the others, was playing cat's cradle with a loop of string.

'Just checking your solicitor has informed you about the ID parade, Mr Morton,' said Satchell.

'Yes, two o'clock tomorrow. No problem.'

Morton spoke without a shred of nervousness, like a man arranging to pick up his gran from the station.

Cindy, without looking up, murmured, 'What, you want him in another parade? You've already done that.'

'Probably because the woman who is causing me all this aggro, accusing me, wants to see me in the flesh – right?'

Satchell ignored the question.

'So you'll be there?'

'Yes, I'll be there.'

Morton adopted a mock-injured tone.

'Do I get compensation for taking all this time off work?'

But Satchell was not answering any questions today.

'See you there then,' he said.

But before Satchell could leave, Cindy suddenly piped up, almost straining to make sure he heard.

'Sunday 26th April . . .'

She had Satchell's attention. She wasn't speaking directly to him, though, but to her husband.

'You're never at home on a Sunday night. You were with . . . Cheryl!'

Damon smiled coldly.

'That's right, Cindy.'

He turned his ice-blue eyes on Satchell.

'I'm never home on a Sunday. When you said I was, you must have been mistaken – right?'

He shrugged his shoulders.

'Women!' he said to Satchell.

* * *

Marilyn Spark left the hospital in an ambulance. She presented a shrunken, shrouded figure as she was pushed in a wheelchair into the Kilburn police station, which housed the ID suite. Her face was heavily powdered, rouged and lipsticked; clown-like was the word that sprang to North's mind when she'd first seen her witness.

'Yes, I know,' Jill Ashton had said. 'She looks a fright. Just don't panic. She's wearing far too much make-up and she's wearing the scarf because her roots need doing. She's very, very nervous.'

'Sure she's going to be all right?'

'No, not sure at all. She got very distressed when they measured her for . . .'

Jill looked across at Marilyn, who was waiting at the entrance for them to find a ramp so the wheelchair could pass up a couple of steps.

'For what?' asked North.

'The breast,' said Ashton quietly.

Inside the ID suite a group of young men were sitting around reading tabloid newspapers, chewing gum and chatting quietly together. Damon Morton and Maddox were conferring over the volunteers, from whom the members of the parade would be chosen. As the accused, he had a certain amount of discretion and he used it.

'I don't like that guy on the right,' Morton said.

The man was excused and the identification officer said, 'Anyone else?'

'Yes. The youngish guy at the end. I want him next to me. And as I'm the only one wearing black, can I swap jackets with him?'

The officer asked the volunteer if he would mind exchanging jackets.

'Empty your pockets first,' he warned.

Marilyn was then wheeled in by another officer to hear the ID inspector's opening spiel.

'On 26th April at ten fifteen p.m. you spoke to a man driving a white Sherpa van on the Caledonian Road. He subsequently attacked you. That man may or may not be on this parade today. But I would ask you not to make any decision . . .'

But Marilyn had already done it. She could barely speak but there was nothing wrong with her eyesight, or her recall, and she had dismissed eight of the men instantly, none of them was anything like the man she wanted above all to put the finger on. And there he was, wearing the brown suede jacket, looking confident and smug as he stared at what, to him, looked like a large mirror. But of course, he knew she, Marilyn, was there, behind it, looking at him. He knew what he'd done to her. And what was more, he knew *she* knew it was him. But oddly she was not afraid. Bastard. That was what she wanted from him. Fear, pain. Just as he had inflicted them on her.

In a separate video control room, North was watching events on the monitors. Another officer was sitting in front of the recording equipment, adjusting the cameras and sound levels. Walker came in and whispered to North.

'I've just been back to the CPS. Good news.'

The Crown Prosecution Service was very often the bane of Walker's life. Although not his employers, they were nevertheless able to control his work, making decisions about what he could and could not do in ways he sometimes felt should be reserved for the police alone. But the CPS had to be kept sweet and informed, above all because they had the power to commence or to stop proceedings against Damon Morton.

'They say if she picks him out now for the attempt, we can have him for the other two women as well.'

North looked concerned.

'You sure, guv? Charge him just on similar facts? Don't we need hard evidence to link him with Lennox and Harrow?'

Walker shook his head.

'Not according to CPS. For once they appear to be on our side. The offences are practically identical. The facts of one will prove the rest. All Marilyn has to do is put him in the van with her that night and we can charge him with one, two and three and see how Ms Maddox likes it.'

Things were happening in the identification room. Marilyn was signalling for a pad of paper and pencil. Gripping the pencil as if it would save her life, she carefully wrote a number down on the pad before handing it to the identification officer. Then she went back to her savage contemplation of the man in the suede coat.

'Marilyn Spark, you have identified the man at position number six. Is that correct?'

A triumphant guttural croak emerged from Marilyn's voice-box while, from the rear of the room, Corinna Maddox pushed forward.

'May I see that?' she demanded.

She took the paper and saw the number six written in a shaky hand. Then she looked again at the man sitting at position number six. Although he could not have seen them through the one-way glass, Damon Morton seemed to be aware of their eyes on him. The faintest ghost of a smile played over his mouth and was gone.

* * *

Walker had the suspect brought with his solicitor into the adjoining interview room. There would be an immediate arrest.

He knew that a charge brought on identification alone always ran the risk of coming unstuck in court, but there would be plenty of time to get more evidence – even a confession. So, although it was a gamble, this for Walker was the only game in town.

Morton showed no sign of cooperating, however.

'Marilyn Spark has identified you as the man who attacked her, Mr Morton. What do you have to say?'

Morton shook his head, glancing confidently towards Maddox. In Walker's experience, prisoners on whom the identification trap has just closed often become confused, edgy and vulnerable. Not Morton. He was still perfectly in control.

'I have nothing to say. She must have been mistaken.'

Walker pulled himself up to his full height.

'Brian Andrew Morton, I am going to charge you with the attempted murder of Marilyn Spark.'

Morton still did not look alarmed, concerned or even uncomfortable. He expressed only contempt.

'That's ridiculous.'

But Walker hadn't finished.

'You will also be charged with the *murders* of Susan Harrow and Carol Lennox.'

He looked at Morton again. The man's jaw had dropped fractionally, but it did not stay like that for long, firming up as he remembered he was the great Damon Morton. He assumed instead an expression which suggested he might just spit.

Corinna Maddox's face, by contrast, was a picture of conflicting feelings. At one level she had failed, since her client was being charged on evidence that was (in her view) fairly flimsy. But then again, these charges meant that Maddox's locum stint at her husband's practice was turning into something considerably more substantial than the usual half-hour's bob before the local juvenile bench that she had been handling most often in recent years. This would be a big trial, with big publicity. There would be pressure, but there would also be excitement. She could hardly wait.

CHAPTER 20

WEDNESDAY 20–THURSDAY 21 MAY

In the offices of the Crown Prosecution Service a preliminary meeting between Walker and Clive Griffith, one of the special casework lawyers for the CPS, was taking place to review the evidence against Damon Morton. Griffith wanted to know first of all how the cases already commenced against Jimmy Garrett and the Bellini brothers would be affected by the fact that their employer was being charged with a matter they had pleaded guilty to.

'It's obvious,' Walker told Griffith. 'Now Marilyn's identified Morton, all the admissions the other three have made are suspect.'

Griffith nodded sagely. He always found Walker impetuous, but the man was not a detective superintendent for nothing and often talked sense. Griffith knew the best tactic was simply to let him speak his mind and use what he said as the basis for discussion.

'So what about the cases of Harrow and, um, Lennox, isn't it?'

'On Harrow and Lennox,' said Walker, 'we've got firm DNA evidence tying in Garrett and the Bellinis.'

'But you think Morton was there as well.'

'I reckon he wasn't just there, he was running the show. You only have to meet him, and then take a look at them. It's like a cult. He's got total control over those guys. Total.'

Griffith rubbed his chin.

'What we need is to give counsel the chance to get all that muck out of them in open court. In other words, we need them all as co-defendants.'

Walker was thinking that these lawyers sometimes seemed to imagine policemen had little more than a soggy J-cloth between their ears.

'Yes, Mr Griffith, we just about worked that one out. The trouble is, it's a bit difficult when they admit all the charges and he doesn't admit any of them. There's two different trials, right there.'

But Griffith wasn't a bit fazed by Walker's tone. There was a cunning light in the lawyer's eye.

'You need another charge. A charge which it is impossible for them to admit, yes?'

Walker frowned. What was this joker saying? From where was he going to conjure a charge like that?

'Like what?' he asked. 'They'd say they'd shot JFK if he told them to.'

'Like conspiracy to pervert the course of justice – in respect of the Marilyn Spark attack.'

Griffith had Walker's full attention now. He got up and paced to the mantelpiece, where he kept a silver box containing after-dinner mints. He picked one out.

'They say they did it and Morton didn't. If you can show that these admissions are false, and concocted deliberately with a view to exonerating Morton, there's your conspiracy to pervert. If these men want to go on protecting Morton, that is the one charge they will feel they absolutely have to deny. If they should admit it, it can only be because he's guilty.'

He bit on his mint and chewed with satisfaction.

'I seem to remember there was something in history called Morton's Fork, a question which damned you whichever way you answered. Well, here's Morton's Fork Two.'

Walker liked the idea. Liked it a lot. It was the perfect solution to his problem. Maybe these lawyers did have a few useful tricks up their sleeves after all.

'Will those charges be tried together with the ones against Morton?'

Griffith nodded.

'Absolutely. You'll get all four in the same trial and counsel can drag out whatever dirty linen he likes. If these men are as you say, they're not very likely to stand up to cross-examination, are they?'

Walker had heard what he wanted to hear. One trial. Now he got up.

'Two of them might be OK in the box. But Jimmy Garrett wouldn't stand up in a stiff breeze. Thank you, Mr Griffith. I think it's possible you've made my day.'

*   *   *

Of the almost 600 inmates at south London's Brixton Prison, only four out of ten are convicted men. The rest are awaiting trial on remand. These men, all technically innocent, receive considerable privileges within the wing to which they are allotted, including long visiting hours and non-compulsory work. So Vincent Nailer, himself awaiting trial for burglary, thought it strange that his cellmate, Jimmy Garrett, was acting as if he was on twenty-four-hour lock-up.

From almost the moment the word came through to Garrett that Damon Morton was to join him in Brixton he sat on his bed trembling. He refused to come out for his food, though he complained incessantly that he was hungry. Eventually Nailer offered to get Garrett's food trays for him, in return for a consideration of course.

Today, carrying in a tray with stew, potatoes, apple pie and custard, he found the kid more terrified than ever.

'You're going to have to come out for association, you know, Jimmy. Here, eat this. Make you feel better.'

'Did you see him?' asked Garrett.

'No, no sign at all. Saw the Bellini brothers, though. Your pal's probably segregated. Evaluation and all that, seeing the padre and the shrink.'

The meat on Garrett's plate was swimming in grey gravy. He loaded his spoon and shovelled it into his mouth, worked his jaw for a moment and suddenly made an inarticulate sound of disgust spitting the food back onto his plate and pushing the plate off his knee and onto the bed. Pieces of stew dropped to the floor.

'It's disgusting. They put something in it. It's shit.'

Nailer stood regarding Garrett with a look of amazement.

'Don't be stupid. It always tastes like that. Pick it up. PICK – IT – UP, you fat git!'

But Garrett had dropped to the floor and, clutching his fleshy throat, was making retching noises. Nailer kicked him, not viciously but hard enough for his foot to sink into Garrett's ample flesh.

'You don't think I'd do anything to the food. You're paying me two quid a tray, you prat. You're a nice little earner for me, Jimmy boy. Oh, well, sod it! Have it your own way. Eat off the floor if you want.'

He sat on his own bed and began steadily to eat his portion as Garrett started to cry. Nailer shook his head as he chewed.

The food was disgusting, but Garrett's snivelling behaviour was even worse.

* * *

Damon Morton had asked to be put on the wing with his mates, the Bellini brothers and Jimmy Garrett. The request was granted, but he still had another day – Thursday – of evaluation before he would be moved. His visiting rights remained unaffected, but he had told both Cindy and Cheryl to stay away. Corinna Maddox was another matter – he demanded to see her.

At Brixton, official visits are carried out in a complex where the interview rooms are ranged along a corridor, patrolled by prison officers who can see but not hear what is going on through a wall of toughened glass. Damon chose to try to dominate Maddox from the start, with no concession to the fact that he was being held on charges about as serious as they come.

'I'm not staying here, you know.'

It was an incontrovertible statement as far as he was concerned. But Corinna Maddox had already taken on board that he would be a handful as a client and was undaunted. She sat down at the table and opened the case file.

'That's exactly what I came to discuss. We can apply to the Crown Court for bail, of course—'

'That's not what I mean.'

Morton swung round. He was wearing his usual black clothes, but had been deprived of the array of clunky silver and steel jewellery he normally wore.

'There's no reason for me to be here. There's three men in this prison who know – *know* – they cut up those women and I didn't.'

Maddox held up her hand.

'Let's not discuss your defence now. We should wait until we've seen the CPS papers and know what they say. It's best not to try to address issues the CPS haven't raised yet.'

Morton could see the point of this. He made no objection.

Maddox then said, 'Do you want me to see if I can get you moved?'

Morton leaned forward across the table, close to her face. His tone was icy.

'Absolutely not. I want to see those men. I want them to give evidence for me.'

Maddox frowned and shook her head.

'That's a very big risk, very,' she said. 'They've got to sustain their guilty plea first and you honestly never can tell what they'll say in court.'

Morton held her gaze with his most penetrating stare.

'I *know* what they'll say. Just like I know that the whole police case hinges on that slag's ID. Prove she's lying or mad and they've got nothing. Whereas three blokes, all of whom work for me, will say *I* wasn't involved. Not in anything!'

He straightened up and strolled to the glass wall, insolently watching the white-shirted prison officer standing opposite him.

'Anyway, the other reason not to move me is there's no point. I'm going to get bail. I know it.'

Maddox shrugged. There really seemed very little to discuss. He was instructing her to make the bail application, that much was clear.

'I just want you to understand that it'll have to go before a judge. And, with a case of this kind, he may well refuse.'

'He won't refuse.'

Maddox began to gather her papers.

'I wish I could be half as sure about all these things as you are.'

Morton spun around and jabbed the air with his finger.

'Well, you get sure. That's how life divides – there's people that are sure and people that are not. And I want a lawyer who's a winner. Now let's talk about how you're actually going to get me out on bail.'

* * *

That afternoon, back at the office, Maddox rolled into her husband's room and caught him biting into a huge veal schnitzel covered in melted cheese and wrapped in a ciabatta sandwich. She looked at this mid-afternoon meal askance as he feebly tried to conceal the evidence.

'Derek, you may deceive me if you wish. But you know that, with your history of blood pressure, by eating fried food you are only deceiving yourself.'

She twirled off her cape and hung it behind the door.

'Now, I need counsel immediately for Damon Morton. He wants to apply for bail.'

'Ah, yes,' said the chastened husband, swallowing the last delicious mouthful that he was likely to extract from that particular snack. 'I've been thinking about Willis Fletcher for the trial. For the time being, what about a junior from Trench Court? Sunil's very good.'

His wife was looking into the mirror, tidying her hair.

'Oh, I rather fancy we want a leading counsel for the bail application, Derek. These are very grave charges.'

Derek Waugh shook his head and clicked his tongue. He needed to recover the ground he had lost over the veal ciabatta.

'*You'll* never get one to agree. But I could have a word, if you like ...'

But she was already pressing the keys of the phone.

'I think I can recall how to overcome leading counsel's resistance, dearest. I shall simply mention that this is a case which will appear in every newspaper in the country. And that if Mr Willis Fletcher feels unable to do the bail, we may find ourselves unable to instruct him for the trial. Oh, hello! May I speak to Barry, please ... Barry? Corinna Maddox here, Clarence Clough ... Yes, fine, thank you ... Yes, very much back, thank you. And I'd like to book Mr Fletcher for a murder case ...'

* * *

The more Walker looked at Morton's defence, the more he saw it depended on the personal control he liked to exercise over the people around him. Usually in these cases, control slackened off when the controller was not there: the mice-will-play syndrome. He wondered if Cindy might be prepared to play, now that her lord and master was away, and sent North and Henshaw down to the house to find out.

They found her distracted, distant, feeble. North wondered if she was needing a fix. Maybe without Damon she didn't know how to get gear. No, that was wrong, junkies always knew how to get what they needed. More likely, if that was the problem, she didn't have the money.

'Cindy, how is it that you remember so very clearly that Damon was at home on 16th and 27th April?'

Charmaine was sitting beside her mother, letting her foot swing. It touched her mother's leg.

'Don't kick, Charmaine. Stop it,' said the mother, and turned listlessly to North. 'You were saying?'

'What made those nights stand out from any other night?'

Cindy reflected. 'I just know he was here, that's all.'

'Though he's not here some nights. Quite a lot of nights recently, for example, he's been with Cheryl Goodall, hasn't he?'

Cindy smoked. She seemed more interested in the next drag on her cigarette than in North's questions.

'That's right, he has his routine. But he doesn't go out much other times. Saturday, Sunday he was usually with . . . Cheryl.'

Cindy's lips curled with dislike as she said the name. Charmaine's foot, still swinging, tapped her leg.

'Charmaine! Stop kicking me!'

She slapped Charmaine's leg and the child whimpered.

'I wouldn't have thought,' said North, 'that Damon was the type to stay in every night. He seems to like people around him.'

'He does. His friends come round here. All the time, yeah. They do.'

North sensed something in the way Cindy spoke. She tried a long shot.

'Cindy. Has Damon ever made you do anything with his friends, you know . . .'

Cindy gave her a hard look. 'No.'

'And he had no friends over here on either – or both – of those two nights?'

'No.'

Charmaine had slipped off her chair and was sidling up to North. Suddenly she reached out as if about to plant her hand flat on the detective inspector's left breast.

'Charmaine!' yelped Cindy when she saw this. 'Enough. Come here!'

The child went back and wound her arms around Cindy's thin body. North had seen Charmaine looking weirdly at her, like someone playing a stalking game. What, she wondered, were the favourite family games played in the Morton household? She shuddered inside.

She said, 'Damon's a very dominating man, isn't he, Cindy?'

But Cindy just shook her head, the blonde hair gently brushing against her daughter's identically coloured mop.

'No, that's not true. He's very loving. He's been very loving to all of us.'

CHAPTER 21

MONDAY 25 MAY

Preparation for the trial of a person on serious charges is an extended, complex and technical affair. Most accused prisoners apply to be granted bail while they wait to go to court, a decision which must be made by a judge, sitting alone. In Morton's case the judge had the happy name of Judge Jeffries.

Jeffries was assisted by submissions made to him by counsel on either side. He was surprised to see the distinguished QC Willis Fletcher appearing in the case at this early stage. At bail hearings he was far more used to dealing with juniors, such as young Camplin, whom the prosecution had briefed to oppose the defendant's bail application. Able chap, young Camplin, but Fletcher was top drawer.

'Mr Fletcher?' intoned the judge when the preliminaries were over and his court settled.

Fletcher rose magisterially. Bearded, he was a large man who amply filled his barrister's gown.

'May it please Your Lordship, I appear for the applicant. My learned friend Mr Camplin for the respondent. I understand there are objections to bail.'

He glanced at Camplin and sat down. The junior rose, looking nervous.

'The Crown oppose the grant of bail, primarily because of the seriousness of the offence. This is a case of an extremely serious nature concerning two allegations of murder and one of attempted murder, all involving mutilation of an extremely, er, serious kind . . .'

Camplin went on to outline the two killings, so that it was clear, if not in so many words, that this was a matter of a serial killer at work. He also mentioned the fear that the accused, facing such serious charges, might abscond before the trial. These were good enough arguments, but he reserved what he considered his best point for last.

'As Your Lordship will also be aware, much of the prosecution case depends on the evidence of an identifying witness, who is a woman living alone at an address within three miles of the applicant's home. We say that the likelihood of his interfering with this witness, or with other witnesses, is high.'

Jeffries now invited Fletcher to reply to the Crown's objections.

'My Lord,' he said, rising to his feet and selecting a piece of paper from one of the bundles in front of him, 'while I would not attempt to deny that this is a serious case, it is one which is fully contested in every respect. The applicant is a man of good character, with no previous convictions, who will be calling evidence of alibi in respect of all these charges. Mr Morton is a family man, with all the ties to the community envisaged by the Bail Act, and his presence at home is required, particularly at the moment as Mrs Morton has suffered from incapacitating bouts of clinical depression for some years, greatly reducing her ability to meet her domestic responsibilities. There are no other family members to care for the two small children under eight and these, if the applicant remains in custody, will have to be placed in the care of the local authority. For these reasons, I would ask Your Lordship to grant bail on appropriate terms.'

* * *

In Brixton Jimmy Garrett had forced himself to leave his cell.
He wanted to use the payphone. It was one of the few times
he had been out of his cell since hearing of Damon Morton's
arrest and now that Morton was actually on the wing, Garrett
had been even more reluctant to venture out. Vincent Nailer's
meal charges had gone up accordingly. He was now levying
three pounds a tray.

Yet Jimmy Garrett desperately wanted to talk to the one other
person in his life who mattered: Jean Dora Garrett, his mother.

'Hello, hello? Mum, it's Jimmy.'

There was silence at the other end, but he could just hear his
mother's quiet breathing.

'Speak to me, Mum. It's Jimmy . . .'

Mrs Garrett still did not – or could not – say anything.

'I want to talk to you, Mum, only you haven't been in to visit
me. Why haven't you been in, Mum? I sent you a visiting order.
I'm your son, I—'

'You're no son of mine.'

The words came out almost as a cough or a choke. To disown
your child is the most terrible act for a mother, the words difficult to think, let alone speak. But Mrs Garrett knew now what
horrors Jimmy had committed. Was this the baby she gave birth
to, the toddler she had taught to sit on the pot? Was this the
infant who had learned the alphabet at her knee and the boy
she had taken to the zoo? Rather than think it was, she had cast
Jimmy out of her life. She would never let him back in.

Coldly she listened to him on the other end of the line, the
voice sounding familiar. It was all too like the snivelling, pleading tone of her six-year-old begging for an ice cream and her
twelve-year-old who wanted a skateboard. But it was not him,
it could not be him.

'Mum, please. I want to explain. I lied, Mum. I lied.'

Yes, thought Mrs Garrett. He lied. He lied about being my son. She put down the receiver.

'Don't hang up on me, Mum. *Don't.* I'll tell the truth now. Oh, God! Mum? *Mum?*'

He sagged against the wall-mounted telephone unit, crying. He heard some laughter – more like sniggering – a few feet away. He looked up. It was Roberto. And a moment later Antonio joined his brother.

'Hey, Jimmy,' said Antonio, jerking his head in the direction of the television room. 'Come on, he's been wondering what happened to you. Now he wants a word.'

Garrett's mouth was wide and his eyes registered naked fear. But like an obedient dog, or a deserter marched back to where his commander was waiting for him, he fell in between the two brothers.

'Sit down, Jimmy,' said Damon. 'On this nice sofa, next to me. I want you to tell me truthfully and exactly what you were going to explain to your mother.'

Garrett swallowed hard and looked at Damon. The early appearance of fear had not left him. But it was now mixed with awed reverence as he said, in a dull monotone, 'I was going to tell her . . . I was going to tell her . . .'

He was shaking while Morton smiled his icy smile.

'You're going against my wishes, Jimmy, you know that, don't you?'

Garrett bobbed his head downwards once.

'And when you go against my wishes you know what you get, don't you, Jimmy?'

Garrett bobbed again.

'Kneel down then, Jimmy.'

As Jimmy Garrett knelt, as if in supplication, Morton stood up and, with a violent pull, wrenched the arm away from his chair. He raised the piece of wood above his head and brought it down viciously on Jimmy Garrett's back, once, twice, three times. Then he kicked him hard two, three times in the ribs and handed the makeshift club to Roberto Bellini, who followed Morton's example before passing the weapon without a word to his brother. Antonio in turn beat Garrett three times and gave the club back to Morton, who took his second turn. And so it went on until Morton was satisfied.

Ten minutes later, Garrett lay on the floor of the television room, his face and body covered in weals and swollen, tender areas where the flesh would swell and bruises would come yellow, black and blue over the following days. This is the state he was in when Prison Officer Fowler found him.

'Who did this to you, Jimmy?'

Garrett snivelled.

'Nobody.'

'Come on, Jimmy. Don't give me that. Tell me, I can help.'

'Nobody did anything to me. I fell over a chair, that's all.'

Fowler leaned down and hooked a hand under Jimmy Garrett's armpit to help him up.

'Come on then, sunshine. If you don't want us to get you justice, we can at least try and get you comfortable.'

* * *

After getting Jimmy Garrett painfully back to his cell, Fowler set off to find Damon Morton.

'Morton, did you beat up Jimmy Garrett?'

Morton was reading a copy of *The Sun* in his cell. He looked up.

'What?'

Fowler repeated the question and Morton folded his paper.

'Hey, you're out of order. You can't just accuse me of beating another prisoner. Besides, it would be ridiculous of me to so much as threaten Jimmy Garrett. My bail application's up today. It wouldn't do to jeopardise my release now, would it?'

'You must think I was born yesterday, Morton.'

Fowler looked down at Morton with distaste.

'I'd love to get the chance to keep you here, young man. Find out what's really going on. But, luckily for you, your bail has been granted.'

*　*　*

Walker had hardly been able to believe his ears, storming into the Incident Room.

'Makes it all worthwhile, doesn't it?' he said savagely to Satchell. 'We fucking knock ourselves out to bang this nutcase up. We throw God knows how many thousand quid at the case. The witness practically kills herself identifying him and now the bloody judge in his God-like wisdom sends him straight back out on the streets.'

'Who was it then?' asked Satchell.

'Need you ask? Bleeding-heart Judge Jeffries. Doesn't live up to his name, does he? Funny how defendants in front of him get bail just because they're married to suicidal wives, like he was!'

He approached Pat North's desk, where she was typing a memo.

'Have you told Marilyn about Morton's bail yet?'

North said bitterly, 'Yes, I've told her. I've also told her she'll be rehoused under the witness-protection scheme as soon as she's discharged from hospital.'

'When's that?'

'Tomorrow morning, bright and early!'

Walker rubbed his chin.

'Morton's going to try to go after her, I know he is. He's got to. Without her, the whole case will pack up. Put Jill with her. Some of those Victim Support people need support themselves in my experience.'

Satchell as ever tried to inject a little optimism into the situation.

'The bail conditions are very tight,' he said. 'If he goes into the same postal district as Marilyn we nick him.'

Walker was pacing around, digging a cigarette out of his pocket.

'You know what's wrong with these judges? They start out as lawyers.'

He ripped the tip off the cigarette, as if it was a lawyer's head.

'Pompous tight-arsed bastards who spend years at university learning just one thing – how to lose touch completely with ordinary bastards' lives.'

He swept towards the door and banged out.

Satchell pointed after him.

'He's been on another bloody planet lately.'

'Yes, it's called Planet Solicitor and he's hating it. He was seeing one this morning.'

'Well, Corinna Maddox would make anyone lose their rag.'

North smiled.

'No, David. He was seeing a family lawyer.'

Satchell stared at her for a fraction longer than was natural.

'A what?'

'About, you know, separating – from his wife.'

Satchell was thinking, How the hell does she know this and I don't?

'I see – well, that's it then, isn't it?'

North had started typing again, but she stopped as a new thought struck her.

'Have we run a check with social services, see if there's been any problems with Morton's kids? If they happened to be on the At Risk register we might be able to use—'

'Been done,' said Satchell quickly.

He'd done it himself while researching Morton's background, and it had been the first thing Willis Fletcher had asked about too.

'The Mortons are fine, according to the local authority. An ordinary happy family.'

'About as happy as Walker's!' said North sourly.

* * *

'Damon?' asked Cheryl, lying beside him in bed at Ridbelow Road as she passed him the post-coital joint.

'Yeah?'

'The police were round here again while you were inside.'

Damon Morton propped himself up on his elbow and took a drag, inhaling deeply.

'Oh, yeah? I told you they would be.'

'Well, they talked to my mum about that statement I made. She says she'll throw me out if I go to court and say all that.'

'She's said that before.'

'This time she means it, nasty cow.'

Morton flopped back and linked his hands behind his head.

'Well, we can save her the trouble. It's simple. You can come and live with me.'

'Oh, yeah! Brilliant, Damon. You're going to leave Cindy.'

He shook his head.

'Not yet. I want us all to stay together until this trial's over. You, me, Cindy, the kids – all of us.'

Cheryl couldn't prevent her lip curling in disappointment.

'I don't want to do that, Damon.'

'Doesn't matter what you want, Cheryl. *I* want you to. We're all *family*, Cheryl, and we stick together.'

She was twisting a trailing lock of hair around her index finger.

'But you and me can't do the things we do, with her watching and listening and everything. And we can't do them here either.'

'So what? We'll do them in the office. Cindy never goes in there. Go on! Get your things packed, Cheryl.'

The look he gave her was not to be disobeyed. She nodded.

So it was that, two hours later, Damon and Cheryl arrived at the Morton house with a fish and chip supper and Cheryl's suitcases. Cindy hardly seemed to react to the news that Cheryl would now be living with them. Charmaine had heard their arrival and got herself out of bed. She was interested. She saw her father feeling Cheryl's bum as they crossed the hall.

They all sat down to eat the chips. Cindy was listless, her sulky indifference annoying Damon, while Cheryl bustled around, hoping to anticipate his wishes. She fetched him a beer and leaned over for a kiss.

'I've got no knickers on!' she murmured.

Morton snorted with laughter and reached out to grope her bottom again.

'Hear that, Cindy?' he said.

Refusing to respond one way or another, Cindy picked at the chips in their paper in front of her. But Charmaine had heard and thought it was funny.

'She's got no knickers on,' she said, with a giggle.

Cindy suddenly swept the chips from the table with a movement of her forearm. Tears were starting to flow from her eyes. Morton jumped up.

'Pick that UP!'

Cindy sat there numbly. She did not move as Morton grabbed the plastic ketchup bottle and stood behind her. Slowly and deliberately, he upended it and squeezed. A thick spurt of sauce hit Cindy's head and flowed down her cheeks and onto her shoulders. When she saw this Charmaine exploded into sudden laughter.

CHAPTER 22

TUESDAY 26 MAY

In the darkest hour of the night, lying on the upper bunk, Vincent Nailer was having trouble getting back to sleep. He'd been woken up by a howl from his cellmate below and now he was listening to a series of random bulletins from the tormented unconscious mind of Jimmy Garrett.

'No, no, Mum! See, Mum, see, Mum, he *told* me to! He gave me that thing and I had to . . . I had to . . . It was him who did it . . . *him* who did it all, Mum!'

Nailer sat up and called out, hoping to wake Garrett up.

'What did you say, Jimmy?'

'*He* killed them, Mum. He picked them up and told us what to do. Couldn't say no, Mum. Just . . . just looked at me and I couldn't say no.'

'Oi, Jimmy!' called Nailer sharply. 'Your mum's not here. Wake up, son!'

'He can – he can – he can just look at you, into your eyes. And you have to do what he says. Have to. Have to. Terrible bad things. Never, never tell anybody.'

Nailer had had enough. He vaulted out of bed and shook Garrett.

'What you talking about? Who can do that?'

To Nailer's surprise, Jimmy Garrett's eyes were open, but he seemed hardly aware of Nailer, or of his surroundings. He was lost in a trance, some inner dimension of guilt and terror, into which Nailer's questions penetrated like disembodied messages from another world.

'Damon,' he replied. 'Damon can. He cut their titties off, Mum. Their titties off. Put them in a box.'

He giggled.

'He said that Susie one had a big tart's box but the teacher was a tight little—'

'Shut up, Jimmy! SHUT IT!' yelled Nailer, slapping Garrett as hard as he could across the face. 'I don't want to listen to this. Shut it!'

Garrett flinched at Nailer's slap but did not appear to wake up. He rolled onto his stomach and presented his bottom like a sow expecting to be mated.

'All right, all right,' he snivelled. 'Just you, Damon.'

Nailer looked down at his cellmate and shook his head, sighing. 'What *did* he do to you, Jimmy? What did that bastard do? You're crazy.'

'Just you first, Damon. Just you. Just you.'

Nailer went to the door and hammered on it.

'Oi! Get someone in here! I don't want to listen to this sick prat no more!'

Behind him, Garrett was snivelling like a child.

'Damon, no! Please, not Charmaine! Not Charmaine! No, no, no, no, NO!'

* * *

Later that morning, Damon Morton arrived at the premises of Clarence Clough in the usual black clothes, with his leather jacket and bootlace tie. The business of the morning was to draw up his defence statement.

'Would either of you like tea or coffee?' asked Derek Waugh, hovering around the conference-room door. 'Judith's just making.'

His eyes were popping almost more than usual as he eyeballed the client. His wife wafted her hand in the air to dismiss him.

'It's extremely kind of you to offer yet again, Derek. Not for me, thanks.'

Morton smiled charmingly.

'Not for me either, thank you.'

Disappointed, Waugh drifted away from the door and Maddox resumed her pose opposite the client, elbows on the table.

'OK, your case has been committed for trial, Damon, and the prosecution have now furnished us with a certificate of primary disclosure of unused material. That means we have fourteen days to serve a written notice on them of your defence.'

Morton frowned.

'What does that mean exactly?'

'It means we have two weeks to get your defence ready.'

Morton shrugged.

'Well, what's all the fuss? It's simple. I wasn't there, I don't know anything about all this. Which I've said all along.'

There was a noise outside in the corridor and Derek Waugh put his head around the door, looked in, and then left again.

Morton noticed her irritated look.

'Do you mind him doing that?' he asked.

Maddox cleared her throat. She ignored the question.

'So, we've also got to say which parts of their case we take issue with and why.'

'That's simple too, isn't it? It's that woman, the one who says she identified me. I take issue with that bitch!'

'Well, I have something else important to tell you, Mr Morton. Further charges are to be brought against both you and your former employees.'

Morton stiffened, frowning. 'What charges?'

Corinna Maddox looked at him keenly. She had seen her client's manner change, seen the surprise on his face. He wasn't expecting a hitch.

'The extra charge is conspiracy to pervert the course of justice.'

'What? That's ridiculous.'

'The police are saying that the confessions made by James Garrett and the Bellini brothers in respect of the attack on Marilyn Spark were demonstrably false.'

She still watched him like a bird eyeing a worm. He was rattled.

'That's not true. They weren't.'

'The prosecution will also maintain that those confessions were made on your prior instructions.'

Damon relaxed slightly, forcing himself to lean back in his chair.

'What – that I told them to? That's just a load of rubbish. They can ask them about it in court, if they like.'

Maddox was shaking her head, tut-tutting.

'No, that's the last thing we want. But I'll tell you one thing. It strikes me as very odd that the Crown should bother to pursue – at considerable expense – this perversion charge against three men who have admitted murder and are clearly already facing two life sentences each.'

'So why are they?'

Maddox smiled. She had begun to get the measure of Mr-cocksure-Morton at last. He was hanging on her every word.

'Well, if you ask me it's a tactical manoeuvre, rather clever. They're doing it because they clearly want those three men in your trial at all costs.'

'So they can cross-examine them?'

'Absolutely, about . . . well, all aspects of their relationship with you.'

'What's the best thing for us?'

Maddox began to look uncomfortable.

'The best thing they could do, from our point of view, is in fact to plead guilty. Then they won't be in court with you. Do you see my point?'

Morton was nodding. He saw the point all right.

'Then that's what they'll do.'

At that moment Derek put his head round the door yet again. This time he had a message.

'Detective Superintendent Walker on the phone for you. Line two. He says it's urgent.'

* * *

At around the same time Marilyn Spark, with Jill Ashton to help her, was walking gingerly into her old flat, looking with a sense of nostalgia at her things, few though they were. It was a small basement, basically a bedsit with a kitchenette and a phone-box-sized shower. Marilyn was not staying long. The purpose of this visit was merely to collect her belongings prior to settling into the safe house.

'You'll have a bit more room in the new place anyway. It's got two bedrooms.'

'And he won't know my address?' said Marilyn nervously. Her voice was subdued, still hoarse from her injuries.

'He won't know this one – it's just to be on the safe side.'

Marilyn went to her wardrobe and pulled out a battered suit-case. She opened it on the bed and started putting clothes into it.

Jill looked with curiosity at the wardrobe of a hardened street-walker – multiple pairs of stiletto shoes, mini-dresses, cheap underwear, chokers.

'It's nice of you to come with me and everything. I wouldn't have liked coming back on my own.'

She paused with a lace suspender belt in her hand.

'Never thought about it before, but that's what I am now, on my own again.'

Marilyn took less than twenty minutes to finish her packing. She stood at the barred window, looking out into the narrow area and up into the street, sipping a mug of tea. Shortly a police car – unmarked, Jill had reassured her – would be there to take her to her new address.

'It's not that I'm not grateful,' she was saying. 'I just can't believe it's necessary. I mean, why's he not locked up?'

'I'm sorry, Marilyn,' said Jill. 'We were surprised too. I mean, *surprised* isn't the word, actually!'

Marilyn's eyes tracked up towards the street. A man with short fair hair was walking along the pavement outside. He stopped right in her line of vision to light a cigarette. He wore a black leather jacket and a dark shirt and there were rings on his fingers of silver or stainless steel. Then he looked down at her and her grip on the mug of tea relaxed. The mug broke with a splintering sound but Marilyn did not hear it. The liquid was hot and splashed her leg but Marilyn didn't notice the pain. She was giving out a long, hoarse cry.

'Jill! Oh, my God! He's out there! He's *found* me!'

But by the time Ashton had reached the window, the man had gone.

* * *

Walker felt vindicated. Out on bail less than a day and Morton was already harassing Marilyn. Immediately upon receipt of Ashton's radio call from Marilyn Spark's flat he gave orders for Morton to be picked up.

The trouble was the police couldn't find him. He was nowhere to be seen in the vicinity of Marilyn Spark's place and Cindy, when they called on her, just said he'd gone out. On business but she didn't know the details. That was when Walker made the decision to call Corinna Maddox.

It was one of the biggest mistakes he was to make in the whole investigation.

'Ms Maddox, I wonder if you could tell me the whereabouts of your client Damon Morton?'

'Yes, I certainly can tell you, Detective Superintendent. He's sitting at the other side of my desk right now.'

'I see. I am very anxious to know where he was this morning, about forty-five minutes ago. Would you mind telling me how long he's been with you?'

'Oh, over an hour. Would you like to speak with him?'

She heard a muffled curse from Walker's end and he said, 'No, thank you, Ms Maddox. If it's all the same to you, I'd rather eat live frogs.'

'As you wish.'

But Walker had gone.

'Well?' asked Damon. 'What did he want?'

Corinna sat for a moment, drumming her fingers on the conference-room table.

'He didn't say . . . But I'm wondering if he thought for some reason you were doing something you shouldn't – something in breach of your bail conditions, shall we say, such as making some kind of approach to Miss Spark.'

'Well, I wasn't!'

'Oh, I know that, Mr Morton, because the period Mr Walker was interested in was forty-five minutes ago. You were here. But if Marilyn Spark says you were near her place, then your counsel's going to send her a large bouquet of flowers.'

'How's that then?'

'Because if she told the police another man was you, it will help greatly to discredit her identification of you at the Kilburn ID suite. Won't it?'

'Yes,' said Morton slowly. 'Yes, I suppose it will, won't it?'

There was something just a little sinister in the way he then laughed, Maddox thought. But the case was going well. *She* was making it go well.

CHAPTER 23
WEDNESDAY 27 MAY

Control and discipline had to be maintained and Morton had told Antonio Bellini to phone him at nine thirty every morning for reports and instructions. Today he explained patiently about the new charge of conspiracy to pervert the course of justice in relation to the attack on Marilyn Spark. He then told him what he, Damon, wanted the Bellinis and Jimmy Garrett to say: that, yes, they had been lying. He now wanted them to plead guilty to conspiracy.

'But I don't get this, Damon,' whispered Antonio into the wing payphone. 'We agreed what we'd say. Why don't we just stick with it?'

'Because I'm *telling* you to say something different now, that's why.'

'Well, OK, Damon, if you say so. But I still don't see why we got to change our story.'

'Tony, listen to me. Don't worry. Nobody's recording this – yes, I know they're supposed to but I know they don't really. Now you've got to trust me. If what you've said never gets heard by a jury, it doesn't exist. So if you don't go to trial it's what the lawyers call inadmissible evidence. It doesn't matter a fuck what the police think.'

* * *

Half an hour after this conversation another call was made out of Brixton, this time through the switchboard of Metropolitan Police One Area AMIP to South Lambeth Street. Pat North, who was talking to Duty Sergeant Morris at the desk, took the call.

'Yes ... Any idea what he's saying? ... OK, yes. I'll have a word with Detective Superintendent Walker right away ... Yes, very interested, I'd say.'

Finding Walker on his mobile, she caught the tail of his conversation.

'She's changed the locks now! And I need to get into the house. Can't you get her solicitors to ... Yes, I know, but I need a clean shirt and some socks! Well, just arrange a time, will you? ... Yes, when it's convenient to her!'

He disconnected and looked truculently round at North.

'Yes?'

'Sorry, guv, but there's a call from—'

Shutting his eyes, Walker butted in.

'Don't tell me. Marilyn Spark's seen Damon again, up a tree this time.'

'No, guv. It's the security department at Brixton Prison. Apparently the inmate sharing Jimmy Garrett's cell has asked to see someone.'

'What? Don't tell me he's admitted to being our slasher as well.'

North said nothing for a couple of beats. The man was being a pain this morning – nothing too unusual there.

'No, not that. But apparently Jimmy Garrett talks in his sleep – and maybe not just in his sleep.'

Mike Walker came round instantly. He did that. One moment he was wallowing in cynicism and despair, the next he was more gung-ho than Joan of Arc. He checked his watch.

'This is it. This is our breakthrough. Get Satchell and Brown over there.'

'Don't you want to do it yourself?'

'Love to, but we're overdue at chambers with CPS and counsel. They've briefed Rupert Halliday and he's no small-potatoes merchant. See you downstairs.'

North walked over to Dave Satchell's desk. The detective sergeant was filing off a ragged nail on his little finger.

'When you've finished your manicure . . .'

Satchell looked up. His smile was not a little competitive.

'And when *you've* finished earwigging the Super's personal calls . . .'

North ignored this sally.

'Will you and Brown get over to Brixton as fast as you can? You got a Vincent Nailer to interview. He shares a cell with Jimmy Garrett.'

'Uh-huh.'

Satchell put in a finishing stroke to his nail and dropped the emery board on his desk.

'Interview him about what?'

North passed him her note about the telephone call from Brixton security.

'Garrett talks in his sleep. He's been saying some interesting things.'

* * *

Approaching the narrow street in which the barrister's chambers were to be found, North's way was obstructed by a black taxi, whose fare had got out and was arguing with the cabbie. Fuming impatiently in the passenger seat, Walker leaned over and jabbed the horn.

'Come on, come on!'

The man in the road, bristling with self-importance, seemed to be objecting to the way the driver was conducting his business. The driver, on the other hand, was not impressed. It was a stand-off.

'Bloody toffee-nosed bastard. Thinks he owns the road,' said Walker, winding down his window. 'Get out of the bloody *way*! Come on, Pat, drive round them, drive round. We're late!'

North backed up and began to edge forward onto the pavement to get past. It was narrower than it looked. Walker quickly lost patience with this manoeuvre too.

'No, no, no. Go back! Go back!'

North put the car into reverse.

'There's space on a meter twenty-five yards behind us,' she said.

'Park there!'

She started to move rapidly backwards but Walker would not wait.

'No, just let me get out. Stop the car.'

She braked and Walker slammed out of the car. He strode towards the portly, grey-haired man who was still arguing with the cabbie in a loud, theatrical voice.

'If you had come over Lambeth Bridge instead of Blackfriars you'd have missed the traffic. The fare's double what it should be and don't think I don't know it!'

Walker went up to the man, jabbing his finger.

'You're causing an obstruction. Do you realise that?'

The man turned and looked at Walker as if from on high.

'I suggest you mind your own business.'

But Walker was already striding away, towards the entry to chambers, muttering to himself, 'I could *make* it my business, pillock!'

Halfway up the carpeted stairs of the elegant chambers building he waited for North, who caught him up breathlessly.

'Guv, the guy outside with the taxi who you had words with – he's Rupert Halliday, our prosecuting counsel!'

Walker did a double-take as the eminent QC arrived at the foot of the stairs. Halliday looked up sarcastically at Walker.

'Hurry along there,' he said. 'We don't want to cause a further traffic jam, do we?'

* * *

So Walker's conference with Halliday began awkwardly. For Halliday the incident had merely served to confirm his view of policemen, which was that they were always in too much of a hurry and always trespassing on the rightful territory of lawyers.

Griffith made the introductions ('The detective superintendent and I have already met – in a traffic jam,' smirked Halliday) and outlined the case against Damon Morton as it stood at present.

'How's your identifying witness?' asked the QC, looking at Walker. 'She's out of hospital, I believe.'

'Oh, er, yes. She's been rehoused, witness-protection programme. She's recovered very well, considering.'

'Yes,' said Halliday, nodding his head slowly. 'And you're confident enough she'll hold up under fire? It's her they'll be having a go at, obviously.'

Walker and North looked at each other. It was the cue to mention the moment of panic at Marilyn's flat, but he and North had agreed in the car to say nothing of this.

'Yes, she knows that. She's very . . . I mean, highly motivated to go to court. Very keen to get him.'

Halliday approved.

'Good. And what about these other three scallywags, the ones charged with conspiracy to pervert? That was on the basis of what? The police interviews? The Garrett fellow's obviously not the world's greatest intellect. What about the Bellini brothers?'

North said, 'One of them, Roberto, is intelligent. He should be able to stick to his story. His brother's more the thug. I'd say he'll trip himself up as soon as he opens his mouth.'

Halliday looked over his half-moons towards Griffith.

'Neat manoeuvre, adding in these conspiracy charges. We'll have the chance to cross-examine now. We wouldn't otherwise.'

Griffith glowed with pride at the compliment.

'Thank you, Mr Halliday. I thought it the best way to proceed.'

'As I see it,' continued the counsel, 'the more we can discredit these confessions, the more support we have for Miss Spark's evidence that there was only one man in the attack.'

He shuffled his papers, coming to one which he had marked with a pink highlighter.

'As I have already suggested, James Garrett's statements look the most promising from our point of view. They're by far the least consistent, both internally and in relation to the others.'

He stared at Walker, that hawk-like look over the half-moons.

'How did you find our Cinderella?'

Walker did not connect Garrett with the pantomime character and looked at a loss. Halliday helped him out.

'This jumper of many colours dropping fibres everywhere – did it fit or not?'

Walker couldn't answer. The thought hadn't occurred to him. And then he remembered a phrase from the O. J. Simpson trial: 'If it does not fit, you must acquit!' Well fat Garrett and slim Morton would take very different sizes of sweater, wouldn't they? Or would they? Sweaters stretch . . .

At this point his phone bleeped. Griffith and Halliday looked at him with irritation. Walker doubted that they even needed mobile telephony. But he was damned if he was going to turn off this wonderfully time-saving piece of kit just to suit their sense of good manners.

'Excuse me, it's my detective sergeant,' he said. 'I'll take it outside.'

It was Brown on the line and he sounded excited.

'Guv? Vincent Nailer's got information, really good it looks. But he wants us to put a word in for him. He's up for trial next week, burglary.'

'OK, OK, I hope you promised him everything, including a free holiday in Marbella. Come on, give, Detective Sergeant, give! What did he overhear Sleeping Beauty saying?'

'That Damon was with them when they killed the women. It was Damon picked the victims out. And he said something about tits being kept in a box.'

'In a what?'

'A *box*, guv. It sounds like Jimmy might want to talk anyway.'

Walker nodded, clenching his fist.

'It does indeed. And I'll be over there soon as I can.'

* * *

It was North who drove Walker to Brixton, but when they got there she discovered Satchell was not about to allow himself to be pushed into the shadows, not by a female detective inspector and especially not by this one. He greeted them with a handful of Mars bars.

'They're bringing Garrett back up now. These' – he indicated the confectionery – 'are to make him happy.'

Satchell then murmured to Pat North, part confidential, though loud enough for Brown to hear what he said.

'I hope you don't mind me saying this, but we think it'll go better if you're not here.'

Miffed, North withdrew.

With Satchell alongside him, Walker eyed the big kid across the table of the official-visit room, watching him fill his face with the gooey amalgam of chocolate and toffee.

'Jimmy,' he said at last, 'we won't take a formal statement from you until you've pleaded guilty, but understand you know where there's some other evidence against Damon Morton.'

Garrett had been chewing so long he was out of breath. He sucked air into his mouth and worked his tongue along his gum-line, eking out the sticky substrate of Mars bar that had stuck there.

'You have to protect me,' he said.

'No problem. You can be segregated in here, Jimmy.'

Garrett took another bar and in one movement expertly stripped off its wrapping. He chopped it in half with a single bite.

'What I said . . .'

He chewed furiously to clear the way for his words.

'. . . when I was interviewed wasn't true. My solicitor said you were charging me for perverting justice. Doesn't really matter, though. I'm getting life whatever.'

Satchell came in with, 'It would matter to your mum though, wouldn't it, Jimmy? She'd be ever so pleased if she knew you'd broken with Damon for good. It was him got you into this.'

Jimmy swallowed and lowered his voice confidentially.

'If I tell you something that will get him, will you tell my mum? She won't speak to me.'

Satchell nodded.

'We'll tell your mum you've been very helpful to us, if you *are* helpful, Jimmy.'

Jimmy considered. It was not hard to see that there was a tussle going on inside his head, a duel between the evil one, Damon Morton, and his mother. Finally, he seemed to make up his mind.

'I lied about the sweater. It wasn't mine, it was Damon's.'

Satchell and Walker said nothing for a moment, allowing it to sink into Garrett's brain that he had told a truth for once – he'd done something at last for his mum.

Then Walker, speaking gently, asked, 'Do you know anything about a box, Jimmy?'

Garrett's mouth gaped. They could see deposits of chewed Mars bar inside.

'You mean Damon's box?' He spoke hesitantly. 'You didn't find it, did you? You didn't look up in the ceiling, that's why. It's up in the ceiling.'

*   *   *

Walker immediately phoned the Incident Room and asked Morris to arrange an immediate search warrant and to send it down with Hutchens and some more back-up plus a photographer.

From Brixton to Damon's yard was not far and it took Walker, North, Satchell and Brown no more than twenty minutes. Access to a fast-track search warrant had enabled Hutchens, Baxter, Palmer and the photographer to arrive almost simultaneously.

Morton was in his office, coming to the door all courtesy.

'Good evening, Detective Superintendent. What can I do you for?'

'We require a further search of these premises. We have a warrant.'

He wafted the printed document, signed by a magistrate, in the air.

'You are, however, entitled to have your solicitor present if you wish.'

Morton smiled, throwing open the door and spreading his arms wide.

'I don't need my solicitor. Start wherever you like.'

Walker looked grimly at him and pointed to the ceiling.

'OK. We'll start with the concealed attic up there above your office.'

And the smile melted from Morton's face like snow on a hot plate.

The first thing the officers encountered was Cheryl, looking dishevelled. She wore her leather skirt and an unbuttoned baggy denim shirt which she pulled closed across her chest, folding her arms tightly. Pat North immediately noticed her glazed look and dilated pupils.

'We do videos too, if you're that interested,' Cheryl said sarcastically.

Walker looked at North and pointed through to the workshop.

'Take this young lady next door, will you?'

Their hands gloved in latex and standing on chairs, Baxter and Hutchens began methodically testing the ceiling for loose tiles.

* * *

Meanwhile, in the inner workshop, North stood with Cheryl, whose arms were still tightly closed over her chest. They listened to the bumping and banging from the office. Then something occurred to North and she turned and stood in front of the girl.

'You've got something under your top, haven't you, Cheryl?'

North made a movement of her hand and Cheryl flinched away.

'Don't touch me. I know my rights, you know.'

'I suspect you of being in possession of controlled drugs, Cheryl, which you are hiding under your top. I'd like you to unfasten it, please.'

Cheryl gave North her most sarcastic smile and suddenly with a flinging motion pulled open the cardigan. She was bare-breasted. A screw-in clamp was fixed to her right nipple, bobbing up and down as the pressure on it was released. On her left breast there was something worse: three long steel cobbler's needles driven through the flesh, in and out so that both ends were visible. North flinched. Cheryl saw the reaction and sneered.

'So – he gets off on tits. You going to arrest him?'

North could see not just the present needles but the marks of old puncture wounds in and around Cheryl's breasts.

'Did he do this to you, Cheryl? Did he put these needles in you?'

She shook her head.

'No, I did it myself, while he watched.'

*   *   *

'Here's one loose,' cried Baxter, still on top of his aluminium stepladder.

He was referring to the tiles which lined the entire ceiling. He pushed upwards, met resistance and banged hard. The tile flew up, revealing a hole in the plasterboard ceiling. Baxter eased first his torch and then his head into the cavity.

'Guv – it's here!'

His voice was muffled but the excitement was unmistakable. He came clambering down and a photographer took his place on the ladder. Flash photographs were taken of the inside of the roof cavity and, a few seconds later, Walker and his officers were looking at a wooden chest which had been brought down and placed on a low table. It was a couple of feet square, reinforced at the corners with metal and pierced with air holes. The clasp was closed but the box did not seem to be locked. The photographer moved around it, taking more shots.

Baxter looked at Walker, who nodded. Baxter picked up a chisel and levered the lid open, lifting it gently. The first thing they noticed was that the box contained two large screw-top jars and a paper package. There were also a sharp wide-bladed knife and two arrow-like weapons, fixed into clips on the inside of the lid. The arrows were between a foot and eighteen inches long, had wooden shafts and six vicious triangular knife or razor-blades fastened, like multiple arrowheads, into one end. They looked remarkably like the rough sketch John Foster had made, more than a month previously, of the implement used for the internal mutilations of Susie Harrow and Carol Lennox.

The policemen looked at these weapons blankly. The hatred that had spawned such devices was almost impossible to comprehend.

But Baxter was concentrating on doing his job. After the photographer had recorded the grim weapons in the box lid, he picked out the paper package, unwrapping it to reveal three thick tufts of hair, with lumps of skin still adhering to the roots where they had been torn away. Then, one after the other, he raised the specimen jars, holding them up to the light. To their horror, the policemen realised that each jar contained, suspended in some preservative, the severed remains of several female breasts.

CHAPTER 24
THURSDAY 28 MAY

The Plea and Directions Hearing, the next hurdle to be cleared in the trial's course, was scheduled for the next day. It represented the defendants' first chance to enter their pleas – guilty or not guilty. While the forensics labs were working feverishly on the contents of the box found at Damon's office, Walker and North sat helplessly in the well of the court, unable to influence events in any way until the scientists and lawyers had finished.

Walker watched Morton, sitting on a lateral bench, still a free man. He had been interrogated the previous evening but not a tiny part of his shiny assurance and arrogance was tarnished by the AMIP team's find the previous day.

He had simply told Walker, 'I didn't know the box was there. Do you think it is remotely likely that I would have left them there for *weeks* for you to find? I've told you, I never saw that box before in my life.'

North saw him looking chainsaws at Morton. She leaned over and said, in an attempt at reassurance, 'The lab's bound to get something we can use off the box.'

But Walker shook his head.

'Don't hold your breath, Pat. He wouldn't have left it there unless he'd cleaned it up.'

'You reckon he left it deliberately?'

'Of course he did. A bloody masterstroke. Because that would be such a stupid thing to do, much too stupid for a man of his superior intelligence. So he did it. Another nail in the coffin of our case.' He nudged her. 'Look at him. He's not taken his eyes off Garrett. You see him?'

Garrett and the Bellini brothers were aligned nervously together in the dock. Morton had been staring fixedly at Jimmy Garrett ever since they'd been brought up. Garrett, wanting to look anywhere but into those icy-blue eyes, looked beseechingly for his mother in the public gallery. She was not there.

'Is Mr Morton in court?' intoned the clerk lugubriously.

Morton identified himself and was asked to surrender himself to the dock officer. He was ushered over to join the other defendants in the dock. As soon as he took his place, Jimmy Garrett began to shake uncontrollably.

'Would you all stand, please?' asked the clerk.

All stood as the judge entered and the charges were read without delay.

'Brian Andrew Morton, Antonio Bellini, Roberto Bellini, James Garrett, you are charged with murder in that on 16th April 1998 you did murder Susan Zoe Harrow. Brian Andrew Morton, how do you plead, guilty or not guilty?'

Morton looked quickly around. He wanted everyone to see his self-assurance.

'Not guilty,' he pronounced.

'Antonio Bellini, how do you plead, guilty or not guilty?'

Bellini did not pause for effect, but seemed to rush it, his cry of 'Guilty' almost colliding with the end of the clerk's question.

After Roberto had also pleaded guilty, with a shade more confidence, Jimmy Garrett was asked. He had trouble getting it out.

'Guh-guilty.'

The clerk then repeated the same charge, with the name Carol Alexandra Lennox in place of Susie Harrow and the date, 27th April. Damon's plea of 'Not guilty' rang even more resoundingly around the court, while the 'Guilty' pleas of the others were low-key mutterings.

The clerk then turned to Morton for the third charge.

'Brian Andrew Morton, you alone are further charged with attempted murder, in that on 26th April, you did attempt to murder Marilyn Spark. How do you plead, guilty or not guilty?'

'Not guilty.'

As the clerk reached the final charge, Walker leaned forward in his seat expectantly.

'Brian Andrew Morton, Antonio Bellini, Roberto Bellini, James Garrett, you are each further charged with conspiracy to pervert the course of justice, the particulars being that between 28th and 29th April 1998 you conspired together that Antonio Bellini, Roberto Bellini and James Garrett should make false statements of confession to the murder of Marilyn Spark, with the intention of thereby perverting the course of justice. Brian Andrew Morton, how do you plead, guilty or not guilty?'

Again, that confident, purposeful statement.

'Not guilty.'

The clerk turned to Antonio Bellini, asking him the same question, and as he did so the court, expecting another denial, was shifting about, whispering and shuffling their feet. But Antonio stunned them by saying, quite distinctly so that everybody could hear, 'Guilty.'

There was a moment of startled silence and then a whisper of conversation in the public gallery which the judge had to stifle. The court settled down again, all ears for the pleas of Roberto Bellini and Garrett. They heard both men following Antonio in admitting their guilt to the charge of conspiracy.

'What?' whispered North. 'I don't believe this, guv. You hearing what I'm hearing?'

* * *

Pat North, back in the Incident Room, had no idea where this left their case. They'd been told Garrett and the Bellinis simply wouldn't plead guilty to conspiracy but they had.

'How does he do it?' she asked Baxter, who was boxing up a bundle of documents. 'Fresh fish? He's got them trained like bloody seals! They all pleaded guilty. But the good news is Jimmy Garrett's giving his statement right now.'

'So Morton stays out on bail?' asked Baxter.

'Yep. Let's hope he doesn't go out and kill someone else.'

Baxter scratched his head.

'But I don't get it. What about all the evidence we found in that box over his office?'

North shook her head.

'We can't prove he ever handled them, though. Forensics say there are no prints. Everything was cleaned with surgical spirit. But they do have matching DNA on the hair for the three victims.'

* * *

Over at Brixton Prison, as North had told Baxter, Garrett with Cookham in attendance was indeed supplying Walker and Satchell with a new statement about Morton's part in the attack on Marilyn Spark. He was in a state of abject terror but his evidence was everything they had hoped for.

'I wasn't there because it was my mother's anniversary. Bellinis weren't there because it was Tony's birthday or something. So yes, Damon, he done the King's Cross tart by himself.'

'So why did you say you attacked Marilyn Spark?'

'Because it's what we all agreed, isn't it? You see, after the schoolteacher, we was back in the yard, right? We was covered in blood and that, so Damon made us strip off and he turned the hose on us. Real laugh it was. He used the jet spray.'

Garrett's face was for a moment in repose as he thought about the scene. Walker felt sick, but he invited Garrett to go on.

'All right. Anyway, that's when he told us about the King's Cross tart he done, and if there was any comeback he told us we was to admit it. Like he said, we was all in it together anyway. Only it was more important that he stayed free because he couldn't do nothing for us – to help us like – if he was in prison along with us. That's basically what he told us and we agreed.'

'Why, Jimmy? Why did you agree to lie for Damon?'

'We were scared of him. I was, we all were. But we worshipped him too, you see? That's why. We . . . we, loved him.'

Walker and Satchell exchanged glances. It was enough. Surely now they'd got Damon.

CHAPTER 25

MONDAY 16 NOVEMBER, MORNING

Six months later, in spite of the best hopes of those prosecuting him (*per*secuting him, according to his own story), Damon Morton was to be tried alone. And he came to his trial jauntily, attended by his unorthodox ménage of wife and teenage girlfriend. Damon expected, and received, considerable attention from the media and posed with both women for the photographers, though he allowed them only a brief session. It was important to give everyone a fair crack of the whip, but equally important not to jeopardise his exclusive contract with a popular tabloid. They had bought provisional rights in Damon's story for a very secretive £250,000, payable in the event of him being acquitted. The other 'red-top' papers were pursuing Bibi Harrow, Colin Lennox, old man Bellini and Mrs Garrett, but these were also-rans, their stories sad or seedy. The glory – and the power – seemed to be all with Damon.

There was hysterical media interest and Damon Morton had famous Rottweiler tabloid hacks eating out of his hand. The paper that had signed him up had hours of interviews in the can, although because of the laws concerning contempt of court none of it could be printed until after the trial. Damon, the hacks and hackettes believed, was innocent, of course. He had never claimed to be a conventional sort of guy, but that didn't mean he was a serial killer. The story of the kid with the poor background, the unconventional lifestyle and the startlingly articulate philosophy of life ('There's people that are sure and people that are not. And the people that are sure are the ones that control things.') was going to sell a lot of newspapers. No less interesting was the remarkable contrast between his wispy wife and that junior biker's moll of a girlfriend, both of whom now lived with him.

Once he had finished with the hacks, Damon had to cast off his persona as a media darling and put on a fresh one, that of injured innocent. He did this easily. He was already using a more-in-sorrow-than-in-anger face as he walked towards the court. The usual rigmarole of surrendering himself to the justice system had to be gone through. But soon he would be free for ever. He knew.

Halliday arrived with his junior, Camplin, and walked past the Morton group. He saw Willis Fletcher ahead of him and caught him up, matching strides.

'Are those our Satanists over there, Willis?'

'They certainly are.'

'I read dark rumours about ritual sex acts,' said Halliday.

'Really?' said Fletcher, not to be drawn.

'Yes, but what is a ritual sex act anyway?' put in Camplin.

Halliday took this as a cue for humour.

'You have to say you've never done anything like this before, take her to Covent Garden and swear three times you're leaving your wife.'

Camplin and Fletcher laughed heartily.

'Well,' added Camplin, 'from what I gather, our very own Dr Faustus is very much staying with his wife – but he gets to keep thc teen flesh into the bargain.'

'Must really be getting help from the Evil One then. As indeed they are hinting in the lower reaches of the press.'

'Who should know, of course.'

They went on their way towards the court building, carrying their bundles, each feeling the tingling adrenalin that accompanies the start of every high-profile case. It is an addictive buzz which never quite leaves you, however high your eminence at the Bar.

Corinna Maddox was also feeling the same wonderful high. In her customary flowing cape and manifold bangles, she hailed Willis Fletcher across the lobby like a long-lost friend.

'And is this another of them?' murmured Halliday to Fletcher as Maddox bore down on them.

'Not exactly,' said Fletcher. 'My instructing solicitor.'

'Good morning, gentlemen,' trilled Maddox. She seemed to be on her way to the main door of the building.

'Going the wrong way, aren't you?' asked Fletcher.

'No, I'm coming back shortly. Just sending Mr Morton's harem home. They don't seem to realise witnesses can't spectate.'

A short distance away, a small knot of parties connected to the case (as distinct from mere spectating members of the interested public, who were waiting their turn elsewhere) had assembled in the care of an usher, prior to entering the court's public gallery. Bibi Harrow was there, as was Salvatore Bellini. Colin Lennox was in his corduroy suit, which presented quite a contrast to the baggy black T-shirt, satin snowboarding trousers and blizzard-white trainers worn by Nicky Burton, who stuck close by Bibi.

'You here for the Morton trial too?' Colin asked him.

'Yeah,' said Nicky. 'My girlfriend was one of the – you know.'

Colin nodded his head. He knew.

'Same here,' he said. 'My wife.'

Nicky looked at Colin. He'd never before felt fellowship with a middle-class teacher-type like this one. He burst out, with new warmth, 'Well, they better get this bastard, huh? Nail down the lid.'

Colin nodded again.

'That's what we're here for.'

'Yeah, right. And it's been a long, long wait, brother.'

* * *

Marilyn Spark thought the suspense would never end. In the witness waiting room she was strung out, couldn't stop pacing and perpetually twisting her scarf around her hand. For once, Jill Ashton's presence failed to calm her.

'Will I have to go first?' she wanted to know, lighting her fifth cigarette since they'd got here.

'Yes, you will.'

'God, I wish it was over.'

'It won't be for a while yet, I'm afraid.'

'The two other women who died. I keep thinking about them. Can't get them out of my head.'

Jill shook her head sympathetically.

'I'm not really allowed to discuss the case, Marilyn.'

Marilyn continued to smoke and prowl the room.

'I just want to get it over with.'

* * *

Walker and North had heard that Garrett, on the way to the court in the security van, had been bawling that he wanted to be taken back to Brixton Prison. He was stark terrified of the ordeal ahead of him, but whether it was the prospect of facing Judge Winfield and the court or Damon Morton was unclear.

Walker knew it was the latter. In any case, Garrett was telling everybody he wasn't going into the witness box after all.

Walker immediately headed off to the custody area, moving so fast that North could only just keep pace with him.

'Maybe it would be better,' she was saying breathlessly, 'not to call Jimmy. We know Halliday doesn't want to.'

'Yeah, I know he doesn't. Thinks he can do it all off his own honeyed tongue. But I will be very pissed off if Garrett's perfectly good thirty-page statement, spilling all the dirt on friend Damon, goes down the toilet.'

They had reached Jimmy's holding cell. With his fingers on the door handle, Walker turned to her and said, almost furiously, 'So just leave the talking to me!'

They found the witness sobbing, and his face bearing pulpy, blotchy witness to the fact that he'd been crying for hours.

'I don't want to say anything! I don't want to give evidence! His eyes will be looking at me, accusing me. I can't take it. I can't do it!'

Walker rested his hand on Garrett's shoulder, as if to calm the boy's strung-out nerves.

'Now listen to me,' Walker was saying. 'Just listen up and calm down. Your mother can't come in here now because there's no time. But she will be down to see you afterwards.'

From behind Garrett's wide, shuddering back, North looked at Walker doubtfully. As far as she knew, Dora Garrett had no intention of coming near her son today – or any day. But to Walker the end justified the means. This was not some frivolous lie, it was absolutely necessary to get Damon Morton convicted.

'Yes,' he said. 'I guarantee it. She's very proud of you, standing up against Damon like this.'

Garrett's tears had subsided. He heaved in a stuttering breath.

'I don't know. I don't want to see him.'

'Do it for your mum, Jimmy. You will do it for her, won't you?'

'I'll try.'

Pat North was already moving towards the door.

'I'll let them know upstairs,' she said.

'Yes, you'll try, won't you, Jimmy?' urged Walker. 'Really try. Really do your best.'

Jimmy mopped his eyes with his fists and looked up pathetically.

'I'll do my best.'

Walker said, 'OK, son. Dry your tears. That's good enough for me and I'd wager it'll be good enough for your mum too.'

* * *

In court, proceedings had begun, the clerk intoning to the jury, 'The defendant, Brian Andrew Morton, is charged on an indictment containing four counts. On the first count he is charged with murder, and the particulars of that offence are . . .'

While he was speaking, North came in and beckoned Halliday outside. Walker was waiting to explain the little problem he'd been having with Garrett's reluctance to give evidence and how he'd overcome it.

'*Little* problem! That would not be my word, Detective Superintendent!' said Halliday.

'But he'll hold up all right, he will!'

Halliday shook his head decisively.

'I think I've heard all I need to hear. If Garrett's not absolutely rock solid, I'm not touching him. Didn't want him in the first place.'

'But his statement's absolutely comprehensive. It's bloody dynamite – you've read it. Cult, control, Morton's involvement in the murders – the lot.'

He smiled disarmingly at Halliday.

'It'll make the jurors' hair curl tighter than your wig.'

But Halliday was as completely immune to Walker's attempted charm as he was to his blustering. And he, not Walker, was in charge of prosecution decisions in court.

'Take my word for it, Detective Superintendent, we are better off without him. He's a liability. He's been all over the place since the word go. The last thing we want is hysterics in the witness box, with a witness breaking down and retracting his statement. It's happened before! The defence would have a field day. I've got enough to worry about with the emotional Marilyn Spark. Don't give me Jimmy Garrett's psychiatric instability as well, please.'

Leaving them, he swept back into court. Walker clenched his fists.

'I – don't – *believe* – this!'

*　*　*

Mr Justice Winfield, satisfied that all preliminaries had been properly conducted, peered down at his court like a racecourse starter about to press the lever and send the runners catapulting from the stalls. The simile tickled him. Willis Fletcher to his right and Rupert Halliday to his left were certainly a well-matched pair of runners. Both were of excellent pedigree and had good form. Both were thoroughly professional, although Halliday was inclined on occasion towards the histrionic. Yet now, though ready to begin, neither was pawing the ground with nerves. Rather, both were calmly picking through their bundles and consulting with their juniors and instructing solicitors.

He looked over towards the jury: the usual motley collection of men and women, although several of them, he thought, looked reasonably alert and intelligent – not that you could tell by looking, as long experience had taught him. His glance next fell on the press, away to the right. Untidy, unfit-looking bunch. Heavy drinkers, no doubt, putting their livers and pancreases in grave danger. Winfield had given up drinking sixteen years earlier and had never regretted it. Finally he looked back at the relatives and the public. They, not the press, were his audience, the people to whom he felt he was accountable. Some of them were certainly grieving. Others might be in similar pain by the end of the trial. If this was not a fairly run trial, if there should be a miscarriage of justice, they would hold him responsible. He would not be thanked of course if everything went well – but that was a judge's burden. Very well then, he thought, let the race begin.

He drew himself up into an attitude of attention and said, 'Mr Halliday.'

And they were off.

CHAPTER 26

MONDAY 16 NOVEMBER. MORNING

'May it please Your Lordship, members of the jury,' said Halliday, 'I appear together with my learned friend Mr Camplin for the Crown. My learned friends Mr Fletcher and Mr Mehta for the defendant.'

He swivelled half left and eyeballed the jury.

'This case concerns a series of offences against women committed earlier this year. All of these, the prosecution says, were committed by this defendant. You will hear about three different attacks. On two of them the defendant was assisted by three other men, who will be mentioned in this trial but will not appear before you.'

Halliday took a drink of water. The jury were concentrating anxiously. Were they beginning to suspect what they were involved in? Maybe. But how could they have any idea of the unmitigated evil Halliday was about to unfold before them?

'The first of these attacks occurred on 16th April, when Susie Harrow, a prostitute who worked in a massage parlour in Fulham, south-west London, was accosted late in the evening by a man driving a white van . . .'

* * *

The witness waiting room was very quiet, now that Marilyn had paced herself to a standstill. Although she still smoked – the place reeked of her butt-ends – she had first stood and then sat still, staring into unfocused space.

The door scraped and the pathologist, Dr John Foster, came in. He sniffed, delighted to have at last located an area where smokers were not regarded as pariahs, and lit up. Jill Ashton recognised him.

'Good morning, Dr Foster,' she said.

Foster acknowledged her with a bow and said, gesturing towards Marilyn, 'Is this the lady in the Morton case?'

Ashton stood up.

'Yes, this is Marilyn Spark. Marilyn, Dr Foster.'

Foster extended his hand, but Marilyn just looked at it. She was not accustomed to shaking men by the hand. Foster smiled.

'Very glad – if you see what I mean – never to have made your acquaintance.'

'You what?'

Marilyn did not see what he meant. Her face was a complete blank. Ashton intervened.

'Marilyn, Dr Foster's our pathologist – that's what he meant.'

Marilyn took Foster's hand awkwardly and tried to return his smile. She had some idea that he had attempted a little joke, but she certainly didn't get it.

* * *

Bibi Harrow could not see the whole of the court. She could see the judge up there in his long wig and the first two of the jurors, who looked surprisingly ordinary. She could see the barrister who was standing up and talking, Halliday, with his little wig perched on top of his head. She didn't really care for him, especially the way he had so casually described her Susie as a prostitute, for everybody to hear. What did he know? Susie hadn't deserved what happened to her. She was always a good girl.

Bibi glanced at Nicky next to her. He was a bit of a wild lad, but he'd been kind in the end. He'd finally acknowledged Justine as his kid and even got his own mother to help out sometimes. It lessened the burden a little. It would never go away, but it was easier now, Bibi could say that.

She was hardly listening to the lawyer, but instead she studied the man in the dock. Suddenly Morton glanced up towards her and met her gaze. His eyes were cold and blue, like splinters of ice. She shivered.

* * *

'It is the Crown's case, as I have mentioned,' Halliday was saying, 'that four men were involved in the murders of Susie Harrow and Carol Lennox. I can tell you that James Garrett and two brothers, Roberto Bellini and Antonio Bellini, have all pleaded guilty to charges of murdering these two women and are awaiting sentence. However, it is the Crown's contention that the principal attacker and the author of the distinctive pattern of injuries present in each of these distressing cases was the defendant you see before you, Brian Andrew Morton.'

Halliday took another sip and, over the rim of his glass, made a brief survey of the court and, in particular, the demeanour of the accused. He appeared to be twisting round in the dock to look behind him, at the public gallery. Not trembling and cowering before the power of Halliday's authority at any rate. Not yet. Halliday cleared his throat and went on.

'It is not, I think, in dispute that he employed these other three men in a small business which he owns. We say that the actual attack on Marilyn Spark, which I have described to you as the second of the three attacks, was carried out by Morton alone. You will hear from Marilyn Spark in evidence how she described her attacker to the police in spite of horrific injuries to her throat which affected her ability to speak, and how she later picked Morton out at an identification parade.'

Colin Lennox had avoided reading the newspaper accounts of the case and was hearing many of the details of the attack on Marilyn Spark for the first time. When Carol had died he was vaguely aware of a murder in the previous fortnight, but nothing specific. Afterwards the police had told him that there had been two attacks on prostitutes and they were similar to Carol's murder but Colin had blocked much of this out. Even now that he was having counselling through the Support After Murder and Manslaughter organisation, he still found it hard to equate the death of his wife with that of one prostitute and the assault on another.

In his long address, Halliday described the dominance this man Morton exercised over his three employees, and how they helped him murder Susie Harrow and Carol, though (according to Halliday) he attacked, raped and tried to kill the other woman on his own. He then ordered the others to confess to this crime as well as the other two, so that he could go free.

Then some photographs were shown to the jury.

'You will find these photographs distressing,' Halliday warned. 'However, it is important that you are aware of the similarity of the injuries that these three victims suffered. In these photographs you will see the victims' left breasts were removed . . .'

Colin shut his eyes. He didn't know how to bear the thought of all those strangers looking at the mutilated, abused body of his darling.

'. . . and you will hear from Marilyn Spark how she was forced to inflict the same injury on herself.'

Halliday said these words with considerable force. From somewhere to Colin's left there was a gasp and someone else whispered, 'God, no!' The jurors, who had the task of actually looking at the photographs, seemed terribly shaken – even more so when Halliday told them of the discovery of the box in the attic above Damon's office, explaining that it contained severed breasts and clumps of pulled-out hair. There was a pin-dropping silence in the court as Halliday finished his opening remarks.

'You will be driven, will you not, to conclude that these are the activities of a tightly knit and evil cult? The prosecution will show that it was led by the defendant, Brian Andrew Morton, known to his associates as Damon, and that these three men were controlled by him throughout, carrying out quite repulsive crimes under his direction and then lying in order to exculpate him.'

*　　*　　*

Cindy's senses were disorientated. She could see and hear all right. But what she saw seemed far away, as if beyond the mouth of a deep hole into which she had fallen, without hope of rescue. What she heard similarly reached her dimly and echoing and, when she spoke, her voice sounded loud in her head, though she doubted others could hear her. If she had been asked about it, she'd have put these symptoms down to tiredness. After all, she had hardly slept for weeks.

Now that the day had arrived and the trial begun, she did not know what to do. So she followed when Cheryl had gone back to the court at lunchtime to try and see Damon. Cheryl had given Cindy an earful at the time for tagging along with her.

'Look at yourself, Cindy. I mean, the last person he'll want to see is you. And I don't want to see you neither. So just piss off, will you?'

But Cindy had hung around. She had nothing else to do. Sitting anonymously on a bench opposite the court, she saw the reporters and lawyers come out at lunchtime, using their mobile phones and making for the pubs. She had lost sight of Cheryl for a while, but then there was a commotion as a car started to push out through the crowd, away from the court. A couple of police, whom she recognised as having worked on the case, were inside and a thin-faced woman with short peroxide hair. Suddenly she heard Cheryl's voice piercing the hubbub. Despite her blurred hearing, Cindy could have located that harpy-screech anywhere.

'Is that the one they say sucked him off?'

Cheryl was running towards the car, her heavy boots clumping along the pavement. She reached the car, which was held up at a security barrier and pressed her face close to the rear window.

'He wouldn't get 'is cock out for *her*!'

There seemed to be a struggle inside as the blonde tried to get past the policewoman beside her and out of the car. She was screaming at Cheryl, her face contorted. She was no doubt calling her all the names Cindy would like to call her, if she had the courage. Cow. Slag. Scum. Tart. Dirty bitch.

Then the barrier went up and the police car was released. Cheryl was left screaming abuse in its wake, while the people strolling past stared at her. Cindy might have smiled in triumph to see the public disgrace of that horrible, foul-minded child. But she had forgotten how to smile.

* * *

To give Marilyn a break, North had taken her to lunch at a small pub she knew, a respectable distance from the court. The incident with Cheryl had been deeply regrettable but Marilyn calmed down when North allowed her a gin and tonic as a bracer.

'Just the one. You'll be on after lunch. You mustn't overdo it.'

It was an encouraging sign when Marilyn laughed.

'What do you think I'll do? Fall down the steps of the witness box? It'll take a lot more than a couple of gins to get me pissed.'

CHAPTER 27

MONDAY 16 NOVEMBER. AFTERNOON

Back in court, Halliday called Marilyn straight away. She walked to the stand, on the judge's left-hand side, without hesitation. Her posture was erect and she did not tremble as she took the oath.

'Is your name Marilyn Spark?' asked Halliday.

She drew a deep breath and prepared to give her evidence.

'Yes,' she said.

'Miss Spark,' continued Halliday, in a gentle voice, 'I would like to ask you some questions about the night of 26th April this year. Would you tell us in your own words what happened to you that night?'

Marilyn cleared her throat.

'Well, I was working as a . . . a prostitute at the time. I was standing in a street at the back of King's Cross station. And a man drove up in a white van. He pulled up next to me and asked me if I was working and I said yes. He told me to go round the back of the van, which I did. I got into the back and he called out to me that he was going to drive around the corner. Anyway he did. I mean he drove off, but it wasn't around the comer, it seemed further.'

'How far would you think?'

'I don't know, sorry.'

The strain was beginning to show on Marilyn now, but, from the police benches to the side of the court, North felt she was going well enough. She crossed her fingers anyway.

'What happened next?'

'He stopped the van. There was no windows, so I couldn't see where we was. He got in the back of the van with me straight from the driver's seat. There was a curtain he came through.'

'I see. And then?'

'He got hold of my arm and he put ... well, a handcuff on it and he fixed the other handcuff to this rail on the side . . . you know, on the inside of the van. Then he got out a knife and he . . . he asked me to, well, he *made* me do oral sex with him because if I didn't he said he'd cut me up. So I did that. And then . . . and then . . .'

Halliday waited while Marilyn took a slug of water from the glass beside her. He did not try to lead her.

'And then,' she said, straightening up and facing Morton, though not looking at him, 'he ripped open my shirt and put the knife down where I could get it and he stepped back out of reach. Then he . . . he told me to pick it up and . . .'

She was shaking now, her knuckles white as her hand gripped the witness-stand rail. She swallowed hard and shut her eyes to regain control.

'He told me to cut off one of my breasts with it. My left breast. And so I . . . so I did.'

There was a sudden, unnerving shriek from the back of the court and everyone turned. It was Bibi Harrow. Her eyes shut, oblivious of the people around her, she was reliving each moment of the ordeal on behalf of her daughter. Mr Justice Winfield didn't know this. To him it was just noise and it had to be stopped.

He said sternly, 'Silence in court, please!'

Marilyn's eyes were darting around now, trying to locate where the scream had come from. There were beads of sweat on her face. Halliday gently prompted her to come back on track.

'And then?'

'If I hadn't been tied to the rail thing I would have fallen down. He pulled off my . . . you know, the clothes on my bottom half and he stuck this thing in me. I don't know what it was. Something metal and sharp at the end. He . . . he twisted it. I never ever felt pain like it. I don't know how long it went on, though, because I fainted. That's all I can remember.'

There was more noise from the public gallery as Salvatore Bellini, breathing heavily and loosening his tie, stumbled towards the exit.

Halliday took no notice. He said soothingly, 'Thank you very much, Miss Spark. The court realises how very difficult that evidence must have been to give. May we pass on to the man himself. Did you give the police a description?'

'Yes.'

'And can you tell *us* about the man who attacked you?'

This part was easier. Marilyn had it off pat.

'He was a white man with short, mousy-blond hair. He was between five foot eight and six foot and medium build. He had a London accent.'

'Was there anything distinctive about his clothes?'

'Yes, there was. He was wearing a sweater, the colours were very noticeable, red, green and blue. And it had a hood.'

'And what about the van?'

'The van was white like I said, but it had a kind of red zigzag line painted across the rear doors.'

'All right, Miss Spark. This man who attacked you, are you absolutely sure he was alone?'

'Yes, I'm positive. There was no one else there.'

'And have you seen that man since?'

'Yes, I have.'

'Where?'

'At an identification parade, I picked him out.'

'When you say picked him out . . .'

'I mean, I picked a man out because I recognised him. He was the man who attacked me.'

'There is no doubt in your mind about that?'

'None. I'd know him anywhere.'

Halliday now turned from Marilyn to the jury.

'And members of the jury, there is no dispute in this case that the man who Miss Spark picked out was, in fact, the defendant. Thank you very much, Miss Spark. That's all I have to ask you, but . . .'

He gestured towards Fletcher.

'. . . there may be further questions.'

He sat down but, before Willis Fletcher could rise, Winfield asked Marilyn if she would like a short break. Briefly the idea of a cigarette flashed across her mind, but she rejected it. Better get this over, then have a smoke. She shook her head.

'No, I'm all right.'

* * *

At the Morton house, after she'd wandered back from the court, Cindy found a calmer Cheryl sitting watching television. Cindy had a pile of Damon's clothes to iron and mechanically she set about the task. Cheryl's programme was one of those tale-telling chat shows from America – this one about people who lived in a state which permitted marriage at puberty. Cheryl half watched while cutting out an article from the paper headlined: IS THIS THE FACE OF EVIL?

'I don't think Sally Jesse Raphael's nearly as good as Oprah or Jerry Springer,' she was saying. 'I love it when they beat up on each other. Huh – look at that! Imagine getting married at twelve.'

Cindy was thinking about something else.

'Cheryl,' she said. 'Do you think Damon actually knew that woman? The one in the car.'

'Nah, she's just making it up, isn't she? He never had sex with her, never would've wanted to. I know him. I mean, stands to reason. He won't screw you, so why should he screw her?'

Cindy looked at Cheryl and shook her head wearily.

'Cheryl, *you* weren't the first babysitter, you know. And you won't be the last.'

She walked out of the room. It took a moment for it to sink in, what Cindy had said. Then Cheryl shouted, 'Oi! Come back here.'

Cheryl chased Cindy up the stairs and found the bathroom door locked.

'What you doing in there, eh? What you mean about the babysitter bit? You're a bloody liar. You'd say anything to wind me up, because you're jealous, you silly stringy bitch!'

Without warning, the door swung open and Cindy stood there, her shirt unbuttoned and a bottle of disinfectant in her hand.

'There's no cotton wool. Have you got any? I'm hurting.'

Cheryl's voice changed fractionally. It wasn't warmth exactly, but some kind of sympathy which made her step towards Cindy and say, 'Here, let me have a look.'

*   *   *

Fletcher began by giving appropriate expression to his deepest sympathies for the dreadful experience described by the witness.

It had been an appalling attack and, he said, having to recount it cannot have been easy. He then turned to his own allotted task – the systematic destruction of that same witness's testimony.

'The reality is, is it not,' he was saying, 'that you never had much of an opportunity to observe the man who attacked you on 26th April?'

'I did, I did. I said I'd know him anywhere and I would.'

Fletcher held up his hand calmly.

'Would you kindly just answer yes or no to the questions I shall put to you? Let's go back to when the van stopped. You regarded the driver as just an ordinary client. As such you wouldn't have paid him any particular attention, correct?'

'Yes, not at that stage, I mean, I—'

'You went straight to the back of the vehicle when he asked, did you?'

'Yes.'

'And it was dark in there, is that right?'

'Yes.'

'And once inside you were subjected to a horrific attack as you have described?'

'Yes.'

'You were frightened?'

'I was terrified.'

'What I mean is, your concentration was centred on self-protection.'

'Of course.'

'Throughout what must have been a fast-moving series of events?'

'Yes.'

'In circumstances that were inevitably making identification difficult?'

'No, I know it was him.'

'Who – the man you picked out?'

'Yes.'

'Couldn't it have been someone else?'

'Never. It was him!'

'You're quite certain?'

'It was him! I'd know him anywhere.'

She was looking squarely at Morton now, sitting in the dock, his back straight, his face a mask of arrogance.

Corinna Maddox had leaned forward and attracted Fletcher's attention. The barrister inclined his head and she whispered in his ear. He simply nodded and continued.

'Well, Miss Spark, I put it to you that there was another occasion when you saw – or *thought* you saw – your attacker and you reported that sighting too to the police.'

'Yes, that's right.'

'Tell us about that sighting.'

Marilyn looked at him, trying to work out what to say. She barely remembered the incident now – just the shock she'd experienced at the flat when she saw that bloke who looked like . . . But the police had persuaded her to try and forget the whole incident. He was just a passer-by, they said. She glanced at Detective Inspector North, sitting over there on the police benches.

'Could you answer the question, please.'

'That's a . . . a police matter.'

Fletcher turned the pages of his bundle of paper and extracted one sheet, from which he refreshed his memory.

'Let me help you, if I may. I understand that it is not unknown in the aftermath of a violent attack for an individual who looks even slightly like the attacker to trigger a strong emotional reaction in the victim. Do you think this may be what happened in this case?'

'I don't know.'

'Perhaps I could help you again. You said you saw the man who attacked you out of your window and you also said he was Brian Andrew Morton. But Mr Morton was sitting in his solicitor's office at the time. So your sighting of him must have been wrong.'

'Yes.' She uttered the word in a near-whisper.

'You see, my concern is whether this phenomenon, which seems to have occurred when you thought you sighted him outside your flat, might also have occurred when you picked Mr Morton out at the identification parade.'

'No. I am sure, I'm positive it was him. That man was the one who attacked me.'

'But you were positive, you were sure, that it was him outside your flat.'

There was a pause. Marilyn could think of nothing to say. Corinna Maddox, sitting just behind Fletcher, twisted around and looked with satisfaction at Morton. Things were going very well.

Fletcher waited for a few beats and went on.

'What is your occupation now, Miss Spark?'

She looked alarmed towards the judge.

'Do I have to answer that?'

Winfield leaned forward. 'I'm afraid so. Please answer counsel's question, Miss Spark.'

'Well, I'm doing the same thing, more or less. On and off . . .'

'You are still a prostitute?'

'Yes. I am.'

Fletcher bowed slightly and said, 'Thank you, Miss Spark.'

Halliday rose.

'I have no further questions, M'Lord.'

Judge Winfield peered at Marilyn.

'You may leave the witness box, Miss Spark.'

Marilyn walked much less steadily away from the stand than she had gone to it. She felt bad – she felt Fletcher had made her *look* bad. She felt she had let herself down.

'Mr Halliday,' asked Winfield, 'is your next witness likely to be giving evidence for some time?'

'Yes, M'Lord.'

'In that case,' said Winfield, 'I shall adjourn now for today. Ten thirty tomorrow morning.'

The usher told the court to be upstanding while the judge withdrew to his chambers.

* * *

'It's infected,' said Cheryl, dabbing with a piece of cotton wool soaked in disinfectant at the red and swollen area on the upper part of Cindy's left breast. 'You need antibiotics. I hope it's not catching. You know, something off that filthy slag. If he did go with her and he's brought back her fucking germs to me, I'll bleeding well kill him!'

Cindy stepped back and did up her shirt. Cheryl screwed the top back on the disinfectant.

'He should've finished the job.'

Cindy frowned. She wasn't sure she'd heard right.

'What did you say, Cheryl?'

'He should've finished her off proper that night. Saved us all this trouble, eh?'

Cheryl's voice was so casual, as if describing something Damon had done at work – to a fridge or a television set.

'But it couldn't have been him,' said Cindy. 'He was with you all those nights.'

Cheryl looked with contempt at Cindy, as one with no illusions looks at a dupe.

'You dumb cow, Cindy. He was never with me, not on any of those nights.'

Her face a sudden ghostly pale, eyes wide with fear, Cindy froze. A look of horrified enlightenment followed. Cheryl shook her head, tut-tutting.

'And unless he was with *you*, where do you suppose he was? Damon was doing what he likes. Damon does that, Damon can. No one says "no" to Damon because, if they do, they get punished. That is what Damon was doing those nights. Didn't he tell you?' She smiled. 'He told me.'

* * *

When Damon let himself into the house he found Cindy standing in the hallway waiting for him. She looked even more haggard than usual, but Damon didn't want the fact that his wife was turning into a living ghost to spoil his triumphant mood.

'My barrister made mincemeat of her.'

He swung the door closed and slid the safety chain into place. When he turned again Cindy had not moved.

'You lied to me,' she said, shaking.

Her voice was quietly fierce. She hadn't spoken like that for – oh, years, he thought. Damon looked at his wife, surprised. Beyond Cindy he saw Cheryl, chewing gum, and Charmaine behind her. They were waiting to see what would happen, how he would handle this. Whatever *this* was, it was a situation, but he didn't know what it amounted to yet. He remained icily calm.

'I lied? What did I lie about, Cindy?'

'You killed those women, didn't you?'

Cindy jerked her head towards Cheryl.

'She told me!'

Damon took a step towards her and raised his hand. Cindy flinched.

'Charmaine, upstairs!' she shouted.

Charmaine darted for the stairs, but even faster Damon's fist lashed at her mother's face. Cindy went down, flailing. Then she was cowering, as she had done so often before. Charmaine, crouching now at the top of the stairs with her face pressed between the banisters, took it all in.

'No, Damon!' cried Cindy.

Damon stood over her, breathing heavily.

'You question *me*?' he whispered.

He stepped across Cindy and went into the kitchen, wrenching open the drawer. He pulled out a white-handled, serrated knife. Returning to Cindy, who was now scrabbling backwards until she met the wall and could go no further, he leaned over and pulled her shirt. The buttonholes tore open.

'No, Damon, no!' she cried.

Cheryl stood there, still chewing calmly. She watched as Damon reached out to cut Cindy. Only then did Cheryl choose to comment.

'Don't kill her, Damon. You need her, remember?'

Charmaine had shut her eyes and covered her ears. But she could not keep out her mother's screams going on and on.

CHAPTER 28

TUESDAY 17 NOVEMBER. MORNING

Corinna Maddox was sitting in her place in the court and the time for Damon to present himself had arrived. But he wasn't here.

She hurried outside and, to her relief, saw him hanging around in the corridor.

'Come on! You should be in there.'

'I know,' said Damon, drawling a little. 'I need to tell you. My wife's been taken ill. I don't know if she'll be able to give evidence or not.'

Maddox clicked her tongue. One thing after another.

'I'll tell Mr Fletcher. It's been quite annoying. Salvatore Bellini died last night.'

Damon didn't give a toss what had happened to old man Bellini.

'What's going to happen if Cindy can't come to court?' he asked impatiently.

Maddox stopped. Morton was trying too hard to be casual. Something was bothering him.

'Her statement could be read out in court, I suppose, if the judge agrees. But the prosecution won't like it. And having her evidence read won't do you any favours. There is nothing quite so effective as a wife getting up in court to stand by her wronged husband.'

She looked at Morton curiously.

'Is there something the matter?'

But before the man could reply, an usher came out to summon all parties for the case of Morton.

Halliday's next witness was Dr Foster. The pathologist had already taken the oath and was ready to give evidence, holding a collection of laminated sheets.

'Tell me, Dr Foster, what do you say about the pattern of injuries sustained by Susan Harrow, Carol Lennox and Marilyn Spark?'

Foster did not hesitate.

'The pattern is so similar that I would say it was virtually impossible for this to have occurred by coincidence.'

At this there were murmurs in the public gallery, quelled by a severe look from Winfield. During the interlude Maddox took the opportunity to attract Fletcher's attention, informing him about the doubt over Cindy Morton's ability to testify.

'What's the matter with her?' he whispered testily.

'I don't know.'

'Well, I don't care how sick she is. I want her in court. Or, at the very least, a doctor's note.'

Meanwhile, Halliday was explaining to the judge about Dr Foster's diagrams.

'My Lord, this is a complex matter and the photographs which we have seen are of such a graphic nature . . .'

'Quite so, Mr Halliday,' interrupted Winfield. 'But I believe you and Mr Fletcher had agreed on which photographs to use.'

'Yes, My Lord. However, Dr Foster has prepared a series of diagrams which might be a more suitable way for the jury to compare and contrast the injuries.'

Winfield nodded magisterially.

'I assume you have no objection, Mr Fletcher?'

'Ah, no, My Lord. I have no objection,' agreed the distracted Fletcher, who was wondering what he would do if he had to explain Cindy's indisposition to the court and read out her statement instead. It would make a poor substitute for direct evidence.

Foster left the witness box and walked down into the well of the court, where a white board was set up with the outline of a woman's torso drawn on it.

'Using your diagrams, Dr Foster,' Halliday continued, 'could you explain exactly what that pattern was?'

'Yes. I shall tell you first what I learned from the post-mortem examination of the two dead women and then what was revealed in the doctor's report on the attack victim, Marilyn Spark.'

Foster produced three large transparent sheets, each of which, when laid over the whiteboard, showed the position of the injuries sustained by one of the women, marked in a different colour for each victim – red, green and blue. When the three transparent sheets were placed on top of each other, as Foster did after explaining each one in turn, everyone in court could see the marks were almost exactly aligned. The court hung on every word, appalled, shocked, fascinated.

'So I am led to believe,' the pathologist was saying, 'that the same kind of knife and torture weapon was used on all three women.'

'Thank you, doctor, you may return to the witness box.'

He did, leaving the three transparent sheets in place, one on top of the other, to stay on view throughout the rest of his testimony – sustained evidence of a powerfully consistent pattern of psychopathic behaviour.

'May I ask you again, Dr Foster, would you say that the injuries you have clarified for us bear what one might call a common authorship?'

'Yes, I would. It is impossible of course to say categorically that a single person inflicted them, but it is undoubtedly the case that the pattern – if you will, the *design* – of these injuries proceeded from a single mind. Which leads me to believe that the injuries were carried out by the same kinds of weapon in the same way.'

'In summary, doctor, what you are saying is that they were caused by the same person?'

Fletcher leapt to his feet.

'My Lord, my learned friend should know better.'

Halliday smiled and withdrew the question at once. He glanced at the jury. They looked precisely as distressed and as impressed as he hoped they would.

'No further questions,' he said and sat down.

* * *

Outside the courtroom, Cheryl was ranging along the corridor, trying to find someone who could get her in to speak to Damon.

'No, miss,' said an usher firmly. 'Your friend is still in court and at lunchtime he'll be in custody.'

'His wife's really ill. How can I get a message to him?'

Then she heard another voice behind her, one that she recognised.

'Can I help at all?'

It was Dave Satchell on a cigarette break. He'd heard the unmistakable tones of Cheryl Goodall and wandered over to see what was happening.

'If you give me the message, Cheryl, I can see he gets it at lunchtime.'

But Cheryl was not, it seems, that desperate.

'You! I wouldn't give you my used chewing gum.'

Interesting, though, thought Satchell. Trouble in the Morton camp – couldn't be a bad thing.

* * *

Halliday called Michael Walker to the stand. The detective superintendent gave a straightforward account of the inquiry which had led to the arrest of Morton in typical Walker style – clipped and succinct, with no flourishes.

Halliday finished and Willis Fletcher rose to cross-examine. Fletcher and Walker were not friendly, but they knew each other tolerably well since, on a previous occasion not long ago, they had been on the same side – the prosecution of the child killer Michael Dunn. But you would not have guessed at any prior acquaintance at all from the tone of Fletcher's questions, nor from Walker's answers.

'Detective Superintendent, you interviewed the defendant extensively, on a number of occasions spread over several weeks, did you not?'

'Yes, I did.'

'Mr Morton had no previous convictions, is that right?'

'Yes.'

'And has he consistently maintained on all these occasions that he knew nothing about all these offences and that he was with other people when these attacks occurred?'

'Yes, he has.'

So far, so predictable, thought Walker. But if he has any surprises up his sleeve, I should know soon enough.

'You told my learned friend that you came to arrest the defendant because you observed James Garrett driving the van in which Miss Spark said she was attacked. The van belonged to the defendant, he fitted the description given by Miss Spark more closely than Garrett, so he was arrested. You then questioned the Bellini brothers because the defendant said they also drove the van – correct?'

'That is correct.'

'So it has been clear from the outset that there were three other men, men who are certainly guilty of the two murders, who had frequent access to Mr Morton's vehicle?'

'Yes.'

'Is it also true that these three men all had access to the defendant's business premises – at evenings and weekends, even when he was not there?'

'Mr Morton claimed they did.'

'Could the witness please be shown exhibit DP/44?'

The usher picked up from the exhibits table a labelled bunch of keys in a clear plastic evidence bag and handed the bag to Walker. Fletcher explained, 'Exhibit DP/44 comprises the bunch of keys found on James Garrett when he was arrested, is that right?'

'That was what was recorded by the exhibits officer,' he said, stiffly.

Walker looked at the keys and weighed them in his hand. There were at least six keys.

'There are other keys on it besides car keys, aren't there?' asked Fletcher. 'Two Chubb keys, a Yale key and a key for a padlock?'

'That's right.'

'Presumably one of your officers established that these other keys – not the van keys – also opened the doors to the yard and Mr Morton's offices?'

Walker blanked. He couldn't remember . . . and if he couldn't remember, it won't have been done. Shit!

'I . . . don't believe so,' he said uncomfortably.

'Well,' said Fletcher with palpable satisfaction. 'Perhaps with My Lord's permission, one of your officers wouldn't mind going over and trying these keys in the yard and office doors now – and returning to tell us the results?'

Walker could not believe this. He was being made to look an idiot.

'Certainly,' he said.

He spotted North on the police benches and nodded to tell her to get it sorted.

'With access to the yard and offices, would you agree that any of the three men who have admitted to the two murders could have hidden the box containing the – what we have heard called – trophies about which we have heard so much, without Mr Morton knowing?'

'That's not for me to say,' said Walker stiffly.

'Did it *not* occur to you that the owner of the box may have been one of these three men – Mr Garrett, Roberto Bellini or Antonio Bellini – and that it was perfectly reasonable of them to try to explain to the police that Mr Morton had nothing to do with the crime.'

At this point Winfield intervened.

'Mr Fletcher, this really is a matter of comment.'

'I withdraw the question, My Lord.'

* * *

In the corridor outside the court, North now had Morton's keys in her possession and was looking for Satchell.

'Oi,' she said when she found him. 'They're breaking for lunch. Get your skates on and get over to Morton's yard – see what these keys fit.'

Satchell looked incredulous.

'You're kidding – hasn't anybody tried them?'

'No, they bloody haven't.'

This was Walker, following closely behind the detective inspector. Satchell held up his hands.

'Well, don't look at me!'

Walker looked grim.

'I am, sunshine. You should have tested these, because they've made us all look like pricks – which is what Fletcher intended. He knows this has got bugger all to do with anything. I'm going to the pub.'

* * *

When Satchell got to the yard he found one of the keys opened the padlock on the yard gates and knew the others would open other doors – to the office and shed, if not the house. He climbed the steps to Damon's office and, as predicted, one of the mortise keys easily opened the lock. He walked inside, looking around. The place was reasonably tidy, the paperwork done after a fashion and the workbenches cleared and swept, although a first aid kit lay open in its plastic box on one of them. Around the walls, mixed in with the nudes and fetish photographs, were pinned cuttings about the case – PROSTITUTE FOUND MURDERED – SLASHER'S SECOND VICTIM – IS THIS THE FACE OF EVIL?

Community-minded businessman? Stalwart of the Lambeth Chamber of Commerce? Loving father and husband? Give me a break, thought Satchell as he surveyed the scene.

'Oi! Who's in there?' It was Cheryl's voice, calling out as she mounted the steps.

Satchell prepared for battle.

'If it's you press bastards, I'll do you for breaking and entering.'

'Who do you want arrested, Miss Goodall?' said Satchell. 'Police are here to assist.'

Cheryl stood at the door, chewing.

'Just get out of here,' she ordered with a sneer. 'You got no right to come and go as you please.'

'Oh, yes, I do. I've got every right. And how is the fair Mrs Morton? Any better, is she?'

*　*　*

Back in the witness box after lunch, Walker was being cross-examined over the business of the sweater that had been found in the sitting room of the Morton house and which Walker claimed was Morton's not Garrett's. Meanwhile, the garment itself was being shown to the jury.

'As we can see,' said Fletcher, 'the sweater is large, and Mr Garrett is much larger than Mr Morton, is that not so?'

Walker's reply was audibly tetchy.

'A sweater is not exactly made to measure. It's the kind of thing often worn over other clothes.'

Fletcher turned to Corinna Maddox and was handed a colour snapshot.

'Would you please have a look at this photograph, Detective Superintendent.'

The usher brought him the snap and he looked. He blinked. He looked again. No, his eyes had not deceived him.

'Do you recognise the photograph, Detective Superintendent?'

'No.'

'Do you know the man pictured in it?'

'Yes – Jimmy Garrett.'

Yes, Garrett, blast him. In, by the looks of it, the Mangia 'a Mamma restaurant.

'Thank you. And what is Mr Garrett wearing in this photograph, please, Mr Walker?'

He could barely bring himself to say it. He almost stuttered and then controlled his tongue.

'The sweater.'

'The sweater! Yes! The same sweater, ladies and gentlemen of the jury, which you see before you.'

In the dock Morton smiled, and Fletcher too could hardly suppress his satisfaction. The jury was more difficult to read, but he could see that one or two of them were frowning.

* * *

For the second day running, Damon Morton returned home in triumph, chasing away photographers who called out to him. His defence had won the day yet again.

But for the second day running too, bloody Cindy contrived to spoil his triumph.

'There's something bad wrong,' said Cheryl, running out of the house to meet him, clutching Karl. 'Cindy's not moved all day, not spoken. She seems to be asleep but I can't wake her.'

Damon's mood switched from euphoric to savage. If that bitch had tried to take another overdose . . .

He kicked the door of her room open – almost breaking the catch. Charmaine was curled up next to her mother, stroking her brow. Damon fired his daughter out and bunched his fists. But he suddenly stopped himself. No, he thought, this was the wrong approach, it wasn't productive and it wasn't how a superior being went about protecting himself. So instead of smashing his fists into Cindy's already bruised face, he drew in a couple of deep breaths and knelt beside her. Then he placed the back of his fingers against her cheek.

'Hey, little Cindy,' he crooned. 'Cindy, love. It's Damon come home to you. It's Damon come home . . .'

CHAPTER 29

WEDNESDAY 18 NOVEMBER

Walker could not deny it, the case for the prosecution had ended the previous day on a depressing note. Fletcher had got the better of him in the witness box and he blamed himself for sloppy preparation. The matter of the keys was inexcusable – he had been made to look a prat. But in itself it had done no great harm, since the Crown had never suggested Garrett and the Bellinis were denied access to Morton's yard.

The matter of the sweater itself was worse, much worse, and had kept Walker awake, alone now in a crummy Kensal Green flat, for much of the night. He went over again and again what he should have done. He should have tracked down the origins of the sweater via the label, should have interviewed everybody who might have sold it to Garrett or Morton, should have got statements from anyone who saw Garrett and Morton on a regular basis – filling-station people, postmen, customers, suppliers – in case they had seen the sweater being worn and who was wearing it. Walker had been so certain that it was Morton's sweater, he had never gone to the trouble to prove it.

When he got up in the morning he felt sick with anxiety. If Morton was acquitted because of this, it would be his fault. He had miscalculated badly.

Walker drifted as low as you can go that morning. He knew he would never tell a soul about it. For a while, on the way to the Crown Court, driving and listening to Capital Gold and the old hits he used to like as a kid, he entertained the thought of telling Pat North about himself and how he'd pratted it all up – the marriage, the case. She was pretty smart, she was pretty sympathetic and she was, well, just pretty. But North was going with that rugby player anyway. Didn't want to be bothered with him and his problems.

* * *

Damon Morton, on the other hand, felt good today. It would be his day and he knew it. He was going to be the star performer in the witness box. He was going to be acquitted. And *then* he was going to net a quarter of a million quid selling the story. He actually felt happy on the way to court. It was to be a day of destiny.

* * *

'Are you Brian Andrew Morton?' asked Willis Fletcher, when the preliminaries were over.

'I am.'

He was pleasantly aware that every eye was turned on him: the judge, jury, lawyers, hacks and public. They were all there for him – for *his* day in court. He was particularly aware of the attention of the jury, watching his every move, gesture, expression.

'Mr Morton,' continued the barrister, 'you have heard the details of a series of offences set out on a number of occasions in this court. Could you tell the jury now, at the outset, whether you were in any way involved in any of those offences, at any time or in any way?'

'No, no, I was not.'

The answer was confident, spoken to the jury as much as to Fletcher.

'Had you ever, in fact, seen Miss Spark, the witness who identified you as her attacker, before she gave evidence in court?'

The court Bible still rested on the witness box's parapet. Damon met Fletcher's eyes with an unwavering gaze as he reached out with his right hand and laid it on the book.

'No, I swear on the Bible, I never did.'

It was something he had thought of the day before, this swearing on the Bible. Now let them say he's one of the Devil's disciples.

'Can you tell the jury,' said Fletcher, 'where you were between eight p.m. and midnight on 16th and 27th April of this year?'

'Yes, I can. I was at home with my wife and family on both those nights.'

'You did not leave the house at all?'

'No.'

'And could you tell the court where you were between ten p.m. and midnight on 26th April, also earlier this year, the night on which Miss Spark was attacked?'

'I was with Cheryl Goodall. She's my girlfriend.'

There was a slight stir of interest in court at the admission of a girlfriend, but Morton seemed oblivious to it. He maintained continuous eye contact with Fletcher.

*   *   *

'Come on, Cindy, let's have a look at you. You could be going in any minute.'

It had not been more than a token overdose, twice what she might normally use. Enough to make Cindy semi-comatose for a few hours. That for her was perfect bliss. Waking up was the continuance of nightmare.

'I just want to go home,' she whispered.

They were in the witness waiting room and Cheryl was fussing over her. Having discarded all her facial rings and bolts and the worst excesses of her black and green eyeshadows and lipsticks, and wearing a powder-blue suit and pearls in her ears, Cheryl now appeared clean, fresh and full of vitality: wholesome, even. Cindy by comparison looked like the living dead. The impression was accentuated by a thick layer of face make-up, which she never normally wore. It gave her an unnatural, embalmed look.

She put her hands to her face and tiredly rubbed at her cheeks, forehead and eyes. The powder and greasepaint came off in sticky swathes where she had touched herself.

'Don't do that!' ordered Cheryl sharply.

She reached for her make-up bag and placed herself in front of Cindy, then, steadying her by taking hold of her chin, dipped her fingers in the make-up and dabbed it on. Meekly, Cindy sat there, allowing the damage to her face to be concealed. She had stopped caring.

* * *

Fletcher was now asking Morton about the sweater, which had been put in front of him.

'Can you,' the barrister asked, 'give any explanation of how this sweater came to be found by the police at your house?'

'Yes. Jimmy must have left it there that Tuesday morning. He often came in for a cup of tea. I felt, you know, sorry for him.'

'Would you describe what your overall relationship with your employees was like?'

'We were all friendly, not so much that I'm the boss and they're the workers. We were all, like, on a level.'

Again members of the jury noted the candour in his eyes and his easy posture as he went on.

'I'm married, of course, and the lads aren't. The three of them went out together, more as a group. I reckoned it was, you know, meeting girls, having a laugh. That's why I used to lend them the van.'

'You knew they did things without you as a group?'

'Yes. It wasn't like they had big secrets all the time. It was just I knew there was stuff I wasn't . . . included in.'

Fletcher nodded his head and sat down. From his point of view, everything had gone well. Morton had given a good account of himself under friendly questioning. How would he do when he came under attack?

* * *

Rupert Halliday had decided on a relatively aggressive approach from the start. Walker, sitting at the back, noticed the way Halliday's head jutted out when he was angry: it had been just the same, he remembered, during the spat with the taxi driver, when he and Halliday had first met. Was he really angry or just putting on a good show? You simply could not tell.

'Mr Morton,' said Halliday coldly, 'you present the three men who worked for you as individuals whom you considered you knew well.'

'Yes.'

'Are you easily fooled, would you say? Deceived?'

'Not particularly.'

'Yet you ask us to believe that these three admitted sex killers whom you say you knew well, who worked for you, who came and went familiarly in your house, all the time were using your van and your office for the commission of their disgusting and abhorrent crimes – and yet you *never* had an inkling of what they were doing?'

'Well, I didn't know. I had no idea. Like I said, I was deeply shocked and . . . troubled when I found out, when the police came.'

'Mr Morton, would you say you had leadership qualities?'

'Yes, in a way. I run a business, so you have to.'

'Do people look up to you?'

'That's not for me to say.'

'Let me put it this way. Do you enjoy the admiration of others?'

Willis Fletcher was on his feet as soon as he saw the tendency of the questioning.

'M'Lord, with respect, are these questions relevant?'

Winfield looked down sternly at Halliday.

'Please make the appositeness of your questions clear, Mr Halliday.'

Halliday nodded submissively.

'As Your Lordship pleases. Mr Morton, would you say you had a special interest in dominating other people?'

'I don't get you.'

'Some people are dominant and others are easily dominated, wouldn't you say?'

'I suppose so.'

'And which are you, Mr Morton?'

'I wouldn't know.'

'What about each of the three men you employed? Which are they, dominant or able to be dominated?'

'I couldn't say. It would depend on the situation.'

Fletcher was on his feet again.

'My Lord . . .'

He needed to go no further.

Winfield came in with, 'Mr Halliday, I have warned you, you must get to the point.'

'Yes, M'Lord. I put it to you, Mr Morton, that you are lying and that you knew perfectly well that the Bellini brothers and James Garrett were susceptible to your power and influence.'

'No, it's not true.'

'And that you let them work for you for this very reason.'

'No.'

'You said you were sorry for Garrett, didn't you?'

'Yes, but only because—'

'I put it to you that you are a man with a sadistic, frightening and inflated personality who *habitually* dominates the people around you, aren't you?'

'That's completely untrue.'

'And I also put it to you that you were in fact the ringleader of the gang which tortured and killed Carol Lennox and Susan Harrow, and it was you who cut these grotesque trophies from the women's bodies and concealed them at your yard, wasn't it?'

'No, it was not. I had no idea what they did when they borrowed the van.'

'You certainly dominate both your wife and your mistress, though, don't you, Mr Morton?'

'I do not! How could I keep five people under my control like this? This is complete fantasy!'

Halliday took a drink of water, a deep breath and tried another tack.

'Did you know there was a concealed attic above your office?'

'It wasn't an attic, just a roof cavity.'

'I stand corrected. Did you know about the roof cavity and the concealed trapdoor giving access to it?'

'Obviously I knew there was a cavity. Not the trapdoor.'

'In your *own* premises?'

'I never had any reason to go up there.'

'When you saw this box, had you ever seen it before?'

'No, never.'

'Jimmy Garrett told the police it was yours.'

'He was lying.'

Halliday was in trouble, everybody could see it. He was like a man driving a powerboat along a rocky coast in the dark. He was not sure of his direction; his craft did not have enough fuel. He nosed along, probing for ways of getting at Morton. He did his best to shake his evidence over the sweater, the knife and the arrow-like weapons. But all the time he was, as Walker whispered to Satchell, only making pissholes in a glacier.

* * *

When it was Cindy's turn to come to the stand, she duly gave her husband his alibi. Her voice was almost a whisper and she had to be asked to speak up. The jury saw her as very nervous, very flaky, and perhaps teetering on the edge of her trolley. Halliday, when he rose, could plainly see her fear and vulnerability and was determined to take advantage if he could.

'You are quite certain that your husband was with you on these dates, Mrs Morton?'

'Yes, I am.'

'And on the intervening date, the 26th, where did he tell you he was?'

Cindy's reply was inaudible.

'Mrs Morton, I realise this is difficult,' said Winfield kindly. 'But you really must speak up so that the jury can hear your evidence.'

'He was with his girlfriend.'

'His girlfriend!' crowed Halliday with the same note of sarcasm Walker and North had experienced on the stairs outside his chambers. 'A very understanding relationship, you and your husband must have.'

* * *

Next, in total contrast, came the girlfriend herself. Cheryl looked fresh, healthy and mature beyond her years as she gave Morton his alibi for the night of 26th April.

'Brian was with me that night. I can't lie about it. It was till well after twelve. Every night we had together was special, even though what we were doing wasn't right . . .'

* * *

Cindy came into the public gallery and sat down to watch and listen. She felt an angry tap on her arm. It was the woman with the peroxide hair, the King's Cross prostitute.

'Why's she lying? Why did *you* lie for him?' Marilyn hissed.

Why did she? Cindy didn't know. It was automatic, it was just expected of her.

'I know Damon – sorry, Brian,' Cheryl was continuing sweetly. 'I know he couldn't have done those terrible things.'

Walker sat on, and on, listening to all this rigmarole and knowing that they had failed to secure sufficient evidence for a solid conviction. After Cheryl had finished, he swept out into the corridor. North followed him.

'What can you *do*?' he stormed. 'They're lying under oath, and if the jury don't see through them . . .'

North shook her head. She didn't believe what was happening either.

'Yeah, well. It's out of our hands now. You coming back in for the closing speeches?'

'No. They'll go on for hours. I'd rather be in the pub. Come and get me if anything happens.'

CHAPTER 30

THURSDAY 19 NOVEMBER

If he was going to pull the case out of the fire, Rupert Halliday knew he would have to do it with his closing speech. When he began, on the Wednesday afternoon, he was prepared to speak well into the next day. He did not care. The defence had been having it all their own way and he felt he was due some indulgence.

He had spent the rest of Wednesday going over the evidence of the prosecution witnesses – forensics, the pathologist and Marilyn Spark. On resumption this morning, his first point was to match the description Marilyn gave of her attacker – which the defence had not disputed with the owner of the van which she had equally accurately described and which forensic evidence proved had been used for the attacks.

'Members of the jury,' he said, 'please remember that the actual van indisputably used in these attacks was owned by an individual who perfectly fitted the victim's description, given in hospital, of her attacker and that this was also the man, a total stranger to her, whom she later identified in a police parade. Is it remotely credible that this could be a coincidence?

'Can you possibly believe it is another coincidence that the sweater found at Brian Morton's house was the same as that worn by Marilyn Spark's attacker?

'There are too many incredible coincidences in this case. Another is that, on each of the three nights when his own van was being used for these vicious attacks, Mr Morton was spending the evening either with his wife and children or with his girlfriend. He can produce no further corroborating alibi evidence for any one of these nights.

'What kind of a man is this, who can persuade us that his life is forever blessed by the hovering wings of benign coincidences? The prosecution believes in this case that the defendant is a manipulative and devious person who easily gains purchase over others, bending them to his will, terrifying them even . . .'

Walker was not listening. He was due to attend the funeral of Salvatore Bellini and had merely come to court to catch up on events before getting down to the cemetery. But he felt his black tie was remarkably appropriate, since these last days were also seeing the slow death and burial of his case.

Salvatore had not, apparently, believed in cremation. Walker, who had no taste for Requiem Masses and intended only to be there at the graveside, found the mourners gathered around the long slot dug in the ground for the reception of the coffin. The priest was intoning the ceremony.

'May the God of all consolation who, of his love, created man and, in the resurrection of his only son, gave to all men the hope of rising again, fill you with his blessing . . .'

Then, with a silver sprinkler, he moved around the grave, shaking drops of holy water over the coffin. Walker surveyed the mourners. Several stout, black-clad women were weeping.

'And so, in firm and patient expectation of the resurrection of the dead and the life of the world to come, we commit your servant's body to the ground . . .'

The two brothers were standing with the rest of the family group, but markedly distinguished from the rest by the fact that each was handcuffed to a prison officer. A security van was parked not far away.

'In the name of the Father and of the Son and of the Holy Spirit may Almighty God bless you . . .'

And then it was over. As the mourners drifted in different directions in small groups from the graveside, Walker approached the grave, looking at the wreaths laid nearby. One of them simply said '*Ciao*'. He looked at the coffin.

'*Ciao*, Salvatore,' he murmured.

The brothers were still standing there, on the other side of the grave. Walker looked at them.

'It wouldn't have been much of a life, spending the next twenty years visiting you two in prison. Might as well have stuck a knife in him yourselves, while you were about it.'

He tried to hold their attention, but they were not much interested in what Walker was saying. Looking from one to the other, Walker tried again.

'So why – why, for God's sake, have you protected Damon Morton?'

Antonio blinked and said calmly, 'If Papa hadn't gone against Damon . . .'

'He'd be alive today,' supplied Roberto.

Sweet Jesus, thought Walker as the brothers were led away at last to the prison van. It *is* a cult.

* * *

At about the same time Mrs Garrett, after a long tussle with her conscience, and fortified by a private word with her vicar, had gone in to see Jimmy. He still looked very ill, with facial bruises and a wild, suspicious look in his eye. But despite these signs of distress, she could not understand why he hadn't testified against Morton and put right his earlier lies. After all, it was that man who had got Jimmy into this situation in the first place.

'I was going to, Mum,' he told her in the visitors' room looking fixedly at the table. 'Honestly, I was all ready. I didn't want to but I said I would.'

'What were you going to say, Jimmy?'

The boy's face was blank. But he still couldn't look at her.

'Just answer their questions, like.'

'Jimmy, you said you had made up your mind to tell them the truth.'

'I'm all *confused*, I tell you. Damon's saying to me one thing, you saying another, the police saying another . . .'

'Jimmy, you'll be sent to prison for those things you did do. Why pretend you did the thing he did? Why lie for him?'

Jimmy frowned. It only slowly dawned on him that she knew the truth. Mrs Garrett was shaking her head.

'That's not your sweater, is it, Jimmy? Why did you lie, Jimmy? Why did you lie to save that . . . *creature*? Thank God your father's not alive, it'd kill him.'

Jimmy Garrett thought about his mother. He loved her, yes. She'd brought him up and been very caring. But how could she be so stupid? He suddenly raised his eyes to meet hers for the first time.

'You don't understand, do you, Mum? It's Damon – *Damon*'s my father.'

* * *

Rupert Halliday had been on his feet most of the day. His throat was dry, his voice hoarse, his legs weary, yet he was still enjoying himself. This, after all, was his element. But now, finally, he started to come to a conclusion.

'In this hugely complex mess of facts, claims and counter-claims, one absolutely positive fact shines through. Marilyn Spark's identification of this defendant as her attacker. Everything else in the case flows from that correct identification. The van, his van. The sweater, his sweater, found at his house. The box, his box, found in his office, that he had cleaned with white spirit. The false confessions of the other three to the attack on Miss Spark made to assist Morton, made to conceal his role in all three murders and made to order – to *his* order.

'For these reasons, let me clearly assert, you may be certain that Brian Morton is guilty of all three attacks, and of conspiracy to produce these false confessions.'

CHAPTER 31

FRIDAY 20 NOVEMBER

The next morning Willis Fletcher, like Halliday, began by summarising the offences for which his client was on trial and the evidence presented. But, naturally, his emphasis was different. He made it his business to stress how little evidence there really was to tie his client to the crimes.

'The Crown have invited you to rely on Marilyn Spark's identification of the defendant. Yet you have had it demonstrated to you that there was at least one occasion when she got it wrong. That was when Marilyn Spark mistakenly identified another man, a passer-by in the street, as Brian Andrew Morton.

'Members of the jury, in view of this gross mistake, how can the Crown say that Marilyn Spark is a reliable witness? How can you be sure that her identification was correct at the time of the identification parade, when she made a different identification on another occasion? Suppose Brian Andrew Morton had not been with his solicitor, or had an equally verifiable alibi, at the time Miss Spark claimed to have seen him. It doesn't bear thinking about, does it? Members of the jury, as you know, your duty will be to acquit in case of any reasonable doubt. I hope when the time comes you will remember this manifest doubt.

'Marilyn Spark is in fact a thoroughly unreliable witness. That is the reality and, I'm afraid to say, what one might expect from someone who makes her living by prostitution.'

As Fletcher was turning a page, about to embark on another section of his peroration, there was a crash from the public gallery and a voice screamed across the court. It was Marilyn Spark. She could not sit and listen to this prick bad-mouthing her.

'No! You bastard, I was telling the truth. That man's a killer. He's a disgusting animal!'

An usher started forward, gesturing and mouthing warnings to Marilyn. At the same time, Cindy Morton suddenly rose and made her way towards the exit. Winfield looked up.

'Silence in court!' he called, then nodded for Fletcher to continue.

'There is no forensic evidence linking Brian Andrew Morton with any of the victims, or with the weapons whose common use in all these offences is a central element of the Crown's case, yet my learned friend has told you Brian Andrew Morton must be guilty. We submit that such an argument is wholly nonsensical.'

Cindy was walking unsteadily out of the court building now. She vaguely heard behind her a pounding of feet and a voice shouting, but she did not connect this with herself until she realised it was the Spark woman, the prostitute who had accused Damon, running after her.

'What do you want?' said Cindy, turning but continuing to walk away from the building. She was breathing hard and with difficulty. 'Leave me alone.'

But Marilyn was determined to have her say.

'You swore on the Bible that he was with you. Why? Why did you *do* that?'

Cindy stopped in her tracks. She was looking at the ground. She couldn't look at Marilyn.

'I didn't know, all right? I didn't bloody KNOW? It's just I thought . . .'

But the strength in her voice drained away. Anyway, what was the point? As she started walking again, Marilyn did not pursue her but instead called out, in a harsh voice.

'Thought? You never thought for a minute! But I'll tell you what to think now. For what you did, the Devil's going to get you.'

Cindy stopped again. She turned and this time she forced her eyes towards the other woman.

'He already has,' said Cindy.

* * *

When Cindy got home she found Cheryl's scrapbook, with the cuttings about the case and the trial carefully pasted inside. She sat on the floor and began tearing it up into small scraps, slowly at first, and then frenziedly until the pieces lay scattered around her on the floor, like confetti.

* * *

Fletcher had a final trump card up his sleeve and he kept it until the end of his speech. It concerned the now infamous sweater, worn by Marilyn's attacker. He asked the jury to look at their bundle of photographs.

'You will see,' he said, 'that on this page is a copy of the police photograph of the interior of Mr Morton's office in which the wooden box was found.'

He looked up to see that the jurors had all got the photograph in front of them.

'If you look carefully at this, can you see the cork noticeboard hanging on the wall, and can you make out that, in the top of the right-hand corner, there is the same photograph of James Garrett that you have been shown in this court?'

It was the picture of Garrett wearing the sweater. Fletcher sounded both triumphant and full of insinuation as he finished.

'The police have in fact always had evidence that Garrett was the owner of the sweater in their possession and have either failed or, who knows . . .

His voice allowed for all sorts of interpretations to be placed on the omission of the photograph from evidence: police carelessness, arrogance, a whiff of corruption.

'What is patently obvious is that it would have materially assisted them in determining the ownership of the sweater at an early stage. Why it did not do so must, however, be for you, not me, to decide. In summary, members of the jury, the Crown's case against my client is a weak one from every point of view. They cannot put him on the scene of any one of the crimes, they have no other scientific evidence against him and his identification by Marilyn Spark is highly unreliable. Finally, of the conspiracy charge against Mr Morton there is not one scintilla of evidence. You therefore have no alternative but to return a verdict of "not guilty".'

With this flourish Fletcher finished and sat down. An outbreak of whispering and small movements passed through the court, like the fluttering caused by a sudden draught of air. Winfield looked at his watch. Fletcher had been far more concise than Halliday. There was time for lunch and then he would sum up.

* * *

It took ten minutes for Cindy to walk home from Vauxhall Station. She was turning something over in her mind: the continuation of what she might have said to Marilyn Spark back there, outside the court building.

'It's just I thought—'

What?

She began very slowly and reluctantly to force herself to say it. The truth – the bloody truth – the bruised, crushed, gashed and battered truth. The truth about Damon. Did she love him? She used to worship him. She allowed herself quite willingly to fall under his spell. He could be violent, like a lot of men, and had controlled her with his weird ideas about sex and pain. But she never imagined he could have carried out these brutal, senseless attacks. Now, she didn't know. Did she hate him? Oh yes, that was the bit she was really beginning to understand.

'It was just I thought—'

What, then?

Thought he was my husband, thought I loved and had to stand by him, thought he would kill me, thought what would happen then to Charmaine and Karl? Thought . . . thought . . .

That woman had shouted out that Cindy had never thought. Oh, but she had. Thought and thought, but never brought an end to her thinking. She went on walking. Love had shut her eyes. It seemed such a pathetic thing to think now, like a line from a stupid song. And now it would be time to open them again. If Damon came home this time it would be all her fault, wouldn't it?

* * *

The summing-up, even more than Fletcher's speech, was a model of concision. Judge Winfield reminded the jury of their duty, having heard the witnesses, to sift out the facts and to decide the case on the evidence alone.

'This is clearly a terrible case,' he told them. 'The details of it are quite frightening and likely to provoke extreme distaste towards the defendant and great sympathy towards the victims and their families, and in particular Marilyn Spark who survived her dreadful ordeal. However, I must remind you not to try the case on emotion but according to the oath you took at the commencement of this trial, that is, according to the evidence. And it is to this evidence that I now turn . . .'

Walker listened to Winfield, unwinding his highly predictable phrases for an hour, then quit the courtroom for a smoke. He walked for a long time outside, trying to empty his mind of all hopes and fears about the case. Eventually he found himself in the courtroom canteen and, half an hour after that, he was pouring sugar into his second cup of tea and tearing the tip off another Marlboro when North came flying in to find him.

'Guv, the jury's coming back!'

'Coming back? When did they—?'

He shut his eyes. The fears came flooding back.

'It's too quick. They'll have gone with Fletcher.'

'You don't know that,' said North.

* * *

The court was unnaturally hot, suffocating in its tension, as the jury returned.

'Mr Foreman,' said the clerk. 'Please answer this question yes or no. Have you reached verdicts on each count on which you are all agreed?'

'Yes.'

The clerk cleared his throat.

'On count one, do you find the defendant guilty or not guilty of the murder of Susan Zoe Harrow?'

There was no pause. The jury foreman stated the result of their deliberations with studied matter-of-factness.

'Not guilty.'

There was a startled, anguished 'Oh!' from the gallery as Bibi bit her knuckle.

'On count two, do you find the defendant guilty or not guilty of the murder of Carol Alexandra Lennox?'

'Not guilty.'

Colin Lennox had been sitting with his head bowed, his eyes tight shut. The foreman's words seemed amplified and distorted in his ears.

'No!' he whispered. 'No!'

For counts three and four the results were the same. Not guilty. Marilyn could not believe, could not even entertain it. All that anguish. All that hope. And the bastard was going to walk free. And then, as the last 'Not guilty' was pronounced, the slag Cheryl Goodall jumped up in the public gallery and shrieked, 'Yesss!' She was almost sick.

The press was running for the exit, mobile phones ready in their hands. Morton had been released from the dock and had shaken Fletcher's hand. Then he had gone out to join Cheryl and pose for photographs on the Crown Court steps, popping the champagne that the newspaper had provided. One of the reporters from a rival paper phoned not his news editor but the number of Damon Morton's house. The opposition might have the exclusive but he would like to be able to say *he* broke the news to – and heard the first reaction of – the wife.

But Cindy didn't seem to react. And she certainly was not celebrating.

'Mrs Morton, just tell me how you feel about the not guilty verdict.'

He could hear Cindy breathing but she still said nothing. In the background he could hear a doorbell ringing, and someone knocking.

'Mrs Morton?' he went on. 'I'm asking you about your husband's acquittal.'

'Leave me alone!' screamed Cindy Morton. Then the phone went dead.

Leaving the courtroom Walker and North watched the party around Morton and his girlfriend. They were standing by a taxi, ready to drive off, and bottles of champagne were overflowing.

'They all lied for him,' said North. 'Why?'

'God knows what kind of hold he has over them,' said Walker grimly.

North had had no experience of this before, no vocabulary even. She shook her head, helplessly.

'Well, whatever it is, it's evil,' she said.

CHAPTER 32

FRIDAY 20 NOVEMBER. EARLY EVENING

The mood of euphoria and mutual congratulation in the taxi lasted as far as South Lambeth. But as they approached Wycliffe Road, Cheryl received a shock.

'Well, thank God it's over, Damon. You can leave Cindy now. Or kick her out. Then it'll be just you and me, eh? Bliss, that'll be.'

Damon Morton yawned.

'You're joking, Cheryl. Why should I leave her? Things are OK as they are.'

Cheryl was speechless. She had just assumed Damon would now dump the useless Cindy. But apparently he had no intention of doing so. As they arrived at the Morton house, Damon got out and shoved a note ungraciously at the driver. Cheryl refused to get out of the taxi.

'Damon!' she shrieked. 'Tell me. Are you leaving her? Just give me a final answer, yes or no!'

Morton was relaxed now, as he leaned against the taxi, taking another swig of champagne straight from the bottle.

'No,' he drawled. 'What about the kids?'

Cheryl bared her teeth.

'You've never given a shit about those kids. You've never given a shit about anyone but yourself. So why don't you just piss off, Brian!'

She yanked the door shut, making Morton jump clear to avoid being hit. He heard her tell the driver to take her to Ridbelow Road.

He shook his head and clicked his tongue as the taxi drove away. Back home to mother, he thought. But it wouldn't be long before she came knocking at his door once again. And shortly after that she'd be very, *very* sorry for her failure to understand his position.

As he found his key, he could hear a voice inside the house. It sounded like Charmaine. He let himself in and he saw her, behind the door. Her eyes were wide and her face pale.

'Cindy!' he yelled. 'It's me! Cindy! Where's Mum, Charmaine?'

Charmaine was looking very oddly at him, he noticed, her face pulled into a grotesque expression, like a gargoyle. He did not yet notice, behind her, the phone dangling off the hook.

He strode to the stairs and vaulted up them two at a time.

'Cindy? You up here?'

He was angry now. He had come home from the greatest triumph of his life and his flaky bloody wife couldn't even get it together to be there to welcome him. He crashed through into the bedroom and the bathroom, then crossed to the little spare room, which Cindy had been using. Finally he checked Karl's and Charmaine's room. His son was sleeping in his cot.

Charmaine sat herself down beside the dangling phone and held the receiver to the side of her face. She started whispering with her mouth as close as possible to the mouthpiece, just like Mummy had told her to. Mummy had very carefully explained what Charmaine had to do.

She had to press the number nine button three times and wait. Then when a person answered she must give her address,

32 Wycliffe Road, London SW8 – she knew that by heart anyway. Charmaine had done both of these things by the time she
heard Daddy outside the door. Then she went back to the nice
lady on the end of the telephone – the nice lady who Mummy
had said would be there to answer her. Charmaine watched
Daddy go storming past her and into the front room, then she
took a deep breath and started reciting the words Mummy had
made her learn, and heard her repeat over and over.

'You better come now,' she said. 'Daddy cut Mummy. Daddy
cut Mummy. Daddy cut Mummy . . .'

'Cindy, you bitch, where are you?' her father roared as he
came back down the stairs.

Charmaine was still sitting on the floor beside the little
telephone table. He yanked the phone from her hand and
replaced it.

'Who you talking to?' he snarled.

'Secret,' she said slyly.

But Morton was already checking the front room, then
the kitchen, the utility room, the downstairs toilet. Finally he
thought of the office. Yes, she must be there.

Going out into the yard, he saw the scrapbook of the trial
cuttings torn to shreds and scattered over the passage floor.

*　*　*

Walker had decided to ask Pat North for a date and he had told
Satchell. Now the two men stood outside North's office. They
could see she was on the phone.

'She's probably talking to Batchley,' said Walker bitterly.

'No, I'm telling you,' said Satchell encouragingly. 'The rugby
player's out of the picture. Just ask her. She can only say no.'

North had not been talking to Batchley, for now she burst out of the office, her eyes wide with excitement.

'Guv! Central control at the Yard just got a 999 call from Damon Morton's house!'

Walker reacted instantly. He turned and was striding towards the exit and the car park.

'Get back-up and then come with me!' he shouted.

* * *

Damon swiftly crossed the dark yard and took the wooden steps to the office door two at a time. He could hear music coming from inside the hut – 'Silver Tongued Devil' was playing on the sound system. What the hell was she up to? She almost never went into the office. He tried the door itself, but it was locked. The key was in his pocket and, as he groped for it he stood at the rail, looking down and around. The van was parked in the middle of the yard, right in the path of a slanting ray from the streetlamp. He was about to turn around again and open the office door when he was stopped by the thought that there had been something about the van . . . something wrong.

He looked hard. The rear door was not properly closed. The latch was not turned down and the two doors hung very slightly apart, so that the red zigzag line was not quite continuous.

'Cindy?' he said.

He walked down the steps, more slowly and cautiously this time, as if he apprehended there was something wrong, something that would have to be handled with care. He approached the van and reached for the rear door handle. There was a sound from inside, a movement and a brief, tiny whimper. He swung open the door.

Cindy was kneeling in the van, close to the right-hand side, facing him. She was wearing a shirt, but unbuttoned. Her left hand was handcuffed to the rail of the van. In her right hand was the kitchen carving knife. And all over her chest was a mass of blood, dripping and spurting down from the place where her left breast had been, as well as from a deep wound in her throat, to form pools in the carpet around her knees. She was watching him now, her eyes almost closed, exhausted, but still she continued to look at him. The old slavish expression was gone from her eyes, though. This was a new face. Her eyes seemed to express simultaneously unbearable pain and cynical laughter.

'Cindy!'

Morton stared into the van and Cindy reached out, offering the knife to her husband, as if presenting him with a gift. Without even knowing what he was doing, he took it, looking uncomprehendingly at the blade.

Life was draining from Cindy's body fast and Morton did not know how to react. This for once was something he couldn't fix simply by an act of will. This was out of his control.

It was then that he heard the police sirens, saw the flashing blue lights reflected off the shiny pools of blood surrounding him and knew it was too late even for the most cunning, most superior of men to take evasive action. Cindy's trap had closed. He looked round and there was Walker, his eyes glinting. He had a torch and he trained it on Cindy, then on Damon, then back towards Cindy. No longer moving, she was slumped lifeless, hanging from her tethered arm. Walker took another step towards this hellish scene. He had noticed something. He flashed the torch beam around the walls of the van. On one side, using her own blood, Cindy's finger had scrawled DAMON in foot-high letters. The beam travelled round to the opposite wall. There, in exactly the same way, she had written another word: GUILTY.

Morton looked from one word to the other. Then he turned back towards Walker and something snapped. His face was aghast, then it crumpled. And his mouth let out words which sounded, suddenly, like the whimpering of a trapped beast.

'It wasn't me!' he cried. 'It wasn't me!'

EPILOGUE

The aftermath of the storm found the roads awash, shimmering under the passing cars' headlamps. A lot of girls had taken refuge from the heavy rain in a small cafe beside King's Cross station, returning to their patches beneath the arches only when it stopped raining. This was a well-known area for toms. Many of the old cavernous tunnels beneath the railway had been converted into garages, good shadowed pick-up areas and close to plots of waste ground that were hidden from the main road and out of sight of passing patrol cars. Some of the girls would get into their johns' vehicles, direct them there, do the business and return to work as often as ten times a night. Only the rain would make them scurry to the safety and warmth of the cafe. Behind the condensation on the curtained cafe window they could smoke their lungs out; in the toilet they could shoot up before getting back to work.

For a few die-hard toms, no amount of bucketing rain could drive them off the street. One of these was Marilyn Spark. She had acquired her prize stronghold position and God help any of the weekenders who dared put a toe across the pavement cracks which delineated its boundary. Marilyn was famous among them now. She had come back tougher and meaner to the only life she felt she could control. Her bleached, cropped hair made her instantly recognisable, as did the black leather jacket with its collar turned up, the hands always on her hips to show off her figure. Her husky raw voice never said more than was necessary and the darkness hid the scar to her throat; the drugs she pumped into herself again hid the terror that lurked behind her angry eyes.

'Hi, Marilyn. Had a good night?' one of the girls called out.

'Had better,' she growled back, then turned to the kerb as a car slowed to crawling pace.

She'd just got lucky . . .

Dear Reader,

Thank you very much for picking up *Alibi*, the second 'Trial & Retribution' thriller. I was so fortunate that the success of the TV series allowed me to continue writing these novels – of which there are six in total. I hope you enjoyed reading the book as much as I did writing it and do keep an eye out for news about the next book in the series, *Accused*, which will be coming soon. And if you haven't yet had a chance to read the first in the series, *Trial and Retribution,* it's out now.

In *Alibi*, the police have captured their perpetrator, but even a survivor's eyewitness testimony struggles under the weight of three false alibis. Everything hinges on the jury's decision. But when witnesses are prepared to lie under oath, how does the jury know who to believe? What did you think of the justice meted out at the end of the book? Was this a fair resolution?

If you love crime and legal thrillers you may enjoy my podcast, *Listening to the Dead*, which I co-host with former CSI Cass Sutherland. We explore the fascinating world of forensics, from the science behind the headlines to the evidence that cinches a conviction – with world-class experts discussing their most well-known and shocking cases. All episodes are available now on all podcast platforms.

You may also enjoy my Tennison series, which is a prequel series that follows Jane Tennison – my iconic character from *Prime Suspect* – through her early career and landmark cases all the way through to the beginning of the show. I've been so pleased by the response I've had from the many readers who have been curious about the beginnings of Jane's police career and it's been great fun for me to explore how she became the woman we know in *Prime Suspect.* If you want to catch up with the Tennison series, the first nine novels – *Tennison, Hidden Killers, Good Friday, Murder Mile,*

The Dirty Dozen, *Blunt Force*, *Unholy Murder*, *Dark Rooms* and *Taste of Blood* – are all available to buy in print, ebook and audio, and the thrilling finale will be coming out soon!

I'm also working on a very exciting new project and writing my memoir, which will be coming out in 2024. I've lived a very full life – I've been an actress, producer, screenwriter and author, overcoming my fair share of challenges along the way, and I have no intention of slowing down. I hope this memoir will not only entertain, but also impart some of the wisdom I've gained along the way. There will be more details to come, and I look forward to sharing my story with you all.

If you would like more information on my memoir, the podcast or my fiction writing – or just want to hear more from me – you can visit **www.bit.ly/LyndaLaPlanteClub** where you can join my Readers' Club. It only takes a few moments to sign up, there are no catches or costs and new members will automatically receive an exclusive message from me. Zaffre will keep your data private and confidential, and it will never be passed on to a third party. We won't spam you with loads of emails, just get in touch now and again with news about my books, and you can unsubscribe any time you want. And if you would like to get involved in a wider conversation about my books, please do review *Alibi* on Amazon, on Goodreads, on any other e-store, on your own blog and social media accounts, or talk about it with friends, family or reader groups! Sharing your thoughts helps other readers, and I always enjoy hearing about what people experience from my writing.

Many thanks again for reading *Alibi*, and I hope you'll return for *Accused*.

With my very best wishes,

Lynda

Keep reading for an extract of Lynda La Plante's
next case for Tennison

TASTE OF
BLOOD

AVAILABLE NOW

Chapter One

DI Jane Tennison arrived at her new station, hoping for a fresh start. She'd been transferred, at her own request, after she had investigated the case of the bodies found in an old air-raid shelter. She had been proud of the way she had handled the complex enquiry, but the DCI had given her little credit and she had found it impossible to continue working alongside him.

Jane had worked at three other stations, on a variety of cases, but none of them had really stretched her. After taking a month's long-overdue leave, she had been eager to find out where she would be posted. She had requested that it be closer to Bromley as the travel had been an issue on the last investigations she had worked on. One case in particular had been centred around Greenwich, which was a long drive from where she lived.

She had become rather disillusioned with her career and had even considered, albeit half-heartedly, quitting the Met. And when she had received the details of her new posting, it didn't immediately make her feel any more positive. Although it was closer to home, the station only had a very small CID section. However, on the plus side, Jane was interested in meeting her new boss, DCI Fiona Hutton. She had never worked alongside a high-ranking woman, and wondered if it would give her career the boost it needed.

Jane was now living with Eddie Myers and they were engaged to be married, although they had not yet agreed a date for the wedding, partly because they had been so focused on refurbishments to the house. Eddie's handiwork had already almost doubled the property's value, and he was now working on the front and back gardens, laying down paving and ordering trees and plants.

During her leave, Jane had enjoyed spending time with Eddie, helping him to put the finishing touches to the redecoration, though at times she had found their lack of a shared interest beyond the house a little bit worrying. But he was so caring and good-natured that she put her doubts aside. And he certainly impressed her with his work ethic. He was becoming increasingly successful as a builder and renovator, and he and his team were working non-stop.

The drive to her new station only took fifteen minutes, and Jane arrived dressed in one of her smart suits, with a white shirt and Cuban-heeled shoes. She had recently had her hair cut shorter at her sister's salon, and Pam had encouraged her to have some more highlights. She was pleased to see there was a parking bay marked 'DI Jane Tennison' on a white plaque, and she was smiling as she made her way to the modern-looking, double-glass-fronted entrance.

Inside, the reception area was small, with a pine desk, typewriter and telephone, and a row of three hard-backed chairs against one wall. The access into the station offices was situated behind the desk and had a security keypad. The door was ajar and as Jane approached, a young, red-haired, uniformed officer walked out.

'Good morning. I'm DI Jane Tennison.'

He smiled. 'Good morning, ma'am, I am Constable Peter Thompson. If you go straight down the corridor, you will see the main double doors for the CID office. I will inform DCI Hutton that you have arrived.'

The young man stepped to one side to allow Jane to pass, holding the door open and then closing it behind her.

The strip-lighting on the ceiling gave the corridor a clinical feel, not unlike a hospital, and it seemed much less atmospheric than any of the stations Jane had previously worked at. Jane hesitated, then opened the door and walked in.

It was a spacious room with a double row of empty desks with typewriters and telephones, all with decent swivel office chairs. Placed along one wall facing the desks was a large whiteboard with various scrawled felt-tipped messages. The office door to one side was closed and had a neat plaque saying 'DCI F. Hutton'. As Jane was taking in the empty room, the office door opened and a middle-aged woman in a tweed suit with a pink blouse came out carrying a thick file.

'You must be DI Jane Tennison. I'm Dora Phillips, head of the clerical staff. I think that desk by the window has been allocated to you. Right now, everyone is gathering for a briefing in the boardroom. Usually, we have a meeting on the first Monday of the month which always kicks off at eight thirty so everyone can have breakfast in the canteen. However, this morning there's a lecture taking place in about ten minutes. Now, if you would like to put your coat in the closet just by the double doors, and leave your briefcase on your desk, I can take you through.'

Jane deposited her coat and briefcase and followed Miss Phillips down the corridor to the boardroom.

Jane began to feel nervous as the door closed behind her. Seated around a large table were fifteen officers, some in uniform and others in street clothes. They all turned expectantly to look at Jane. Two of the officers half-rose out of their chairs.

'Good morning,' Jane said.

One of the officers, a big, burly, balding man, pushed his chair back and stood up.

'Detective Constable William Burrows . . . you must be Detective Inspector Tennison. Let me introduce you to everyone, and feel free to take the seat at the end of the table.'

Burrows went round the table making introductions and everyone smiled and raised their hands in acknowledgment. In all the years she had worked at the Met, Jane had never had an introduction like it and found the formality extraordinary. It was as if they were college students.

The double doors opened and DCI Hutton made her entrance. She was wearing an immaculate suit and high-heeled shoes that accentuated her six-foot height. She had thick blonde hair, held by a tortoiseshell clip, and Jane thought she was quite a formidable presence as she moved around the table to stand by her empty chair.

'DI Tennison, I must apologise to you for not being available to welcome you and introduce you to everyone, but I am sure DC Burrows has already done that for me. I would just like to welcome you and give you a brief outline of how we usually work. We normally have a once-a-month informal morning's briefing, but today there's something a bit different.'

She drew back her chair and sat down, giving Jane a warm smile, before opening a large, initialled, leather notebook.

'Detective Paul Lawrence is due to arrive any moment to give a talk about a major breakthrough in forensic science. I felt it would be beneficial for everyone to listen and take notes.'

Jane knew Paul Lawrence well, and when a moment later he was ushered into the boardroom by Miss Phillips, she was really pleased to see him. Paul had hardly changed from when they had first worked together, when she was a probationer at

Hackney, although his wavy blond hair was now thinning a little. He gave Jane a quick smile of recognition as he went to stand beside Hutton.

Paul opened a thick file, thanked DCI Hutton for the invitation, and began.

'I am sure many of you have heard of the new scientific breakthrough: DNA. DNA stands for deoxyribonucleic acid, which is a complex molecule that contains all of the information necessary to build and maintain an organism. All living things have DNA within their cells; in fact, nearly every cell in a multicellular organism possesses the full set of DNA required for that organism. Although 99.9 per cent of human DNA sequences are the same in every person, enough of the DNA is different that it is possible to distinguish one individual from another with a DNA profile. To make any test, a smear or swab has to be taken from inside the cheek or mouth. Or you can use blood, saliva, semen, vaginal lubrication and other bodily fluids, or even personal used items like hairbrushes, toothbrushes and razors, which can all have traces of DNA, as well as stored items such as banked sperm or biopsy tissues.'

Paul looked up from his notes and asked if anyone had any questions. Hutton was the first to speak.

'Do twins have the same DNA?'

'Only if they are monozygotic, which means identical. Anyone else have questions, or shall I go on to give you an example, which will hopefully help you fully understand this amazing breakthrough?'

'Please go on,' Hutton said, when no one spoke up.

Paul nodded. 'When a sample such as blood or saliva is obtained, the DNA is only a small part of what is present, so before DNA can be analysed it has to be extracted from the cells and purified.'

It was Hutton again who raised her pen to indicate she wanted to ask a question.

'Could you give us an example of a case that has recently used DNA to obtain a result?'

'Sure. As I have said, this is still a very new science but very soon it's going to become a vital tool, particularly in solving murder and rape cases. In July last year a young girl was murdered, and from the MO the officers were certain the same killer had murdered another young girl in 1983. The police already had a suspect arrested, and a sample of his DNA was compared with the DNA from blood samples recovered at both crime scenes. He was released because his genetic code did not match.'

There were frowns around the table as the officers wondered how DNA evidence had helped solve the case.

Paul waited for a moment before continuing. 'Hard to believe, but a woman in a bar overheard two men talking – one of them saying he had got away with murder because the police had arrested someone else for the crime. The man was traced and his DNA was found to match both crime-scene samples. He admitted to the murder and also pleaded guilty to previous rapes.'

The conclusion of Paul's story was met with unanimous applause, and the meeting broke for coffee, during which Paul answered more questions before continuing for another twenty minutes, focusing on how important it was to observe a strict protocol to protect DNA samples from contamination, and make sure any samples taken were transferred correctly to the laboratories.

When he finished, Jane was keen to talk to him, but he only managed a quick 'Let's catch up soon' before being ushered from the room by Miss Phillips and on to his next appointment.

DCI Hutton asked for everyone to stay and have their usual update meeting but to keep it as brief as possible. Jane opened her notebook as officers began talking about various cases. Jane was surprised that there seemed to be no murder enquiries or investigations into any other serious criminal offences, and instead most of the discussion was about petty crimes and disorderly conduct. The most serious case involved a teenage cannabis possession arrest. DCI Hutton glanced at her wristwatch, and that appeared to be the unspoken signal for the team to get to work. Notebooks were closed and chairs pushed back as Hutton gestured to DC Burrows.

'I'd like you stay, DC Burrows, and brief DI Tennison on the dispute at Clarendon Court.'

Burrows moved his chair to sit beside Jane as Hutton left the boardroom and opened a file bulging with documents.

'Right, this has been quite a lengthy investigation involving a dispute between neighbours that has been ongoing for many years, and is basically about one of them building a fence around his property and a set of gates allowing access into his garden. There were letters and all sorts of insults and lawyers getting involved, until the planning board eventually gave permission for the fence to be built, which is apparently when the dispute escalated, culminating in an incident that left one man in hospital on a life-support machine. I've spent many hours interviewing the families of both parties to try and find out what happened. I have also had a brief interview with the neighbours living opposite, but they were not at home when the incident occurred.'

After initially being disappointed that this seemed to be a case of neighbours quarrelling over a fence, Jane's interest was now piqued, especially when Burrows explained that the victim was still in a critical state and that it therefore could turn out to be a murder case, even though the alleged assailant, Mr Caplan, armed only with a garden spade, was claiming he'd acted in self-defence. She started looking through the documents.

'His wife claims that he was not in any way intent on using it; it just happened to be leaning against a wall when the two men began to argue,' Burrows explained.

Jane turned a page and tapped it with her finger.

'Is this his statement when he was brought into the station? Did Mr Caplan have any injuries consistent with being hit with an iron bar? I see he claimed that he only used the spade to protect himself, as his neighbour had an iron bar and struck him first.'

'Yes, but there was no bruising or other marks where he said he was struck, and no iron bar was recovered from the scene. So Mr Caplan looks like he's going to be facing an assault charge at the very least.'

'I'd like a map of the area,' Jane said. 'It's difficult to visualise the exact layout of the properties. And also the letters regarding the dispute.'

Burrows collected all his documents and handed them to Jane. Then he pushed his chair back and suggested they go into the CID office where a drawing was pinned up on the board.

The large room was busy and Jane put the file on her desk and went to join him in front of the board, where she saw a rather amateurish drawing in crayon showing a large square marked TARMAC. On one side were the outlines of two substantial properties, along with drives and garages, numbered 4 and 8. On the right-hand side of the tarmac were two smaller properties numbered 10 and 7 respectively, with MARTIN BOON PROPERTY written prominently and in brackets VICTIM.

Then, opposite numbers 4 and 8, there was the most substantial property of all. This was number 12 and the owner was marked as DAVID CAPLAN.

'As you can see it's a very secluded courtyard,' Burrows explained. 'We have an estimate of the value of the properties. Numbers 4 and 8 are fairly new builds and we reckon to be worth £500,000 each, if not more, as they both have extensive back gardens. The two smaller ones, numbers 10 and 7, are more likely around £300,000 as their rear gardens are not up to much. The big property, number 12, would have been the original twelve-bedroomed manor house, with indoor swimming pool, two large gardens and a triple garage – valued at about three to four million. I would say that all the properties around it had been built when the land was sold off by the original owner's heirs. It's now owned by David Caplan. He bought it five years ago.'

Jane stifled a yawn, trying to concentrate, as Burrows tapped the number 12 with his pencil.

'This is the fence and the gates that have been the cause of all the bad feeling between them. Mr Caplan had been given planning permission to take down the fences and replace them with a high wall and a pair of electric gates, even though Boon had objected to the wall and complained to the council. Boon also claims that where the fence is now is four inches over the boundary!'

Jane chewed her bottom lip, then pointed to the tarmacked courtyard.

'Who owns that, or do they all share it?'

'They've all got right of way, but they are not allowed to park there. It's owned by number 10.'

'What? The tarmac area belongs to that small house? That doesn't make much sense.'

Burrows shrugged. 'You tell me! It's owned by Mr and Mrs Larsson, and she is a nasty piece of work; very rude and unhelpful. According to Mr Caplan, her husband has threatened his wife because she had parked outside their own double gates. She was also unpleasant when they moved in, and claimed the new double gates would not be allowed to open outwards as she owned the courtyard.'

Jane shook her head. It all sounded like a very odd situation.

'So, this woman, Mrs Larsson, has she got any involvement in the assault?'

'No, but we think that she is pulling Mr Boon's strings. He seems to have been very friendly with her and easily influenced.'

Burrows looked at his wristwatch. 'I ought to be going to the hospital. If Mr Boon dies, obviously it puts a whole new slant on the enquiry. I'll leave you to go through the file, and we'll get back together in the morning to discuss the next steps. I think Stanley should be back soon, and he'll be able to answer any queries you might have.'

Jane went to her desk. It all seemed so tedious, she had not really been paying much attention to what Burrows was saying. She decided to go and have some lunch before returning to her desk and making some notes.

It was after two when Jane returned to her desk and started wading through the contents of Burrows' file. Jane turned her head when she heard the door opening. She could hardly believe it! DI Stanley stood there, wearing a smart dark suit and black tie, his usual wild hair cut neatly, and with no moustache. He looked older, with lines etched on his face. On seeing Jane, he gave her a wide grin and walked over to her desk.

'Long time no see, Jane!'

He leaned over to give her a kiss on the cheek. She could smell the alcohol on his breath, and he looked quite flushed.

THE THRILLING NEW SERIES FROM THE QUEEN OF CRIME DRAMA

Lynda La Plante

IT'S TIME TO MEET DETECTIVE JACK WARR . . .

OUT NOW

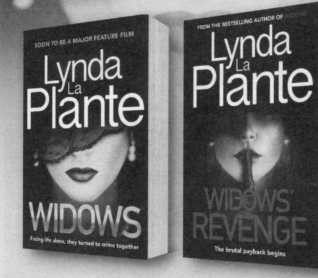